Hidden Agenda

Rochelle Elliot

1

Damn it," Sydney Stone grumbled. She scooped up her empty cup and pushed her chair back. A lack of caffeine was as good a reason as any to leave her useless laptop.

She'd almost made it to the small staff kitchen when Matilda dived on her.

"Please," Matilda begged. "That new intern is late back from lunch. You have to watch the front desk so I can run to the bathroom."

"Did you ask Ben?"

"He's on a training course."

"Tara?"

"She took an early lunch to get her eyebrows tattooed."

"Old Betty?"

"Really?" Matilda cried. "Old Betty, who creeps through my drawers and can't transfer calls because all the flashing lights make her nauseous?"

Sydney was torn. She could smell the fresh pot of coffee just beyond the kitchen door.

"Do it for your bestie," Matilda jiggled on the spot.

"Oh, go on," Sydney waved her away. She pouted at the coffee machine as she walked past the kitchen. Matilda flew down the corridor in her platform Jimmy Choo's. Sydney prayed her crazy friend wouldn't break an ankle.

Although, it would probably serve her right. Reckless running in high heels was probably a health and safety violation.

But I really don't have time for a trip to A&E.

Sydney slid into Matilda's swivel chair at the front desk. The call lights flashed across the computer screen as she hooked Matilda's earpiece over her own head, took a breath and started transferring calls.

"Welcome to Passion Media, you're speaking with Sydney. How may I assist you today?"

What a crazy bloody morning. She'd told them it was a bad idea to install the new accounting software programme the day before Passion Business went to print. They'd been assured it would have no impact on the magazine, or in fact any operations outside the accounting department. Now the number of errors across the whole Passion system were growing, and the pimple faced teenager they claimed was a software analyst was about as much use as Matilda's bladder. Small and annoying.

"One moment Mr Jones, connecting you to finance now."

"Thanks for holding Ms Brenan, I'll transfer you to Tim now."

It was okay for him. He'd be back home by dinnertime, probably with his mummy cooking his dinner and ironing his underpants. *I'll probably still be here at midnight, trying to force the stupid system to accept the last minute changes before print deadline.*

A gentle cough alerted Sydney to someone wanting her attention, and when she looked up from the computer screen, a pair of deep blue eyes stared intently back at her. Her heart thumped a little faster, and she tried to swallow a gasp, that came out as a little squeak. She almost laughed aloud at such a ridiculous reaction.

She watched his smooth lips curl into an inquisitive smile. She'd been staring for a lot longer than was socially acceptable. She swallowed hard and prayed her cheeks weren't flushed. She held a finger up to the best looking man she'd seen in forever, like possibly her whole entire life, including that time she bumped into the England Rugby Sevens team. They'd all been a lot shorter than she'd expected.

"One minute," she whispered.

Sydney transferred two more calls while staring hard at the stapler on the desk. She snuck another peak. Clearly the system issues had pushed her over the edge. She resisted the urge to check her heart rate on her Fitbit. So a good looking man was smiling at her, there was work to be done, and she needed to get back to it.

"Welcome to Passion Media," she nodded at the hot guy. Her heart did a backflip. Bloody hell his eyes were lovely.

Sydney Stone, stop this right now. You are not the kind of woman who goes weak at the knees.

"Do you have an appointment?"

"Do I need an appointment?" he asked with a hint of amusement in his voice. But Sydney had no time for games. Sensible Sydney was back in charge. She took half a second to check if he was wearing a wedding ring. He wasn't. Not that she cared.

She kept a pleasant smile on her face but narrowed her eyes.

"Is there someone you were looking for?" Sydney tried again.

"Who would you recommend?"

"Sir, we're a bit busy today. How about you make my job easier and,"

"I'm Denton."

"Okay. Well Mr Denton, let's start again. How can I help—"

"No. Denton is my first name."

"I apologise. Now if you tell me who you're here to see?"

"It's your turn."

Sydney glanced at the calls backing up on the computer screen.

"My turn for what?"

"Your turn to tell me your name."

Sydney kept a strained smile on her face and gritted her teeth. So the inside didn't match the outside. Disappointing though not unexpected. Dude needed some assistance. She knew just how she could 'help' him.

Matilda barrelled in from around the corner. Sydney closed her mouth, choosing not to call Denton whoever he was, a dickhead, therefore avoiding an hour in the HR woman's office, talking about the importance of customer service.

"Matilda, this man really, *really*, needs some help." Sydney raised her eyebrows a quarter of a millimetre, a conspiratorial micro-look they'd perfected to communicate their frustrations at work. But Matilda's eyes widened.

"Ow," Sydney cried as the earpiece was ripped from her head and she was shoved roughly from behind the desk.

"Thank you so much Sydney, I'll take over now." Sydney watched Matilda glide around the front desk and hold out her hand.

"Good Morning Sir. We've set up a space for you in conference room four. Or would you like to see the office first? Shall I rustle up some coffee?"

Mr Hottie took the hand Matilda had offered. It probably felt smooth and warm. He looked up and winked, throwing Sydney a smug smile.

She returned it with a smarmy nod.

"All yours Matilda."

Sydney stalked back to the kitchen. Obviously this Denton dude was important. But her need for coffee was more so.

She made it to the Nespresso machine this time. She had her hand wrapped around a Ristretto pod when a voice called out,

"Syd, it's crashed again! I can't access the backup either." She didn't need milk. She'd swallow it espresso style.

"Syd, get back here."

"Damn it!" Her coffee mug was back on Matilda's desk.

A panicked voice now echoed down the corridor.

"Does anyone know where Sydney is? I need her NOW!"

Sydney grabbed an ugly brown mug from the shelf.

"I hate crappy coffee mugs," she muttered as she watched the elixir of life pour from the machine. She watched from the doorway as Matilda and the hottie from reception passed by and disappeared around the corner, then she turned in the opposite direction and stomped back to her desk.

2

It was dark outside when she finally looked up from her computer screen. Sydney gently rolled her neck from left to right. She swivelled her chair to face the window and let her eyes relax as she watched the lights of London twinkle beneath her.

It had been such a thrill two years ago, getting that stack of business cards with her new job title. *Investigative Journalist* - Passion Media. She was a someone, at last. Sydney Stone was never going to end up like her mother, sitting at home, dusting vases and watching The Bold and the Beautiful, while her husband took care of all the 'business affairs'.

It hadn't been easy but she had made sure every aspect of her life was geared towards achieving a successful career.

So what was that empty feeling she got when she looked out at the world? What would it be like to work a little less? To spend more time exploring the city and less time looking down on it?

"Sydney Stone."

Sydney turned her chair towards her office door.

"Mr…" Sydney paused. "Denton. Was it?"

"It's Denton Cole." He took a couple of steps into Sydney's office and leaned across her desk with his arm extended. Sydney accepted his hand and the moment he wrapped his fingers around hers, a shot of electricity sent a shiver through her. She needed to calm down.

Her heart rate kept rising. And what the hell was that strange nervous knot in her stomach. That could bugger off and so could Denton bloody Cole who remained leaning over her desk, his hand still holding hers, with those stormy blue eyes she remembered from earlier, gazing at her. It was a good thing she was already sitting down.

"May I?" Denton finally asked, lowering himself into the chair opposite Sydney. Their hands separated, and Sydney rested her burning palm on the cool desktop. She grasped for her usual level of composure.

"It's really late, you're in the office after hours, and I'm beginning to think I'm supposed to know who you are Mr Cole."

"Call me Denton. It was actually quite nice, at the reception desk earlier, to find you had no idea who I was. I work hard, you see, to remain somewhat elusive."

"Ah," Sydney smiled tightly, the light bulb finally went off. "Cole. You're our mystery majority shareholder and our new CEO."

"You sound disappointed," Denton replied.

Sydney re-examined Denton Cole, in light of his new status as her boss. His tie hung loosely at his neck, his sleeves were rolled up. A shadow of stubble made his jawline more prominent.

"Mr Lloyd, the man whose job you've taken, was kind and honest. He was a mentor to many of us at Passion." There was a challenge in Sydney's words and she was pleased her voice didn't waver.

"I know. Dave Lloyd is one of the good guys. I hold him in high regard." Denton smiled. "He mentioned I should look out for you.

'Won't get an easy ride with Sydney Stone.' I think that's what he said."

Like he'd be getting any kind of ride from her. Sydney narrowed her eyes. She tried to put a lid on the intense intimacy she felt when her eyes met Denton's across her desk. She looked down, moved a pen from the left side of her desk to the right, then spoke again.

"It's been suggested that maybe Mr Lloyd's early retirement may have been coerced."

"And what does Dave say about that?" Denton asked.

"He refused to hear a word against you. But there's a feeling, on the ground, that perhaps under a new watch, Passion Media will be less concerned with upholding journalistic standards and reporting the news, and more concerned with bottom lines." Sydney didn't add that the conversations she'd heard in the last week mostly revolved around how soon it would be before the more meaty stories were dropped in favour of reprinting clickbait LOL cats they found on YouTube and asking politicians for their favourite brand of shampoo.

"Are you accusing me of something Sydney?"

"No. I don't know yet, Mr Cole."

"Denton. I don't really care for surnames Sydney."

"And I don't care for arrogant, egotistical—"

"Sydney Stone," Denton Cole interrupted. He rose from his chair and strolled over to the window behind Sydney. "Investigative Journalist."

She swivelled her chair in his direction but immediately regretted the move. It would have made a much bigger statement to keep her back to him. But damn it, she'd look timid if she turned back now.

"Sydney Stone," Denton repeated her first and last names.

"Defender of truth and freedom. How many awards have you picked up this year?"

"Our *team* were awarded four medals at the Media Awards."

"Sydney Stone."

"Mr Cole, it's kind of you to repeat my name, but I think I've got it set to memory. It's hard to believe but I've actually had it since birth."

"You know I thought you were a man?"

"You're not the first, and you won't be—"

"The last?" Denton Cole grinned. Sydney sent him a withering stare, then swivelled her chair back to face her desk. She folded the screen of her laptop down and shuffled papers into a meaningless pile on her desk.

"You know Miss Stone, I think it would be quite an achievement to be your last." And with that he strolled back past her desk and left her office.

Sydney's mouth remained in a stunned circle, her pulse hammering away. Had he really just said that? *Bloody rude!* Her body tingled and hummed and betrayed her displeasure.

She tried to construct words into sentences, but all journalistic credibility failed her.

"It's been a pleasure, Sydney." Denton was already halfway down the corridor, calling out to her. "So much so, I'll be back tomorrow. Let's have lunch. I'll swing by and pick you up."

Sydney scrambled from her desk to her doorway. She watched him walk away, his hands in the pockets of his pants, whistling what sounded like the theme song from MacGyver.

Say something, anything!

"I hate when people whistle," she yelled after him. Denton Cole stopped. He turned back to Sydney and raised a hand in acknowledgment, then disappeared around the corner.

She could still hear him whistling.

3

Denton Cole was in a good mood. Even the monochrome mundane apartment Harvey had rented for him wasn't half as annoying as usual. Harvey apologised as usual and offered to make a quick trip to John Lewis for some throw cushions and a nice floral arrangement.

"Sod off," Denton told him. "I spend half my life in hotel rooms, so sue me if I want a bit of life and colour when I'm somewhere for more than a few weeks. Who knows, this one might stick!"

"That's what you said in Paris," Harvey laughed. "And Barcelona. And when you made me go to all those viewings for apartments in Toronto."

"I bought one didn't I?"

"Yes," Harvey nodded, "and I'll buy you a cashmere throw in the colour of your choosing if you can tell me your address in Toronto, and the last time you were there."

Denton walked past the shiny black laminate on the kitchen walls, grimaced at the chrome and glass coffee table that would show a mark should the slightest fingertip come into contact with it. He resolutely ignored the giant framed '&' symbol that hung on the stark white wall in the foyer, and paid no attention to the matching question mark of equally ridiculous size, hanging above the master bed.

"I'm off the clock now," Harvey held up his mobile. "I'm going to call my mother, decline the opportunity to go on a date with Denise's son's best friend who also happens to be gay. Meet you downstairs in 15 minutes."

"Tell your mum I love her"

"Only if you want to marry me!"

"If only your flair for business didn't come in black and chrome."

"Someone has to bring the masculine energy to the party."

Denton grinned, taking in Harvey's lavender shirt and matching floral tie.

"Meet you downstairs in 15 minutes."

Denton called his message service, switched his phone to speaker and dropped it on the bed. He unbuttoned his work shirt, dropping it over a small black occasional chair.

"You have 16 new messages," the digital voice told him.

He listened while absentmindedly running his hands over his well-defined abs.

"Next new message. Received today at 5:57 pm."

"About damn time," he growled when his best friend's voice filled the room.

"Cole. I'm safe for now. I don't think they've followed me but I don't know how long I've got. I'll be in touch as soon as I've got something solid. I know you'll hate this mysterious shit, but right now the less you know the better. I'll be in touch."

"Damn right I hate it," he grumbled.

Denton erased the message and dropped his pants.

They were the only sweaty bodies in the basement gym below Denton's apartment.

"This woman," Harvey puffed when their synced treadmills eased off the hills and let them jog for a kilometre. "This Sydney Stone. She's sweet on the eye?" Harvey raised his eyebrows and waited for his boss to answer.

"She's fine, you know, to look at. Why is that?"

Their machines whirred and their legs pumped harder.

"I know you're a consummate professional," Harvey puffed.

"But you have not stopped talking about her."

"Whatever." Denton checked the heart monitor on his watch.

"Your eyes met over the desk in the crowded reception area. Then she got all snooty in her office. You're meeting her for lunch tomorrow."

Denton waved Harvey away and increased his pace on the treadmill.

"Fate brought you together. It's like in The Notebook. You and this Sydney Stone woman will be shagging on a grand piano by Friday."

"What did I tell you about those movies Harvey?"

"They're not real." Harvey upped his pace, "But I can't help it boss. You deserve a happy ever after. *After* my victory dance."

Denton put the two bottles of beer on the table with only a little animosity.

"I'm still jet lagged."

"You were in Moscow. You're calling jet lag on a two hour time difference?"

"It counts," Denton grumbled. "The hotel you put me in didn't have a gym so I missed a couple of days. I assume you did that on purpose."

"Of course I did," Harvey grinned. They clinked bottles and drank.

"She'll have googled you by now. Your Sydney Stone."

"Do you like your job Harvey?" Denton asked.

"Let's see what she'll see." Harvey lifted his phone from the table.

"Siri, who is Denton Cole."

"Siri," Denton spoke to his own phone. "define constructive dismissal?"

Harvey ignored him.

"Here we go. Miss Stone now knows the Cole Family were American, originally from Connecticut. Your great-grandfather was a copper baron, made millions. Lived a privileged and very public life. But when part of that family fortune trickled down through your grandfather to your father, he moved to London, married an unknown English woman and lived happily ever after, building up his own business empire in relative anonymity."

"You know I'm aware of these details Harvey, what with it being *my* family and all."

Harvey waved a hand at Denton,

"What did people do before the internet? *This* article mentions you and your sister, but there's no real detail. The writer, Eugene Bliss her name is, she's more interested in the old Coles. She must have been 90 when she wrote this, she's a geriatric historian *slash* American gossip columnist. She seems shocked, and quite distracted by your mother. Listen to this,

'Violet Cole, maiden name unavailable, came with no title, had no societal connections, and though British, she was not related to the Queen in any way.'"

Denton sipped his beer and Harvey kept reading from the screen.

"'This must have been of enormous disappointment to the Cole family. *What a waste of good breeding and money!'*" Harvey put his phone down and took a long drink from his pint glass.

"So the Cole's are like American royalty?"

"Hardly," Denton scoffed.

"Eugene Bliss seems to think so. Is there a stack of bones rattling around in the Cole family closets?"

"I've never looked," Denton dismissed Harvey, "I've never met any American Coles, but there are some cousins floating around I think."

"They'd probably run a mile, your father having compromised your breeding like that. How terribly middle-class you are, Mr Cole," Harvey beamed.

"I think I'll have a burger," Denton picked up the menu.

"Do you think they were like an American version of Downton Abbey?"

"I have no idea, Harvey. All that society stuff is ridiculous. See why I hate those red carpet invitations you make me accept?"

"I sign you up for one in five. And if I didn't you'd be a lonely, frustrated, cranky old man, talking to a goldfish."

"I see people every day."

"People?"

"People."

"People like Sydney Stone?"

"No one quite like Sydney Stone."

Harvey grinned at his boss.

"I wonder if she's related to the Queen? Have you investigated her assets?"

Denton Cole shook his head.

"I'm rather more focused on my own right now.

4

Sydney sat on the train to Blackwall Station feeling grumpy. She prided herself on always being a step ahead. Always knowing what was coming around the next bend. That's what made her a great journalist. But Denton Cole had blindsided her. She'd been caught out, and she didn't like it. The new majority shareholder of Passion Media was supposed to be an older man. A stereotypical, Murdoch-style mogul. She hadn't thought for a second that a younger, more intriguing man would have been behind the sudden shake-up at Passion.

At a guess, Denton Cole was in his mid-thirties, a few years older than Sydney at 29. But other than the way he'd made her heart hammer, twice in one day, he was a completely unknown entity. She hated that.

Sydney got out her cell phone and opened Google.

The internet search proved unremarkable. She followed a few links to information about Denton's family history. Some old lady in Connecticut had written what amounted to a gossip page, suggesting Denton Coles father was an uncouth man who had no sense when it came to good breeding and societal expectations. Denton was mentioned only briefly. He was 36. He had a sister, Darcy, two years younger, and they were both educated at prestigious schools. It appeared that Denton Cole's father had retired a few years ago, and handed to his son and daughter a small but wealthy group of businesses. Denton had taken over the business interests and was highly skilled and well respected in his own right. The family business had grown in wealth and breadth since he took the helm. His youthfulness and success at such a young age were mentioned a couple of times. And there were plenty of photos of Denton shaking hands with other men in expensive suits. Not to mention the smattering of black tie events with the odd celebrity in attendance. There was a photo of him in a group with Ed Sheeran, but otherwise, the events were distinguishable only by the differing staircases or floral arrangements in the background. Denton wore the same suit and black bow tie in each shot. But Sydney saw a different woman on Denton's arm each time. One woman looked like she'd had her dress spray painted on. Her shoes were so high she probably needed an oxygen mask to make it through the evening.

The most recent photos on Google were of Denton Cole at a hospital wing opening, and at a retirement village, that he probably owned. She'd investigated a story a while back about the huge money being made in high end old people's homes. Sydney zeroed in on Denton's face. He looked tense, his body turned slightly away from the camera. The man in those photographs was hard to match up with the confident, determined Denton who'd invaded her office an hour earlier.

She tried to find something more interesting about Denton Cole. There was a guy Wells, who'd accused Denton of ruining him. Sydney skim read the guys blog about some corporate fraud case where he'd been falsely accused. The guy was pretty pissed off, but it was the only negative piece in a sea of business success stories.

The train pulled into the station and Sydney shoved her cell phone in her bag.

She power walked the short distance from the station to her apartment, the googled images of Denton Cole with beautiful women followed her.

"Probably thinks he can smoulder at any woman and she'll drop her knickers!" Sydney declared to the back of a man waiting for the cross signal. He glanced behind.

"God, sorry. Not you. I just,"— The green man lit up and the man scurried across the road.

Sydney's old boss had always called her out when she'd dig up a story and cause a ruckus. "Here comes trouble with a capital T!" he'd say.

But this time I didn't start it. He turned up out of nowhere! Here comes trouble with a capital D!

When Sydney woke the next morning, she decided it would be crazy to think about what Denton Cole was doing at that very moment. It would be completely nuts to think of him lifting weights or making his morning coffee, probably shirtless. And how insane would she be to imagine Denton Cole slipping into a hot shower?

Sydney finished her own shower with a burst of cold water. She dressed quickly in a white silk shirt, a dark grey trouser suit, and her favourite pair of black heels. She strung a double layer of red beads around her neck and took an extra few minutes to perfect her matching red lipstick.

With an air of determination and a double shot espresso, Sydney hit her usual morning stride.

"Yesterday was mad," Matilda laughed and gave Sydney a quick hug. The two women were in the small staff kitchen between the front desk and Sydney's office at the rear of Passion Media's fifth floor spread.

"Honestly, if you hadn't watched the desk for me, I'd have wet my pants!" Matilda scooped ground coffee beans into a plunger.

"Adult nappies would solve all your problems," Sydney said.

"You can offer that suggestion at the next staff meeting," Matilda stuck her tongue out.

"Hey did Denton Cole find you last night? I know it was late but you were still in your office so I sent him down."

"Oh yes. He found me." Sydney unscrewed the lid from her drink bottle and put it under the spout of the water cooler.

"He's sex on toast. Don't you think?" Matilda leaned against the bench and winked at Sydney. "I mean, I wouldn't say no to his Italian loafers under my bed."

"On toast?" Sydney hadn't paid much attention to his shoes, and she'd promised herself she would be professional. And that meant not thinking about any of his *sexy* attributes.

"He's like a movie star," Matilda sighed. "If only I was single. But you! You'd break your no date rule for him wouldn't you?"

Sydney pulled her drink bottle away from the water cooler despite it only being half full.

"I told you, I don't have a rule." This was old familiar territory.

"Okay, I forgot," Matilda rolled her eyes, "it's not that you don't want to date, it's just you're far too busy for a relationship. But who says you have to marry the guy? Just throw him a bone. Or have him throw you one." Matilda started pumping her hips and Sydney burst out laughing.

"Give him a little nibble Sydney. Put some butter on his sexy toast. You know he came on a helicopter? A helicopter Syd. I wonder where they landed?"

"Helicopters have replaced limos now? What rich men will do to avoid the city traffic toll!" Sydney declared. She lifted her drink bottle up in the air.

"I've left my diamond cufflinks in the Hampton's. Pop down to Tiffany's and pick me up another pair Jeeves. Now fire up the chopper and bring me my loafers!"

"There's a helipad on the roof." Denton's eyes sparkled with amusement. "Now don't give the Mayor any ideas, or he'll apply the congestion charge to helicopters too. Then I'll get kicked out of the rich people's helicopter club."

Sydney knew her face was as crimson as Matilda's. The two women looked at each other, waiting to see who would rescue the situation, but Denton graciously stepped into the silence.

"I'm told there's a supply of chocolate biscuits somewhere, but that it's almost impossible to free a packet from the dark confinement of the double-locked cupboard."

Matilda dug into her pocket and produced the two keys needed to access the biscuits.

"Sorry Mr Cole, but they don't last an hour around here if they're not locked up." Sydney was burning with embarrassment and couldn't think of a single thing to say.

"I'm Matilda. I cover the front desk and lots of the admin around here. We met briefly yesterday? I brought you a club sandwich and a neenish tart." She held out her hand and firmly shook Denton Coles.

"Mr Lloyd, our boss before you, he liked the mint creams and the chocolate bourbons, but if you'd like something different, I can get you anything you want."

"Anything?" Denton Cole raised his eyebrows in Sydney's direction. "I am partial to a hobnob. What about you Sydney? Any weakness we could exploit?"

"Sydney's partial to a bit of trifle," Matilda winked at her friend.

"Extra whipped cream."

"I'll keep a note of that," Denton smiled.

Sydney sent death rays in Matilda's direction. She'd kill her, if she didn't die of embarrassment first. She wanted to crawl up onto the biscuit shelf beside the mint creams and close the cupboard door. If Denton Cole hadn't been blocking the exit, she would have fumbled some excuse and dashed for the safety of her office. *Caught making fun of my new boss and his helicopter, now Matilda's flirting with him on my behalf, while I'm standing right here!* Sydney could feel Denton Cole's amused gaze settle back in her direction. She fed her mind all the sensible messages in a desperate attempt to communicate with her now tingling body.

He's your boss Sydney. Yes, he's very handsome, but he's rich and unscrupulous and he's here because of a hostile takeover. He fired your mentor!

But look at his lovely eyes and I wonder what it would feel like to run my hand through his hair. And oh yes, he's definitely wearing Italian loafers!

"Well, I better get the coffee to the conference room or I'll be very unpopular," Matilda smiled. She lifted a coffee plunger in each hand.

"I'll just squeeze past you there Mr Cole." She slid past, then turned in the doorway and pumped her hips behind Denton Cole's back. Sydney let out a small yelp, then turned quickly back to the job of filling her water bottle.

"See you later Mr Cole," Matilda sang.

Sydney's senses were on high alert. She let herself sneak a peek while Denton unlocked the cupboard. His face was smooth, freshly shaven. She could smell the citrus notes of his aftershave. The urge to lean over and press her face into his neck was almost overwhelming.

Where was this coming from? Since when did Sydney Stone get giddy over guys?

She concentrated on the lid of her drink bottle, twisting it on with deep determination.

Be sensible.

Denton took a packet of mint creams then re-locked the cupboard.

He put the keys in his pocket then stood and watched her. Sydney used a tea towel to dry the water drips from her drink bottle. She quickly made a mental check-list.

Denton Coles flaws:

Did away with Dave Lloyd.

Flirts with the receptionist (okay Matilda was probably the one flirting, but he didn't seem to mind!).

Only been at Passion Media one day, but here he was in the biscuit cupboard, taking a WHOLE packet of Mint Creams and strutting about like he owned the place.

Sydney shushed the voice of reason that told her he did in fact own the place. By a majority shareholding. And that her list might be somewhat lacking in substance.

Has fancy Italian shoes and his helicopter on the roof.

Sensible Sydney definitely did not notice the cool way he'd slicked back his wavy sun-kissed hair, or the way his eyes came to life when he smiled.

Those bloody eyes! Did she want to slap Denton Cole sideways, or have him press her up against the kitchen bench and graze her lips with his perfect teeth. She could feel the heat pulsing at her core. It would only take a moment and she'd have his hair all messed up and his shirt unbuttoned and…

"Sydney, are you alright there?"

Denton's voice brought her back. Sydney realised she'd been holding her drink bottle in the air. She dropped her arm and forced a brilliant smile in his direction. The last thing she needed was for Denton Cole to have the upper hand. He did not need to know the effect he was having on her.

"Make sure Matilda gets her keys back. You really don't want to mess with the biscuit queen."

Sydney twisted the lid of her drink bottle one more time.

Denton leaned in close and spoke quietly.

"Do you always screw that hard?"

The question lingered in the air, long after he'd offered Sydney a sly grin and disappeared from the kitchen. As did the feeling of his warm body so close to her own.

5

There was plenty of work that should have kept Sydney occupied, but Denton had her flustered. The clock at the bottom right of her screen said it was almost noon. Would he remember the lunch invitation he'd extended to her?

"The last thing I want is a lunch date with Denton Cole," Sydney told herself. But she'd just take a quick stroll past reception, just to check for any last minute messages. The stab of disappointment when Matilda assured Sydney her schedule was clear, left her even more confused. And she knew exactly who to blame. He'd arrived at Passion Media and immediately blurred the lines of their professional interactions.

Why am I even calling it a lunch date? Sydney chided herself on the way back to her office. *Surely it's a lunch MEETING. Not a lunch date. A MEETING!* Sensible Sydney was good at meetings. She would happily spend an hour sitting opposite Denton Cole discussing her latest story, or maybe she'd put forward her proposal for a stand-alone Passion Media news website.

But semantics aside, it didn't look like either lunch meeting or lunch date would eventuate.

Ignoring the list of unopened emails, Sydney slouched back in her chair and stared out the window. There was a weird vibe at Passion. In less than 24 hours the easy banter that usually passed in the hallways had all but ground to a halt. Corridor chat was taken into offices, where behind closed doors there were whispers of reshuffles and job cuts. So it didn't seem odd when Matilda snuck into her office and closed the door with a quiet click.

"He's made Old Betty cry." Matilda sat opposite Sydney, in the same seat Denton had filled the night before.

"I'm not bothered, not after that time she complained about the length of my skirt. But my mum loves those articles about her stupid guinea pig. She'll bame me you know."

"Has he fired her?" Sydney asked. Old Betty wouldn't be a huge loss. All fluff and no substance. But Sydney would have a few things to say to Denton Cole if he was already getting rid of people!

"He doesn't seem to waste any time. I know he's got a 51% shareholding, but,"

"62%," Matilda corrected her. "National Business Review just tweeted. Sir Harris Jacobson sold his shares."

"Bloody hell," Sydney growled. "He's taking over everything."

"I know," Matilda agreed. "And don't pretend you haven't noticed him checking you out. I think he might be planning a bedroom takeover."

"Hardly," Sydney picked up her stapler, didn't know what to do with it so put it back on her desk.

"The kitchen this morning!" Matilda exclaimed. "It was like an episode of Suits back there. You're all Donna Paulsen, and he's all Harvey Specter. But with better hair. Maybe I'll get to be a bridesmaid after all."

"Matilda!" Sydney cried.

"I know, I know, you're never getting married, you're too busy to date. And you'd never have sex in the copy room. Even if it meant your *bestest* friend in the whole world might get a ride in a helicopter."

"I swear Matilda, you'll be my *deadest* friend."

"I better dash," Matilda grinned, "I left the new intern minding the front desk. I don't want him stealing my Hello Kitty highlighters. Oh! The reason I came – this came for you." Matilda dropped a white A4 envelope on Sydney's desk then clattered out of the office.

Her name was printed on a white sticker, centered neatly on the envelope. She turned it over and unstuck the seal then tipped the envelope upside down. A USB stick fell onto her desk. Most deliveries came through the mail room and anything a bit suspicious was supposed to go to IT to be checked. But they were still overwhelmed with yesterday's software install. A random USB stick would not be high on their list of priorities. She removed the cap and pushed the stick into the USB port on her laptop.

There was only one file on the memory stick. Sydney let the virus scan run, then double-clicked to open the file. A slightly blurred photo of a business card appeared on her screen.

"Who the hell is Justin Haig?" Sydney asked.

Justin Haig was a Systems Security Analyst. The card gave his work and cell phone numbers, and an email address too blurry to read.

There was nothing else in the envelope and Sydney's interest dwindled. The majority of these anonymous tip-offs went nowhere. Someone believed their neighbours were running a meth-lab in the middle of the night when they were actually bottling jam for the school fete. Or an angry employee made up some story about embezzlement, wanting to see his boss humiliated for not giving him a promotion.

Still, investigative journalism was like that. You had to sort through the rubble to find the gold. Sydney opened a search page on her screen and put in the name Justin Haig. Seconds later she had her man. His LinkedIn page said he'd worked for a number of different tech companies over the years, but most recently at Vanguard International.

Sydney followed a link to the Vanguard website. At face value, it appeared to be a corporate lobby group. The word 'boutique' was bandied about a lot. Sydney clicked on the 'services' tab at the top of the page. So they were more than just lobbyists, they offered a range of services for those wanting to influence Government policy. Campaign coordination, policy experts, legal services, marketing and advertising.

Call us. All enquiries handled with the utmost discretion.

Sydney yawned. She returned to the Google search page and clicked another link.

Justin Haig ran the London Marathon in 3:23. Whoop dee doo. So far, Sydney was bored and saw nothing worthy of a cryptic delivery. She visited Justin Haig's Facebook profile but it was mostly private. His twitter account was active, but his tweets were all about the latest Xbox game release.

Sydney clicked back to the image of Justin Haig's business card. She picked up the phone and stabbed out Haig's cell phone number. It rang through to his answering service.

"Hello Justin, I'm calling from Passion Media. My name is Sydney Stone. When you have time for a quick chat, could you call me on 555 32874. Thank you so much."

Sydney hung up. She checked the clock and gave herself a pat on the back for not thinking about Denton Cole. And how he hadn't stood her up for their lunch date. Because it wasn't a date.

Damn it Sydney. Get a grip!

She returned to the Vanguard website and with nothing better to do, clicked on their contact page.

Sydney arranged the paper clips on their magnetic holder and waited for her call to be answered. She was ready to hang up when a flustered voice rushed at her.

"Vanguard, Minnie speaking, how can I help?"

"Hello Minnie, Sydney Stone here." Sydney worked to keep her voice neutral and non-threatening. "I'm a journalist with Passion Business Magazine."

"If you're calling to complain about the press release, I'm sorry." The girl on the end of the phone couldn't have sounded less apologetic. "The thing is, the boundaries only changed last week, and no one told me there was an issue with the map." Sydney listened to the girl on the other end drone on about council land being reassigned for housing.

"The allocations weren't in dispute until after the map was dispatched and I—,"

"Hold up Minnie," Sydney interrupted. "I don't really give a toss about the zoning boundary thing. To be honest it sounds incredibly boring."

"Oh! Thank god," Minnie sighed, "And it is *so* boring. Some people need to get out more."

"I actually called to speak with Mr Haig. Is he available?" Sydney asked.

"No, because *apparently* he's on leave." Sydney could hear the annoyance in the girl's voice. "Nice for some isn't it. Swanning off on a holiday. Don't worry about telling Minnie. No, she'll just run the front desk, make the coffee, do the typing, fix the photocopier and spend all morning reorganising appointments. Not a problem."

Yes, a problem. Sydney Stone liked other people's problems.

"It's so annoying when that happens," she told her new friend Minnie. Then she waited. Sometimes it was best to let the Minnie's of the world do the talking, without interruption.

"Mr Haig didn't tell me and he's usually so nice. I mean, I guess he's been a bit weird lately, but I thought that was just this snap election stress. All this extra system security stuff the clients asked for. He's really a nice guy, actually cares about the people in the community. Like he helped my friend, Jimmy, at the bakery. Mr Haig helped him do all his accounts, didn't get paid anything. It's all changed now Mr Randall's in the office, with his years of experience and his political connections." Minnie sighed. "Apparently he's worked for Vanguard for years, but I swear he'd never set foot in the office before they set a date for the by-election. Now he's here every day, drinking the good coffee and bossing me around. Like I've got all the time in the world to call up his car cleaning service and go out and get his egg sandwiches."

Sydney laughed.

"Oh shit," Minnie cried. "You're not gonna print any of this, are you? Is it off the record? I'll lose my job for sure if you do. I know I was supposed to say off the record first, but I'm already in trouble for the stupid mapping thing."

"Don't worry Minnie," Sydney assured the girl. "We'll call it letting off steam, and keep it just between us. I've had crap bosses in my time, and I know how stressful it can be."

There wasn't much of a story there anyway. No doubt the hand-delivered USB stick was from some local political nut job creating drama about the electorate boundaries. Probably sent the same USB stick to all the local media. All she'd uncovered was a zoning mix up and this Justin Haig taking an impromptu holiday. Big deal.

The zoning thing was something a community paper might have time to chase. She could flick it on to one of her contacts. But she'd leave her conversation with Minnie out of it. The girl seemed nice.

"Do you know when Haig will be back?"

"Who knows," Minnie said. "He left in such a hurry. I bet Randall blamed him for the zoning thing. Mr Haig blasted in here this morning, wouldn't even look me in the eye. Just asked me to help him find his passport and then he was gone."

"Passport," Sydney mused, "You think he was heading overseas?"

"Well I guess that's what passports are for," the girl laughed.

"Good point," Sydney laughed too.

"All I know is Mr Haig is gone, Randall and some other guy in a suit have been locked in his office all morning, and if I don't get over to the cafe and pick up the sandwiches, my job search will become a whole lot more urgent."

"I hope your desk drawer is full of chocolate – or vodka, and thanks for your help Minnie." Sydney rang off.

She scanned the list she'd scribbled on her desk pad.

Justin Haig
Election
Zoning issues
Mr Randall
Holiday – passport
Vanguard
Jim at bakery

Then she wrote three questions;

Who is Randall?
Where is Haig?
Who cares?

Sydney paused for a moment, then scribbled out the last question and said,

"You care, Sydney. It's your job to sweat the small stuff."

She was working hard on a doodle of a mouse carrying a daisy when a gentle knock on the door was followed by Denton Cole.

"Lunch," he said. A statement not a question.

"I'm a bit busy. I'm working on something. It just came across my desk this morning," Sydney replied primly.

"Work on it while you eat." Denton Cole waited but Sydney stayed in her seat.

"Would you like to come to lunch with me Miss Stone? Of course, Mr Cole, that would be lovely." Sydney smiled her sarcasm across her desk.

"I've told you to call me Denton. And I'm sorry if I was rude. It's been a long morning. Sydney Stone, I would be honoured if you would accompany me to the sandwich place around the corner, where I will buy you the works, minus the onion."

"How do you know I don't like onions?" Sydney asked.

"You're not the only one with investigative skills." Denton reached behind the door and took Sydney's coat from the hook. "Your friend who guards the biscuits told me."

Matilda and her big mouth. With slight trepidation, Sydney came out from behind her desk.

"I don't suppose saying no is an option?" she asked. Denton Cole simply raised his eyebrows and held out her coat.

Sydney let Denton slide her coat over her shoulders. His hands were warm on her neck as he folded out the collar. Heat travelled through her body. Her legs felt weak and for a split second, Sydney imagined leaning back into Denton's arms.

She took her cell phone from her desk and shoved it in her pocket. Sydney turned to face Denton, expecting him to move towards the door. But he held his ground, his eyes locked on the scribbles on her desk pad.

"Cute mouse."

"I doodle when I think," Sydney was defensive. "I really am working on something."

"So am I," Denton replied, looking up to meet her gaze. Sydney locked into his stormy blue eyes and swallowed hard. Denton smiled, then turned towards the door.

"Let's go, I'm starving.

6

Denton was shocked to see Justin Haig's name printed clear as day in Sydney's neat handwriting. She'd missed the few seconds it took him to rearrange his face and act like nothing was wrong.

He welcomed the sharp bite of winter air as they walked along the street in silence. He needed to work out how to handle the situation. But Sydney Stone was an enormous distraction. This edgy, intriguing journalist had drawn him in and stirred him up. Just last night he'd finished his pint with Harvey, gone straight up to his apartment and Googled Sydney Stone. He'd read a few of her stories, appreciated the directness of her writing, the subtle humour she injected into otherwise boring topics. One article detailed her attendance at a particularly dull Government meeting, something to do with tax law, where a toddler had wandered in, made her way to the front of the room, and cried out to the Minister of Finance, 'Stop talking already!'

Denton remembered Sydney had mentioned in her article she'd been moments away from doing the exact same thing.

He watched her as she stomped down the pavement beside him, her chin lifted and her shoulders back. He smiled when she felt his gaze.

"What?"

"Nothing," he grinned. The fire in her eyes gave her an air of confidence and determination. He liked it. Denton didn't doubt for a moment that she'd call out a boring Minister of Parliament who was getting on her nerves.

But if Sydney was investigating Haig, there was going to be trouble. He was her boss. Which meant he should probably not give in to the temptation to press her against the cool brick wall and kiss her perfect red lips.

Denton reached for the door of the cafe, but Sydney got there first.

"After you Mr Cole," she smiled sweetly. He walked in ahead of her and slid effortlessly between the tables and people milling around with dockets, waiting for their orders. He'd cleared tables at Marco's Deli for two summers in high school and loved that it was exactly the same as he left it when he'd gone off to university. The smell of garlic and tomatoes. Pavarotti's smooth voice rising up over the lunchtime chatter, from the same CD that played on a loop all day, every day. Denton paused by the kitchen and beckoned Sydney over.

He pulled open the door and returned her sweet smile.

"After you, Sydney."

The kitchen staff bustled about, and Denton took the sleeve of Sydney's coat and dragged her closer to him, so they weren't in the way.

"Marco!" Denton called out, and the familiar small man with salt and pepper hair appeared from the walk-in freezer. He grabbed Denton in a bear hug and attempted to lift him off the ground. A joke they'd shared since Denton turned 13 and grew an inch and a half taller than Marco.

"You are back here in London. How long this time? You zip in and out. I can never keep up!"

"What can I say, the business keeps me busy."

"Always with the ants in your pants!" Marco grinned. "Tell me, how is your father?"

"He's on a yacht in the Bahamas."

"You stop telling tales."

"He's built a retirement village in Kent, which he presides over like a king."

"That's more like it," Marco nodded.

"But he's talking about buying my mother a yacht for her 65th birthday. So I'd say they're both happy."

Marco slapped Denton on the back and laughed.

"Their very own love boat! And who is this lovely woman?" Marco took Sydney's hands. "You have finally found a wife to make your mother and father proud?" the chef asked.

"I'm not," Sydney started, but Marco carried on.

"I predict many babies, to make your Mamas happy."

Sydney took a startled step back and connected with a tall man carrying a huge metal bowl of grated carrot. It flew skywards and rained down on them all like confetti.

"God, I'm so sorry." Sydney's face turned as red hot as the chilli salsa being prepared in front of them.

"Marco stop being naughty. You know I'm not married. Have you seen a wedding invitation?"

"No, but this is a good omen," Marco winked at Sydney who was shaking grated carrot from her hair, "Like confetti outside a church! Louis will have that cleaned up in no time." And to his credit, Louis was already on his hands and knees and had scooped up most of the mess.

"Don't worry, Signora. Here we don't sweat the small stuff." Louis smiled up at her. "It's okay!" He rose up and went off to find another bowl of carrots, Denton supposed.

"Come on, this way." He took Sydney's hand and felt his breath catch. She felt it too. Her cheeks flushed. He'd only meant to lead her through the kitchen, and really hadn't expected the pleasure of her delicate fingers warming in his hand. How long had it been since he'd held someone's hand?

At the back of the kitchen Denton reluctantly let go of Sydney's hand and they climbed a narrow staircase. At the top of the stairs he turned the door handle and eased it open, revealing the small open-plan loft space he'd always loved.

They were bathed in a warm, familiar glow from the skylight, that filled the middle section of the long thin roof above.

"Marco is an old friend. My father helped him set up this place." Denton shrugged off his coat. Sydney was still hovering in the doorway.

"Come on. Take off your coat. It gets pretty warm up here."

She looked nervous as she scanned the room. The kitchen to their left was state of the art. A large stainless-steel fridge filled one corner, and beside it a matching industrial sized oven sat beneath an oversized bench top.

"I stayed here for a couple of summers when I was younger. Back then it had a butcher's block and a tiny fridge that rattled all night."

One side of the counter was set with placemats, cutlery and long-stemmed glasses, with two leather stools, tucked beneath. Denton threw his coat across the arm of the small couch. It was the only other piece of furniture in the small space.

"I thought you said a sandwich at the cafe around the corner." He watched her as she cautiously undid the buttons on her coat.

"Sandwiches are coming," he assured her. "Drink?" he asked, opening the fridge.

"Look," Sydney sighed, "I don't drink during work hours, and this feels kind of,—" she paused to search for the right word.

"Intimate," she settled on. "And I'm not sure what you've got planned"—her cheeks flushed—"I'm not saying you've got something you know, *not business,* planned. But…"

Denton couldn't help smiling. She was right, the room was intimate, and there was an undeniably *not business-like* feeling that seemed to exist, regardless of where they were. Her office, the staff kitchen. The location really didn't seem to matter. It wouldn't take much to pull her down on to the couch. He pulled out one of the stools instead and sat down. He leaned an elbow on the marble countertop, loosened his tie and undid the top button of his shirt. He smiled at Sydney, and let the seconds lag a little. Enjoyed a moment playing chicken with this intense woman, who in the last 24 hours had filled more space in his thoughts than anything or anyone else.

"What I have planned, Sydney, is to either pour you a soda, or a glass of orange juice, or I may get really wild and mix the two together." He laughed then and shrugged his shoulders.

"Sorry. It's just this," Sydney waved her arm around, "and I thought you were offering me wine," she slid off her coat and placed it beside Denton's.

"Let's try this again shall we?" He'd not met anyone quite like her before, and he really didn't want to make her uncomfortable. "Come have a seat."

She perched stiffly on the edge of the stool beside him. It was the closest their bodies had been, and Denton busied himself pouring soda and juice into the two glasses. *Just be normal mate.*

He took a sip from his own glass and slid the other gently across the counter.

"It's just juice. I promise," Denton grinned.

"Oh for goodness sake," Sydney growled. She grabbed the glass and took a long drink.

When she stared defiantly at Denton, he held her gaze. *You're not getting to me either Sydney Stone.*

A sensational lie. He wanted to undo each button of her silk shirt, slowly and carefully. He let his eyes wander. Imagined running his thumb over the lace edge of her bra.

Where is Haig? The note on Sydney's desk pad popped into his head.

Damn it. Business before pleasure.

"More ice?" Denton asked, adding plenty of frozen cubes to his own glass.

The knock on the door startled them both.

"Sandwiches," Denton laughed, his fingers gently touching her elbow when he stood.

They ate in relative silence. Denton was pleased to have something to focus on, even if it was just chewing and swallowing.

"This is amazing," Sydney mumbled through a mouthful of cheese and chicken. She was dropping blobs of cranberry sauce on to her plate and mopping them up with her finger. Denton longed to take that finger and lick it clean.

"Best sandwiches in the world," he said. *Shall we fold out the couch?*

"Well it's no cheese and marmite," Sydney threw back.

"British or Kiwi?" Denton asked.

"I've never been south of the equator," Sydney admitted.

"I spend a lot of time in New Zealand," Denton explained. "The marmite there is like black tar, but if you can get past that, it's far superior."

"I think I'll take your word for it." Sydney laughed.

"My word," Denton said, "is actually what I needed to talk to you about."

Sydney wiped her mouth with a napkin. Denton tapped his fingers on the marble counter and took a deep breath.

"I have a friend," he started. "He's in a bit of a precarious position."

"I'm listening," Sydney said.

"Is that your work face?" Denton asked.

"Maybe," Sydney laughed. "Matilda calls it my, *I love kittens and small children, so you can trust me* look. It happens automatically now. I used to be a bit overeager," Sydney admitted. "I kind of had to learn to arrange my face in a way that didn't scare people away."

"You want your face to say, I'm interested, but I won't sell my Grandmother for your story."

"Exactly! So tell me about your friend."

"Funny thing, I don't have a story for you." Denton paused for a moment. But there was no other way.

"It's sort of the opposite."

Sydney looked confused.

"You know I'm a journalist, yes? So the opposite of a story really doesn't sound that appealing."

"Okay. This is tricky." Denton chose a spot just behind Sydney's left ear to avoid eye contact.

"I have a friend, someone who needs to keep a low profile for a couple of weeks. He may have come up on your radar. But he doesn't need any media attention."

"You're asking me to keep someone *out* of the news?"

"He's done nothing wrong, I promise."

"Who is he?" Sydney asked.

"Someone who was in the wrong place at the right time. Or maybe it's the other way around. But he's caught the attention of some very nasty individuals,"
Denton explained.

"Who is he?" Sydney asked again. "I can't put your friend in, or keep him out of the news if you don't tell me his name."

"Haig," Denton said. Her face changed as the dots connected.

"Justin Haig. Vanguard. Security Analyst."

"Yes, that's him."

"I got an anonymous tip. Just this morning."

"Yes. I assume they're trying to flush him out."

"Who are?" Sydney asked.

"I'm not sure yet."

"What has Haig done to upset them?"

"I can't say."

"Do you know where he is?" Sydney asked.

"Sort of," Denton admitted. "Not exactly. But—"

"You can't say?" Sydney finished Denton's sentence. The sarcasm was clear.

"Wherever he is, he needed his passport to get there," Sydney finished the juice in her glass.

If Denton wasn't so annoyed about Haig being chased down, he'd probably have been impressed with how fast Sydney worked.

"Can I ask how you know that?"

"I can't say," Sydney threw back.

"Who've you talked to?" Denton asked.

"I can't say," Sydney responded but the small twitch at the corner of her lips gave her away. She was sparring with him. Damn he'd like to play. But now wasn't the time.

"These people aren't playing games Sydney. I don't want to pull rank, especially when I've only been here five minutes. But I am your boss," Denton tried to keep a measured tone.

"You should probably tell me what you know."

"Or what? You'll have me fired?"

Denton hadn't thought that far ahead. He was only just getting to know how Passion Media worked. Last thing he needed was to lose Sydney Stone. But he needed to know if Haig had been exposed. He offered a simple shrug in response.

"You willing to risk it?"

The awkward silence that followed wasn't pleasant. Perhaps it wasn't such a great idea, letting her think he was a grade A bastard who dictated terms and had people fired if they didn't do what he wanted. But Haig was his best mate, a brother through his boarding school years. They'd been each other's guard dog for as long as there were dorks in the dining hall or seniors on night raids. Haig needed Denton to protect him right now. That was all there was to it.

When Sydney finally spoke, there was steel in her voice that Denton hadn't heard before.

"I guess that's how it works in your world." Sydney kept her eyes on her half eaten sandwich. "I spoke to his receptionist. And I'd like to tell you I'm special, but she seems the type that likes to share."

"Damn it." Denton ran a hand through his hair. "Have you talked to anyone else about this?" he asked.

Sydney glared at Denton.

"No. You demanded I join you for lunch so I haven't looked deeper. Yet," Sydney murmured.

"I know it's a lot to ask," Denton said. "But I need you to take a step back from this."

"I don't even know what *this* is." Sydney cried. "I'm an investigative journalist. And you're asking me to kill a story?"

"I can't tell you to stop looking into Haig."

"No, you can't. There's that small problem of freedom of the press." Sarcasm was supposedly the lowest form of wit, but Sydney wasn't laughing.

"I was just hoping you could hold off until I can settle things down, and then we could work something out. I could give you full access," Denton offered.

"Access to what?" Sydney demanded.

"I'm sorry," Denton shook his head. He placed a hand on Sydney's arm but she brushed it away.

"Sydney, this is a serious situation. And I give you my word. I'll tell you everything as soon as I can. I like you Sydney, I feel like there's something here, but I just. I really hate having to do this…" Denton didn't know what else to say.

For a moment he thought he'd seen Sydney's face soften, but without warning, her stool scraped along the floor and she stood up.

"Tell me, Denton, do you bring all your staff to secret rooms for private lunch dates? Or is it just the women?"

"What?" Denton rose from his own stool, "I'm not sure what—,"

"You're charming, I'll give you that. But I don't get my stories this way. I don't make sordid deals in back rooms with arrogant men who think the world owes them a favour. I'm not going weak at the knees, no matter how good looking you are."

"You think I brought you here to," Denton paused for a moment trying to find the right words, "to distract you?"

He watched Sydney grab her coat from the couch.

"I'll take your request under advisement," she told him. "I think I should go now, Mr Cole."

"Sydney," Denton raised his voice. "I'm not who you think I am. I don't play games. This room, yes, I wanted somewhere private. But only because I couldn't risk someone hearing us talk about this."

"What is this?" Sydney asked again. "What is Haig involved in that you won't tell me about?"

"I'm sorry Sydney," Denton dropped his arms. "I can't."

"Then neither can I," Sydney shrugged. "I'm leaving now."

"Hey," Denton called to her when she reached the door.

"Just so we're clear, I do not make a habit of wining and dining women in secret rooms during my lunch breaks."

He watched her nod tightly.

Her feet clattered down the stairs.

But for you Sydney Stone? I'd be very tempted to make an exception.

7

Sydney dearly wished she could have thrown a clever retort at Denton Cole. But her flight instinct had kicked in, and she'd run away, back to the office, like a timid schoolgirl.Her breath was short and shallow and she gripped the arms of her office chair to stop her trembling hands. Did he really think she'd believe he wasn't playing her? It had to be Denton Cole's attempt to keep her focus away from the Haig story. Not that Sydney had any idea what the Haig's story was. Before lunch, she'd been ready to give the whole thing up for dead.

Sydney quickly checked her laptop. The USB stick was right where she left it, poking out from the connection point. She pulled it out and shoved it in her top drawer. Her notes from her phone call with Minnie were still on the desk pad in front of her. Haig's name was right there at the top. She ripped the page off the desk pad, folded it into a small square and stuffed it in her handbag.

"Afternoon boss-lady." Matilda clattered through the door sending Sydney stumbling backward.

"Jumpy much?" Matilda laughed. "I saw you heading out for lunch with Mr Cole," she winked. "Give me the goss and I'll tell you where I hide the quality toilet paper."

Sydney plonked herself down in her chair.

"Nothing much to tell really," Sydney told Matilda. "He's boring. Talked a lot about fiscal responsibility. And revenue streams." Sydney kept her voice even and her face blank. If Denton Cole wanted the Haig story hushed up, she would need to keep any further digging close to her chest.

"No! I could have sworn he looked like the smouldering, eating chocolate mousse off you in bed type. I was hoping he'd taken you for a spin in his helicopter. Instead, you're telling me he's just an accountant in disguise?" Sydney nodded. Matilda would be breathless with delight if she knew Denton had held her hand, and had taken her to a private apartment for lunch. But Sydney was never going to sleep her way up the career ladder. Especially not with Denton Cole.

"What's that orange stuff in your hair?" Matilda asked.

"Carrot," Sydney couldn't help it, a laugh escaped.

"Did you bump into Bugs Bunny?" Matilda asked.

"A busy waiter." Sydney shook her copper coloured curls over her desk and flakes of orange fell around her.

"Denton never said anything," she cried. "I had carrot in my hair all through lunch!"

"Maybe he was thinking about other stuff." Matilda raised her eyebrows. Sydney ignored Matilda's suggestive look and shook the last of the carrot out of her hair.

"The eyes are useless when the mind is blind," Matilda replied flatly.

"What?" Sydney screwed her face up.

"Pinterest." Matilda held her hands in prayer, her fingertips under her chin.

Sydney rolled her eyes.

"He likes you."

"Don't you have work to do, Matilda?"

But work was still the furthest thing from Sydney's mind as she found herself replaying her lunch with Denton over and over again.

She'd seen plenty of really nice, but really desperate people try to cover up a story. And those at the top had the furthest to fall. The room above the deli was a little too convenient, and though Denton's explanation, of needing a private space to talk, was reasonable, it was still an incredibly intimate situation. He'd held her hand, and the way he'd looked at her. She flushed remembering how her nipples had hardened at his lingering gaze. How he'd perched on that bar stool, as if inviting her to slide between his powerful thighs and...

And what?

Sydney felt foolish.

She'd dropped her guard and followed Denton up those stairs like an eager puppy. How could she let her desire get the better of her professional judgement? She had always said the one and only thing she'd learned from her father, was how to spot a liar a mile away.

She hardened her resolve. She would not be that gullible again.

She retrieved the USB stick and plugged it back into her laptop. Then she opened LinkedIn and pulled up the photo from Justin Haig's profile.

It didn't make sense. The small amount of digging Sydney did that morning lead nowhere. Yes, Haig was a Vanguard employee. Politics could be a murky business. But he was a plebe in political circles. He wasn't a candidate or a sitting Member of Parliament. What could he have done to deserve attention from, what had Denton called them? Nasty individuals?

The worst part of it all was that Sydney had enjoyed lunch with Denton. There was something between them, he'd almost said so himself. And she'd started to relax in his presence. But Denton had set her up.

There was no way she couldn't tell him what she knew about Haig. Her career was everything to Sydney. She couldn't risk being fired. Denton Cole would surely know that. He had her cornered. If she killed her investigation, what did that say about her professional ethics? But if she carried on, and withheld that information, Denton Cole could take away the one thing she had worked so hard for.

Sydney straightened her shoulders. *Back to basics. Start with what you know.*

Denton was worried about Haig. But what she didn't know was why. And Sydney Stone had made her career out of asking, and answering the whys.

She knew what she had to do, but for the first time in her career, Sydney felt nervous. When it came to Denton Cole, she knew she wasn't 100% in control of her feelings. But Sydney could iron it out. She was a normal woman, and not completely immune to the effects of a good looking man. Denton Cole, with his moody blue eyes and muscular physique, had roused a physical response in Sydney.

"Purely physical," Sydney told her stapler. Even Matilda, who was practically living with her DJ boyfriend, had swooned. All the helicopter talk and noticing his Italian footwear. But Sydney needed to keep her emotions in check.

But the way he looked at me when I drank his stupid juice. He was smouldering. Sydney let out a shaky breath. Would a shared temptation be harder to ignore?

Sydney rested her head on her desk. Less than a day ago, her life had been simple.

She'd had men before. She wasn't a completely crazy cat lady, *yet.* But Sydney always chose carefully. The men in her life had all understood her work came first, and she was careful to keep her guard up. She did not mix home and office. She did not date fellow journalists. Or photographers, or guys from PR, or media executives for that matter. Regardless of the propositions she passed off at work functions. She always took particular care to avoid the drunk married men, some of whom seemed to think a three-day conference in Manchester and a king size bed at the Holiday Inn gave them a free pass from their wedding vows.

Sydney didn't need a man. She wasn't waiting for someone to come and put a ring on her finger. That was the last thing she wanted. Relationships were best kept simple. She always operated with a clear understanding that any relationship entered into was temporary in nature. Sydney liked to be in control of her life.

Her problem right now, was that anytime she got near Denton Cole, the rules she'd always lived by lost their clout. She closed her eyes.

"I need a plan," she whispered to herself. "Keep it simple sister."

Sydney Stone does not believe in love at first sight. She believes in hard work, success, and self-sufficiency. She does not have office affairs. Denton Cole was her boss and that meant he was out of bounds. She would file any and all non-work related Denton Cole feelings away, somewhere way in the back of her mind. Preferably in a large grey metal filing cabinet, one with an industrial strength lock. He could dwell there, in a dusty back corner.

Denton Cole was under an embargo.

8

"Sydney?" Her eyes flew open, as did the drawer of her imaginary filing cabinet.

Denton Cole stood before her. Her heart hammered and Sydney fought the urge to cry out in frustration.

"Sorry for interrupting. I just wanted to check you were okay, you know, after earlier."

His concern seemed real, but Sydney didn't care.

"I'm fine," she replied briskly. "Busy."

"You don't seem fine," Denton pointed out. "You seem tense."

Sydney straightened her back. She remained glued to her chair, willing her body to receive the message that Denton Cole was off limits. She watched him step into her office and gently close the door. Her eyes followed his every move as he picked up a chair, and moved with it around her desk, placing it down beside Sydney.

Denton took hold of the arms of Sydney's swivel chair and turned her. They sat face to face with their knees touching.

"I think we should have a wee chat about personal space," Sydney cried.

"I agree, Sydney. We should."

Her body craved the closeness of this man, and yet she was filled with anger and resentment. How could he blunder into her office like this, after asking her to put aside her professional integrity?

"Back there, it wasn't what you thought. I came to Passion Media thinking Sydney Stone was some old bloke with grey hair and a little pencil tucked behind his ear."

"Because women can't be investigative journalists? Because we should all be at home having babies and ironing shirts?" Sydney demanded. "Or maybe you think we're all just biding time at our day jobs, not really caring about our careers. Because we're all just waiting for the man-studs to come and make honest women of us."

"Is that the impression I've given you?" Denton asked. "I guess, maybe, I can see how you might have travelled there. I did ask you to a private lunch, and I did ask you to drop the story. But I promise all I'm trying to do is protect a friend."

"You've asked me to put aside my integrity, to do exactly the opposite of what I'm paid to do. To do that you must think I'm playing at being a journalist. You must have been so pleased when you met me. Sydney Stone turns out to be a female reporter, and it's so much easier for you. You don't need to share any information. You don't have to trust her. You can just take her out for lunch, smile at her, make sexy eyes in her direction, and she'll swoon."

Denton grinned.

"Swoon?"

Sydney raised her eyebrows.

"If you think any of this is easy for me Sydney, you're sorely mistaken."

"Tell me, would you have taken a male reporter to such an intimate place? Would you have asked a male reporter to blindly trust you, like you did me? Or would you have popped down to the local gentlemen's club and discussed it over cigars?"

"I don't smoke cigars," Denton informed Sydney.

"Oh for goodness sake. The golf club then?"

"I don't know," Denton admitted. He shook his head. "Nothing I do around you makes any sense."

Sydney saw Denton lean forward, and when his lips gently touched her own, all sense and restraint were completely forgotten. Denton pulled back and paused, millimetres from her mouth. His hand was warm on her thigh; his other gripped the arm of her chair. Her mind a void, Sydney closed her eyes, and Denton's mouth quickly met her own again.

Sydney felt every nerve ending alight as Denton's teeth grazed her lower lip. His hand was warm on the back of her neck, and she clung to the front of his shirt, her lips pressed into his. She could barely breathe and hardly cared. Over and over his tongue found her own, unfurling a passion deep within Sydney that just moments earlier she had been determined to squash. His hand brushed her breast and she heard herself groan, knew she had crossed some invisible line. But Sensible Sydney had no say. She was incapable of anything resembling common sense, so she tightened her grip on his shirt, and kissed him harder.

"Sydney? The door's locked. Come open it." Matilda rattled the door handle. Sydney and Denton pulled apart.

"You locked the door?" Sydney hissed. Her heart was thumping.

"Not on purpose," Denton whispered. "But probably a good thing."

She tried to read his face as he stood and straightened his shirt, quickly moving his chair back to its correct place on the other side of the desk. Denton gave her a nod before he reached for the door and swung it open.

9

"Bloody hell you two, I've only got you the proper coffee and biscuits," Matilda clattered the tray down on Sydney's desk.

"My fault," Denton apologised. "I must have bumped the lock."

"If you'd left me out there much longer, I'd have been fighting off those advertising snobs. And don't think they'd care for a moment that you're their boss, Mr Cole. They'd claw their way over you for a Ristretto. The fact that you look like George Clooney would only make them more excited." Matilda grinned at Sydney, who failed miserably at appearing relaxed.

She twiddled the handles of the coffee mugs on the tray and shifted the milk jug slightly to the left. No one said anything and Matilda loved every second of the silence. She left it a little longer just to bask in the awkwardness.

"Well then," she said at last, "I'll let you get back to it then. Unless you need anything else?" Matilda caught every furtive glance dart back and forth between Denton and Sydney.

"No, nothing else, this is great." Sydney was working hard to sound normal.

"Thanks, Matilda," Denton nodded. "I'll have to walk with mine. Finance and HR are about to throwdown over the errors in that new software install. Sorry to rush off Sydney, we'll continue this later?"

Sydney nodded. Matilda watched Sydney watch Denton spoon two sugars into one of the coffee mugs and take four biscuits from the plate.

"Ladies before Gentlemen," Denton offered and stood back to let Matilda leave the office before him.

"Age before beauty," Matilda smiled and perched on the edge of Sydney's desk. She wasn't going anywhere.

"I asked for that one," Denton shrugged and strolled off down the hallway.

"You talk to all your bosses like that?" Sydney laughed, taking the other cup of coffee from the tray with only a slightly shaky hand. But Matilda caught the wobble.

"Only the ones who've been *kissing* each other!" Matilda transferred her bottom from the corner of the desk to the chair Denton Cole had recently vacated. She took one of the biscuits and split it in two, licking the icing from the middle.

"What are you talking about?" Sydney shuffled back in her seat and made a fuss of adding sugar to her coffee. "We weren't," she tried, but Matilda held her hand up.

"You so were," she declared. "Your lipstick's all smudged."

Sydney put her coffee down and shifted uncomfortably in her chair, resisting the urge to wipe her hand across her mouth.

"No, it's not."

"Oh but it is. And the door was locked, and you both looked all hot and bothered when I walked in. And his shirt was untucked. And your face is all flushed."

"You've been watching reruns of The Mentalist again, haven't you?" Sydney tried.

"I don't need special powers to see what was going on in here Syd. Denton Cole's hot. You're a babe. Don't look so panicked," Matilda tried to reassure her friend. "I won't put it on the staff Facebook page or anything. Your secret is safe with me."

"Nothing is happening. Nothing is going to happen," Sydney rushed to convince her friend.

"Why the hell not? I bet he's a good kisser." Matilda watched the colour rise in Sydney's cheeks again.

So. Syd had finally been bitten by the love bug. Matilda often wondered why her friend hid her heart away, and if anyone would ever be able to break open the lock she'd placed on it. Now Matilda was taking a great deal of joy in seeing Sydney so flustered. She could think of no one more perfect than the sexy and determined Denton Cole, to take a crack at the challenge that was Sydney Stone.

"He's my boss," Sydney tried to reason, "And anyway, it's complicated."

Matilda placed her own hand over her friend's, and smiled.

"It always is Babe."

10

The sun set un-noticed beyond her office window as Sydney worked on the false SPF rating labels on some of the big brands of sunscreen.

She poured over the research Passion had commissioned and worked it into her story. *This is my happy place. Reveal the truth, back it up with facts and figures.* Sydney liked it best when she could help screw over the people who most deserved it. Her fingers stabbed at the keyboard a little harder than usual.

At 9pm she emailed the article to legal, collected her coat from the hook on the back of her door and headed for the lift. She scanned the floor for Denton but was disappointed. He'd left without coming back to see her.

How irritating that she was looking for him at all. It was best to stay away from Denton Cole. She liked to investigate *other* people's complications. She did not enjoy being involved in them herself.

"We must stop meeting like this!" Sydney called to Carmen, the cleaner who worked most nights on the fifth floor. Carmen backed her trolley out of the lift. Their work often brought them together in the hallways of Passion Media, Sydney looking for coffee and Carmen working her night shift job so she could study for her teaching qualifications. But this wasn't Carmen. It was another woman, younger.

"Oh, I'm sorry. Is Carmen not in today?" Sydney asked. The woman shook her head.

"Is she okay?"

The younger woman shrugged and looked around.

"Your first time on level five?" Sydney asked. The cleaner nodded.

"No one's s'posed to be here," she said, looking at her feet.

"Sometimes we work late, we're a media company so there are publishing deadlines. But we're all friendly, and we don't mind working around you." Sydney tried to ease the woman's obvious nervousness.

"Your first day?"

"Yeah, kind of." The girl kept on staring at her shoes.

"Don't worry, we're not slobs like those guys on level four," Sydney laughed while she slipped past the woman and her trolley. In the lift, Sydney held the door open.

"Carmen usually does the reception desk first." Sydney waved towards Matilda's desk, at the stack of coffee cups collected up before her friend had left. The new cleaner looked unimpressed. Her eyes flicked over the wilting banana peel that lay beside the mugs. Sydney adjusted her laptop bag and pushed the ground floor button.

"See you!" Sydney called. The cleaner pulled out Carmen's feather duster and swished it over a fake pot plant. The doors to the lift closed.

Sydney had fallen in love with the industrial style of her apartment building in Canary Wharf the first time she saw it. The exposed brick and steel stairways of its previous life remained, and she loved the way each apartment opened off a large circular atrium filled with tropical plants. Not to mention the huge glass ceiling above the common area, letting in a ton of natural light. Sydney knew she would live at Oasis Apartments before she'd even seen inside her small, one room home.

But today she grumbled as she unlocked her door. She noticed the dust on the butterfly palm by her front door and the bag of rubbish she'd forgotten to take out that morning. She dumped her handbag on the floor, grabbed the rubbish sack and stomped down to the rubbish chute.

When she'd been little, her mother had often referred to Sydney's after school mood as 'tired but wired.' That's exactly how she felt.

Kissing Denton Cole had set a fire deep within Sydney, and though she was determined not to fuel any flames, the memory of his touch, his hand on her thigh, his lips on hers, was all it took to stoke the embers of passion. The mix of pleasure and frustration was intolerable for Sydney. She shoved the bag of rubbish down the chute and slammed the door shut. Her desire was best directed into finding out exactly what was going on with Justin Haig. That was more important than any romantic notion of hooking up with Denton Cole. He was getting in the way and she couldn't believe she was letting him.

Back in her apartment, Sydney closed her front door, then froze.

The lights and heat were pre-set, so it was neither cold nor dark inside, but she felt the urge to stop and listen. Sometimes, living alone, Sydney's overactive imagination ran away with itself. Had someone slipped in while she was putting out the rubbish? Was someone hiding in her closet? Had they pressed themselves in behind the bathroom door? She shivered. Then her coat pocket sprang to life, buzzing and ringing. Sydney squealed and yanked her cell phone out, watched it tumble onto the carpet. She bent down and rolled her eyes at the breaking news notification flashing on her screen. One of the less well-known members of the Royal family was engaged.

"Today can bite my arse!" Sydney scooped her phone up and threw it on the couch.

She kicked her heels off and headed for the kitchen. She grinned. When her neighbour Alfie worked night shifts at the hospital, Sydney hung out with his cat Cornflake. If left alone overnight, Cornflake showed his displeasure by relieving himself in every corner of Alfie's apartment. Except the corner with his litter tray. Sydney liked the company, even if it was four-legged.

"Good evening Colonel Cornflake. All quiet on the Western Front?" She was rewarded with a low growl. Cornflake pressed his ears back and continued glaring out the window. He hated when Blossom, the one-eyed tabby from upstairs, sat on the fire escape and stared at him.

Sydney bent her knees and looked up through the window to the apartment above, where she could see Blossom's front paws and whiskers barely over the edge of the top metal step.

"I'm a bit on edge too," Sydney told Cornflake. "Enemy at the gates. But if you don't mention Denton Cole, I won't mention Blossom. Or that bejewelled collar Alfie's got you wearing."

She reached into the fridge and retrieved a half bottle of Sav, twisted off the top and took a slug from the bottle, then grabbed a glass and a bag of cheese and onion crisps from the pantry.

She plonked down on her very old, very comfortable, faded grey couch. Cornflake, always interested in licking the flavouring off a potato crisp, followed Sydney, turning circles on her lap until he settled on a comfortable position. He purred loudly. Sydney scratched his chin.

She found Graham Norton on TV and used the pizza app on her phone to order dinner.

ROCHELLE ELLIOT
"It's a razzle, dazzle night for us Cornflake!"

ROCHELLE ELLIOT
"It's a razzle, dazzle night for us Cornflake!"

11

In his black and chrome man cave in the centre of the city, Denton Cole stripped off his sweat-soaked gym gear. He stared at himself in the mirror while the steam from the shower slowly filled the small bathroom.

"What are you doing?" He asked his reflection before it disappeared behind a layer of fog.

He could still feel the softness of her lips, the way she'd clung to him, sunk into his kiss. Who knows where they'd have ended up if Matilda hadn't clattered on the door. Terrible timing. Or perhaps she'd saved them both. He'd never been caught with his pants down in the office, but if there was ever a good time for that to happen, he assumed two days after taking over Passion wasn't it.

But Sydney Stone was something else. He could barely be near her without wanting to hoist her over his shoulder and take her to bed. The thought of her stretched out naked almost sent him over the edge. He put his head under the water jets and growled. *What the hell am I doing?*

His cell phone vibrated on the shelf beside his toothbrush. He let it ring to message three times before he stepped out of the shower.

"What?" He demanded pressing the phone to his wet ear.

"Delightful to speak with you too mate," Haig replied. "Now tell me. Who the hell is Sydney Stone?"

12

Sydney had surprised herself with a good night's sleep. She arrived at work early the next morning and smiled when the lift stopped for Carmen on the fourth floor. She held the door open while the cleaner pushed her trolley into the lift.

"Early bird catches the worm," Carmen said.

"It's a calling," Sydney replied.

"It's not just a job, it's a devotion," Carmen said.

"At least you'll have an easy run this morning, I can't think much mess has been made since the new girl cleaned last night. Or are you here to check up on her? Keep her on her toes?" Sydney laughed.

"What new girl?" Carmen asked. The lift pinged, and they manhandled the cleaning trolley out on to the fifth floor. "No one worked last night," Carmen said, pushing her trolley towards the reception desk. "Union called a stop-work meeting. Probably going to strike by the sound of it. Before the election. Lots of publicity."

"But there was a woman," Sydney said, "she was pushing your trolley, she was wearing your uniform."

"Well, she's not done a very good job this lady. Look at Matilda's desk!" Carmen stood with her hands on her ample hips and surveyed the mugs. Sydney could see the banana peel had turned black.

"Who was it then?" Sydney asked, trying to ignore the odd way her stomach flipped. The woman had seemed nervous, but Sydney had assumed it was first night nerves.

"Could be a non-union worker, in the wrong building or on the wrong floor. It happens sometimes."

Sydney had a bad feeling. She walked quickly down to her office with Carmen and her trolley hot on her heels.

The stack of paper in her inbox had been shoved back haphazardly so that it spilled over the side and her neat line of mini Mars bars in her top drawer had been moved.

"What's wrong Sydney? Is something missing?" Carmen asked. "I'll get my Manager on to it right away. Find out who she was."

"No, no." Sydney assured Carmen, "nothing missing. Everything's fine. I'm sure you're right. Someone obviously got started and then realised they were in the wrong place."

"We get some dumb ones," Carmen rolled her eyes. "Don't worry Sydney Stone, I'll have it ship-shape in no time."

Only Sydney was worried. She sat down and waited for Carmen and her trolley to disappear back to the front desk, then she checked her top drawer again. She searched for the USB stick under the Mars bars. Could be in a different drawer? She searched them all.

She ripped into a mini Mars and stuffed it in her mouth. If there was ever a time for stress eating...

She opened her handbag and dug around. Her hand connected with the piece of paper from her desk pad. She unfolded it and read the notes she'd made;

Justin Haig
Election
Zoning issues
Mr Randall
Holiday – passport

Vanguard
Jim at bakery
Who is Randall?
Where is Haig?
Who cares?

It appeared someone cared. Very much.

The story Sydney came up with wasn't a good one. The unexplained cleaner had taken the USB from her drawer, probably for Denton Cole, who was even more trouble than Sydney had realised. He was the only one who knew anything about her Haig investigation, or non-investigation if he had his way. But what was this Haig guy involved in, that would make her new boss rifle through her drawers? Would he really stoop that low?

She could go and confront him. Ask him straight up if he had taken matters into his own hands. But it was a struggle keeping her emotions in check just being in the same room as Denton Cole. Her perspective skewed when he looked at her with those intense blue eyes. Sydney sat frozen in her chair, staring at her stapler. No. She couldn't risk being made a fool of again. Denton Cole may have some physical hold over her, but Sydney Stone was employed to investigate and god damn it, she was going to do her job.

She crept carefully through the morning, fighting the urge to keep checking her top drawer. The USB stick was gone.

This is all completely ridiculous. Carmen would be back any moment to say they'd found the cleaner, and it was all a big mistake. Or Denton Cole would come with a perfectly logical explanation as to why he'd stormed her office and kissed her.

But Carmen didn't appear.

Neither did Denton Cole.

"He's in with legal," Matilda whispered when Sydney passed the front desk for a second time, under the guise of informing Matilda she'd be out for lunch, probably longer than usual. "The wax lady," Sydney explained. Not something that would spark Matilda's inquisitiveness. But it wouldn't have mattered. She was already distracted.

"The door's been closed for over an hour. They all stopped talking when I took in the sandwiches. Head of finance just joined them."

"Redundancies?" Sydney mused.

"It's got to be big." Matilda set about banging staples into pages and moving them across her desk, "Because Denton Cole looks like a sexy thunderstorm today."

13

Sydney escaped the office just before noon. Avoiding Denton Cole in a bad mood seemed like a wise move. Especially considering her destination.

Buttons Bakery was across the street from Vanguard's headquarters.

"I'll have a trim latte," Sydney ordered, "and a chicken sandwich. Oh, one of those chocolate éclairs too please."

She ate slowly while she watched the front entrance to the Vanguard offices across the road. It was visually discrete. Small white lettering on a heavy glass door was the only branding. No one went in or out while she sat and sipped her coffee.

"Another coffee?" the woman clearing tables asked. Sydney's ears twitched.

"A decaf would be great," she checked the name tag on the pink frilly apron, "Jim!"

"I'm Minnie. Like the mouse. My mum had a thing for Disneyland. Jim's my new boss. He has to order me a new one. It's kind of my first day but not really."

"Minnie, don't you work across the road? I think I spoke to you yesterday. I'm Sydney Stone. From Passion Media?"

"Oh. My. God!" Minnie said. "What are you doing here? You would not believe it Sydney Stone. But you changed my life! After I talked to you I was so stressed that what I'd told you would get me in trouble with my boss, so I came over here for a donut and ended up telling Jim the whole story, and he suggested it was better to be upfront with Mr Randall, and that even if I got fired, he'd have me work for him any day. I told Jim I would love to work for him even if Randall didn't fire me! He's really cool," Minnie blushed but continued the flow of words.

"I figured why not? What's the point in spending all day, every day feeling awful? So I went back to the office and wait, just hold on," Minnie said.

Sydney laughed and watched Justin Haig's secretary disappear into the kitchen. She immediately dumped all her carefully crafted excuses for cold calling Vanguard. Minnie had just fallen into her lap. Or at least the seat next to her. With a giant donut and a diet coke.

"Jim said I can take my lunch break now. He's the one Justin Haig helped with his accounts. Jim!" Minnie called out and waved him over.

"This is the reporter I told you about. The one who was asking about Justin. Who sort of got me fired."

"You've been fired?" Sydney asked.

"Don't worry," Minnie laughed, "it was bound to happen sooner or later. That's what I was telling you." Minnie paused to take a long sip of coke.

"Justin Haig is a good guy. He looked after Jim with his accounts. Isn't that right Jim?"

"Good bloke," Jim nodded. "Always used us for catering. Wouldn't accept a cent for helping with my taxes."

"When was the last time you saw Mr Haig?" Sydney asked.

"Couple of days ago. I always make sure I've got lactose-free milk for him. He's a regular so we don't charge extra. One bottle of lactose-free milk won't break the bank."

"When you saw him on Monday, did he mention any travel?"

"No. He usually says when he's going away, saves me getting the special milk in."

"Sounds like a nice guy."

"Exactly," Minnie nodded. "I was really worried after I'd talked to you. See Justin Haig was really the only reason I stayed at Vanguard as long as I did. He didn't mind my bad spelling, or how I always jammed the photocopier. So I kind of felt like I'd been disloyal to him, giving out about him to you on the phone like that. I don't want to get him in trouble or anything."

Minnie somehow managed to bite her donut, chew, swallow and start talking again within seconds.

"I was in a really mad mood you see. I couldn't believe he'd just leave like that, without saying goodbye, when he knows how much old Randall hates me. But honestly, since Randall turned up I've spent more time hiding out over here with Jim than doing my job. So I went back after lunch and I told Randall I'd been speaking to you. We agreed maybe it was time I look for a different job. But," Minnie took another long sip of her drink and a large breath, "an hour later Randall sent me out to get milk, and when I got back some other woman was behind the desk. My desk! And Randall said since he wasn't sure if Haig was coming back, that he had brought in his own Executive Assistant, and that she could handle reception, so I really was surplus to requirements, but that he'd give me a good deal. A month's pay, and even a reference, as long as I went quietly. I cut and run. Right over here to Jim, who got me clearing tables straight away! What with me having been here so much anyway," Minnie giggled and shrugged.

"It's like she's always worked here!" Jim blushed and made himself busy wiping down the next table over.

"Really Sydney, you saved me!" Minnie grinned widely, "I get to come to work at my happy place, and I can use the money Randall is paying me to buy boots. Lots of boots!" Minnie picked up the last of her donut and crammed it in her mouth.

While Minnie went back to the counter to take orders, Sydney finished her coffee and thought about Justin Haig. She got a good vibe from both Jim and Minnie and they were honest about Haig, but she still had no idea why he'd disappeared, or where he'd gone. What they had told her was a series of nothings. Yet it was everything she had.

The cafe was nearly empty when Sydney reluctantly stood up. She had no desire to return to Passion but Matilda would send out a search party, or worse still, Denton Cole would track her down.

"I better get back to work," Sydney told the pair as she buttoned her coat and put her bag over her shoulder. "For what it's worth Minnie, I think you're better off over here with Jim."

"Is he in trouble?" Minnie asked. "Can you find out where he's gone? I worked with him for almost two years, and the only times he went away was for his grandmother's funeral and a couple of boys' trips to Vegas. But if you find out Sydney, even if he's in trouble, will you let me know?"

"Of course" Sydney nodded, "But Minnie, this might just be office politics. If Randall was so quick to replace you, maybe he made a similar offer to Haig?"

Jim shook his head.

"It just feels all wrong. Justin worked so hard for that crowd. To think he stayed all night last week, fixing those computers. Bet he wishes he hadn't bothered."

Sydney reached for the door and swung it open.

"What was wrong with the computers?"

"Nothing much, some networking error," Minnie replied.

"You should have seen Haig when he found the problem," Jim laughed. "He came strutting in here at 7 am, asking for a triple shot. Said he needed a coffee he could stand a spoon up in. Reckoned he'd found the answers to all his problems."

"It was all boring numbers and stuff," Minnie added. "You should have seen the stuff I printed out."

"You printed it out?" Sydney stepped back inside the door.

"By accident," Minnie admitted, "I told you I was crap at my job," she snorted.

"What did you do with the printouts?" Sydney asked, her heart beating a little faster.

"I put them in the recycle bin," Minnie replied.

"Did you tell anyone?" Sydney asked.

"I was always printing out the wrong thing. I probably should have put it through the shredder," Minnie mused.

"Do you think the paper is still there? In the recycling?"

"Probably," Minnie nodded. "Only gets put out once a month."

"Do you think you can get it for me? Discreetly of course."

"I don't see why not, if it helps Justin," Minnie nodded again. "I'm going over there later to clear out my desk and pick up my payslip. But don't get too excited Sydney, it was just a whole lot of garbled numbers and stuff."

"It might be nothing or it could be everything," Sydney said. "Let's roll the dice!"

14

Sydney spent the afternoon trawling through recent press releases from Vanguard. They were rumoured to be working against the more restrictive data mining legislation recently passed in parliament. But she couldn't find a single press release or a direct quote from Randall or Vanguard over the issue. Sydney knew the research department would have more luck, but she didn't like the thought of Denton Cole finding out she was still digging into Haig, after he'd asked her to back off. But she had no real choice. Shutting down an active investigation went against her gut instinct, especially when Denton would not tell her why he needed her silence. It was her job to investigate.

But going against his request made her nervous.

Maybe it was the kiss. Was it clouding her judgement? It lingered in her office, as it had since Denton's lips first touched her own. The touch and taste of Denton Cole was imprinted on her skin. She closed her eyes and immediately felt his fingers on her neck. Her finger tips tingled at the memory of his warm, muscular back. The heat rose through her as she remembered the pleasure of his tongue in her…

"Ahem."

Sydney's eyes flew open and as if she had dreamed him into life, Denton Cole stood before her. Sydney felt her cheeks flush. Denton's chequered blue business shirt was undone at the collar, the sleeves rolled up. His forehead creased as he stared hard at Sydney.

"Tired?" Denton raised an eyebrow, "something keep you awake last night?"

"I slept perfectly fine thank you. I was just thinking about, um," Sydney had to defend herself. She glanced down at her desk, "about botanic gardens. Someone's been stealing plants." The press release she'd skimmed that morning lay on her desk and Sydney immediately realised how ridiculous it sounded.

"That's, well, it's not very interesting, to be honest. We need to see you, Sydney."

"When?" Sydney asked, opening the calendar application on her computer.

"I can do 3 pm, or I've got a gap at 8:30 am tomorrow morning,"

"Now," Denton sighed. "In the conference room . We need to see you now."

Sydney felt a ripple of unease as she followed Denton to the conference room. She caught a glimpse of Matilda behind the reception desk. Matilda threw her a questioning smile. Sydney shrugged in return.

She did not expect the heads of legal and finance to be in the conference room, but it seemed a lot of strange things were going on at Passion Media this week. Sydney sighed, lowering herself into the chair Denton held out for her and felt less than reassured when his hand patted her shoulder briefly before he took his seat across the table.

"I'll cut right to the chase," Vernon Berry, Passion's chief financial officer, said to Sydney. "Miss Stone, the new audit system we installed two days ago as part of the accounting upgrade has flagged you for payroll manipulation." He slid two documents across the table and Sydney picked them up. The claim forms in her hand showed a number of extraordinary items, mostly hotels and restaurants, some very expensive, that Sydney had heard of but never frequented.

"These aren't mine," she laughed. "I've never dined at Chica, closest I've got is a tin of chica-peas at Sainsbury's." Not a single person laughed and Sydney felt herself blush.

"These are not my expense claims Mr Berry."

"Probably not," he nodded. "But the problem is your electronic signature is on the bottom of the files."

"But we have to sign hard copies," Sydney rushed, "If you find the hard copies, you'll see I never filed these," Sydney said, waving the pages in front of her. "This hotel here, it's in Prague. I've never even been to bloody Prague!"

"Sydney," Denton put his hands flat on the table in front of him, relaxed and open. Sydney edged back in her seat and put her own hands in her lap. She glared across at him.

"Sydney." He spoke in a calm and reasonable, very annoying voice. "We trust you when you say you didn't file these. A mistake must have been made. It's to be expected with a new software system."

"But the problem, Miss Stone," Vernon Berry spoke loudly into the room, gazing at the ceiling, avoiding any eye contact. "The problem is that we need to go back into the archives to find the originals. And that's going to take a while."

"How long?" Sydney asked.

"A week, two at most," Berry explained. "In the meantime, you'll have to stand down."

"You're suspending me?" Sydney's mouth fell open. "I haven't done anything wrong."

"Of course not," Berry hurried, "you'll be on full pay of course. Just while our audit team work through and get the problem sorted. As Mr Cole has stated, it's probably just a blip with the new software. These things happen. But we do need to appear to be handling things professionally Miss Stone. The shareholders are watching us closely right now, with Mr Cole taking over the reins. It's best we follow our code of conduct. Standard operating procedures you know." He smiled as if there was nothing to worry about, "You'll get your salary as usual," he assured her. "You could take a little holiday or something."

The woman from the legal department dropped her glasses down her nose and spoke for the first time.

"I believe it's in everyone's best interest if we can get to the bottom of this as quickly as possible." The red from her lipstick had rubbed onto her teeth.

"Let's meet back here with Miss Stone in ten days, unless we have the archived information sooner. It's my legal obligation to inform you of your right to retain your own counsel, Miss Stone, but at this stage we are not looking at any illegalities, but a simple computer error."

"So why can't I continue working?" Sydney cried.

"Protocol, Miss Stone. There are procedures we must follow. It's a good chance to work through our systems and ensure they are up to scratch." Vernon Berry sat back, his hands on top of the pinstriped business shirt stretched tight across his rotund middle.

"I'm a guinea pig then," Sydney stated.

"I'm sorry, we have to follow procedure," Denton Cole spoke to Sydney, his eyes searching hers for some understanding she could not provide.

"So we're all agreed?" the woman and her lipstick teeth asked, ignoring Sydney's comment. "Effective immediately, Sydney Stone will be on administrative leave. She will have no press accreditation under Passion Media while we investigate the situation. But she will remain on full pay, with benefits."

Vernon Berry gave a satisfied nod, and Sydney felt like she'd been kicked in the stomach when Denton Cole gave a gruff yes.

She stood and leaned over the table. She waited for Denton's eyes to meet her own, and with a shaky voice said,

"You, Mr Cole, are a grade A bastard."

15

Sydney left the conference room and stormed to her office. Matilda hustled after her. She closed the door quietly and locked it. Sydney paced the floor, hands on hips, too wild to talk.

"What the hell is going on?" Matilda asked. "Did they make you redundant?" Sydney couldn't form sentences so repeated the same three words, over and over again.

"Bastard. Wanker. Arse-hat."

"Bastard. Wanker. Arse-hat."

"Bastard. Wanker. Arse-hat."

"Let's go get a drink," Matilda said. "For the shock. Put your coat on and wait here. I'll make sure the coast is clear."

Sydney put her coat on with shaking hands. Then raged at Denton Cole.

Did he do this on purpose? Has he pushed me out of my job to keep Justin Haig's problems secret?

Sydney still didn't even know what damn problems Denton Cole and Justin Haig were hiding. But Denton Cole was a master manipulator. She knew that now for sure.

"Come on," Matilda stuck her head around the door and beckoned Sydney out. "I've got someone covering the desk and I've told Jill from advertising that Mr Cole has a few minutes spare. She'll talk his ear off."

The two girls descended all five flights of stairs. Matilda had an Uber waiting, and less than ten minutes later they slid back in time, to a nightclub in 1973, complete with orange vinyl booths and light-up squares on the dance floor.

Sydney sat, and tried to take slow calm breaths so her brain could catch up with her emotions. Matilda laughed with the girl behind the bar, then walked across the flashing floor with two goblets.

"Where the hell are we?" Sydney asked.

"The boyfriend gets the odd gig here. I think it's called Retro Funk or something. Brandy and ginger ale," she said, pushing the goblet across to Sydney. "My Grandma used to say it's great for shock. Get it down you."

Sydney took large gulps. The heat from the brandy hit the bottom of her stomach and burned a little. Then her vision clouded up and a strange hiccup escaped.

"Shit Sydney, are you going to cry?" Matilda grabbed her hand.

"I think so," Sydney tried to fight it, but another hiccup-sob escaped.

Sydney never cried. She didn't mind other people's tears but her stoicism was a source of pride. The emotion was so unlike her. She quickly drained the rest of the glass so she wouldn't have to work out what she was more upset about, being stood down from work, or being stomped all over by Denton Cole.

"Here," Matilda said, sliding her own glass across to Sydney. "You need this more than me."

"He's a wanker," Sydney said, draining her friend's glass and wincing a little. "I need another." The barman barely had a chance to place it on the table. Sydney threw it back between tiny sobs. "My eyes won't stop leaking."

"You want to tell me what happened?" Matilda asked. Sydney nodded. The brandy had entered her bloodstream. She could feel her body slow down. It took a little longer than usual to form sentences.

"He stood me down. Because of a stupid error in accounting. They say my electronic signature is on record, filing expense claims for money I wasn't entitled to. They stood me down."

"So they haven't fired you?

"No," Sydney shook her head, "but they may as well have. I didn't file those claims, Matilda. They're not mine."

"Surely they can get the hard copies and clear it up in no time."

"They're old claims. Apparently, the new computer system picked up the errors, and that means they have to go to archives to get the originals. They say it could take two weeks."

"Is it a one-off error?" Matilda asked, "one document, no trail of irregularity?"

"Nothing but an extra-large month of expenses early last year, including expensive wine, bloody posh restaurants I've never been to, clothes from Floyd."

Matilda gasped, "I tried on a coat there once. It was 1500 pounds. I was so scared I couldn't breathe."

"Well, apparently last February I had a lovely time at Floyd's buying a dress worth 3000 pounds. They can come look in my bloody wardrobe if they want. All they'll find is H&M and Zara."

"If it's a one-off error I don't see why you need to be stood down. Surely they can do the archives stuff and you can carry on," Matilda reasoned.

"Apparently I'm an excellent guinea pig, thanks to the new software they've installed. Legal and that loser Vernon Berry, from Finance, are all excited to test their prothedures. Procedurths, *Procedures.*" It was a tricky word to say after three quick brandys.

"It's all *'we're following protocol.'* Denton Cole was very quick to stick it to me with his 'following pro*ced*ures.'" Ha! She got it that time.

"Oh yes, and it's all pretty great timing for him, the day after he asks me to stop investigating a story about his mate."

"He asked you to step off a story?" Matilda gasped. "Isn't that all kinds of wrong?"

"Exactly," Sydney waved to the woman behind the bar. When the drinks were refreshed she gulped back more of the brandy, paused for a moment, then a sob escaped. "What am I going to do?" she cried. "I can't be off work for two whole weeks."

"You'll be back in no time. Think of it as an impromptu break. You've had holidays before." "I haven't," Sydney shook her head emphatically. Matilda leaned across the table and patted her friend's hand.

"You went to Paris last year on your annual leave."

"I was working," Sydney admitted. "Joel was on that FIFA scandal and he needed someone inconspicuous. I played the slightly uninterested football girlfriend."

"What about Milan the year before?"

"Fashion Week. Big make-up corporations testing products on animals."

"A-ha!" Matilda cried, "You went to Dublin for St Patrick's day!"

"I got STUCK, in Dublin," Sydney replied. "Food poisoning. Spent the night on the bathroom floor and had to call a doctor at 1 am, who gave me a jab in my bum. But thank you, I'd nearly forgotten that awful and embarrassing event."

"Sorry. But at least someone got in your pants," Matilda giggled. Sydney hiccupped and another sob escaped.

"You've really never been on holiday?" Matilda asked. "How could I not have realised this. Have you ever laid down on a beach and listened to music?"

"Sounds awful."

"You've never spent the day skiing, then curled up by the fire drinking mulled wine?"

"Skiing, yes. When that Winter Olympics dude would only talk to me on the slopes. Hot chocolate and fire, no. I had a story to write up."

"And now you have no story to keep you busy." Matilda's mouth dropped in pity.

"There is a story," Sydney's eyes flashed wildly. "There is something going on. I just have to find out what it is."

"Sydney. You're stood down. If they find out you're working they really could fire you."

"Damn it," Sydney cried. She lay her head on her hands. Four brandys in and the room was moving in circles. She'd lost feeling in her lips and cheeks.

"Don't take this the wrong way," Matilda said, leaning her own head on the table so her face was opposite Sydney's. "but this might be a good thing. Take a couple of days to get your head around this. You're allowed to have a life outside of work." Sydney's eyes widened with fear.

"You are not fired," Matilda reminded her. "Go home. Eat toast. Watch bad telly. You could even go to Switzerland for a real mini break. Sexy men in long-johns." Matilda tucked Sydney's curly hair behind her ear.

"Things will look better tomorrow, after a good sleep and a bit of time away from the office."

"Away from Denton Cole," Sydney slurred. "I thought he liked me." A small tear fell from the corner of Sydney's eye, and Matilda dabbed it away with her finger.

"So did I," she said.

16

Four hours, three glasses of water, two cheese and ham toasted sandwiches and one cup of coffee later, Sydney sat staring at the television, trying not to think. The brandy had been soothing but it had worn off. She scratched behind Cornflake's ear. Someone on Twitter had said purring cats could help ease stress and even heal broken bones.

But Sydney had something far worse than a broken arm or leg. In the last two days, Denton Cole had broken her life. He'd stolen her job, and before she realised it was missing, he'd smashed it into smithereens.

She drained the last of her coffee. She tried to stay in the haze by sitting very still, barely breathing, but the wave of shame had grown too big and she couldn't stop it from crashing over.

I'm so stupid. I was so worried about crushing on Denton Cole, I forgot the most important rule - nothing good ever comes from letting your heart rule your head.

The realisation was enough to hurtle Sydney back in time, to the sitting room at her family home, where young teenage Sydney sat with her mother, fighting back the growing rage as she watched her mother defend a man who lied and cheated.

Even worse, Sydney's father's lies were weak and flimsy. In the days after his heart attack, Sydney found emails. Her mother waved her away, so Sydney dug deeper, begged her mother to look at the visa statement on her father's computer.

But she smiled at her daughter, patted her hand, and said,

"No thank you. The funeral director will be here soon. Shall we make some scones?"

Sydney was forced to watch on as her mother grieved for the fake flake of a man who did not deserve such remembrance. All those times they'd welcomed her father home from business trips, made his favourite meals, watched the movies he liked and listened to him telling her mother why she didn't need to go to university or apply for the job at the travel agency. Sure, didn't he earn enough to keep them in an excellent lifestyle? Didn't she have enough stress running the household? He suggested she take a course at the adult education centre. A cookery course so he could bring his co-workers home.

Sydney seethed with anger when her mother did just that, and a steady stream of her father's arrogant banker colleagues poured through the front door to enjoy her mother's gourmet meals.

Not long after the funeral, Sydney and her mother stopped talking about him. He was the butt of constant arguments that never went anywhere. But Sydney made herself a promise. She would never be stuck at home, fluffing flowers and slaving over salmon roulade while some fat prick of a man was out drinking whiskey in dark bars with starved skinny cougars who had nothing to offer but a double D cup and a lack of morals.

Sydney paid her way through university, working at a small community newspaper.

It took a lot of determination and long hours to reach her career goals.

But *'Will you have children?'* was the question her mother always asked.

"You've got time. Lots of women have babies later these days."

Sydney would shake her head.

"I'm not giving everything up like you did Mum."

"I liked being at home. And I would be such a good grandmother."

And Sydney knew she was right. She would knit and bake and babysit.

"Who knows. Ask me again next year Mum," was Sydney's standard reply.

Had she passed on promising relationships? One or two may have resulted in a marriage proposal eventually. Nice enough guys with good jobs and secure futures. But that was exactly the type of man her father pretended to be. Sydney knew the only person she could ever trust was herself. She was determined to create her own secure future.

Sydney felt Cornflake's nose against her hand.

How could my outlook on life have shifted so quickly, from defined and dependable to flimsy and fragile?

Her emotional response to Denton Cole had caused all kinds of drama. She couldn't understand how she'd let herself go unchecked. Denton Cole slid past her defences. And now she knew for sure he was hiding something, but she couldn't investigate. If she followed her gut instinct to chase down Haig, she risked losing her job at Passion Media. No doubt Denton Cole would have her blacklisted with all the big media companies, and she'd end up having to shift to the ends of the earth, probably Alaska, where she would be paid next to nothing to report on road ice conditions.

"I hate Denton Cole," Sydney yelled, startling Cornflake who rose on all fours and growled deeply in return. The intercom buzzer sounded, Cornflake bolted and Sydney yelped as he dug his claws into her lap to catapult to safety. She frantically rubbed her thigh while she hobbled over to the intercom.

"Hello?"

"Hey Syd, it's Alfie. I forgot my key again, can you buzz me up?"

Having heard Alfie's voice, Cornflake pranced over to Sydney and wove around her legs.

"He's coming up now," Sydney told the cat and unlocked the front door, returning to the kitchen to hunt through the junk drawer for Alfie's spare key.

"Hey Cornflake," Sydney heard from the doorway.

"Hey Syd," Alfie called out. Sydney found the key, then returned to the front door and put it in Alfie's hand. "He's been a perfect roommate," she told Alfie, "slept all night and didn't wee on the carpet this time."

"It was obviously the motivational talk I gave him before I dropped him off." Sydney laughed, but someone else chuckled from behind Alfie. Sydney swung the door back further and felt her stomach drop. Her pulse exploded. Her pupils dilated and her mouth went dry.

"You do know this man, right?" Alfie asked, scooping up Cornflake and tickling him under his chin. "Denton was at the door behind me, said he was your boss so I walked him up..." Alfie raised his eyebrows in question. He was waiting and Sydney had to offer some kind of acknowledgement. She nodded her head.

"Yes. He's my boss," Her head was still nodding. She swallowed hard, then held it firmly centre above her shoulders.

"Well, I'll take my kitty and leave you both to it!" Alfie winked at Sydney, mouthed the word 'hot,' then turned to shake Denton's hand.

"Lovely to meet you. If you're about sometime, come over and try that Sea Level Pinot Gris I was talking about."

"Sure thing," Denton replied. Sydney remained where she was, gripping tightly to both the doorknob and her desperate emotions.

17

S hall I come in?" Denton asked. Sydney didn't move, her knuckles white from gripping the doorknob. He waited a few moments, then gently lifted Sydney's hand from the door and pushed it closed.

They stood, with Sydney's hand resting in his own, for what felt like a very long time. As if two hands held together had the power to overcome all the before and after events that had sent them into a spin.

"I've come to say sorry," Denton offered, breaking the spell. Sydney blinked, then snatched back her hand and stalked to the lounge. Denton followed until Sydney held up her hand.

"Too close," she growled. "You stay over there. This is my dance space, that's your dance space."

"Dirty Dancing. My sister was obsessed with that movie." He looked around Sydney's apartment. It had a homely feel he hadn't expected. She had a thing for cushions. And candles. A round wooden tray on the coffee table held half a dozen with their wicks flickering, stretching shadows in the darkened room.

"Nice place," Denton smiled. He put his hands in his pockets because he needed something to do while Sydney stood glaring at him.

"I looked for you, after the meeting. I wanted to say sorry. I mean it Sydney. Can I just apologise."

"No. You just can't!" Sydney threw at Denton. "I knew you were worried about me investigating Haig, but I can't believe you've had me side-lined. I don't know what you're hiding but it must be damn big if you'd go to this much effort."

"I had nothing to do with this," Denton replied. "Did you do what I asked? Did you stop looking into Haig?"

"No." Sydney put her hands on her hips. "I did what I'm paid to do. What I'm trained to do."

Denton shook his head. "I'm sorry Sydney. Someone out there must have heard you were investigating. I talked to Haig last night. His receptionist emailed him to tell him if he was in trouble he could trust Sydney Stone. This isn't on me. If you'd only done what I asked and backed off."

"It's my job!" Sydney rallied, "You can't ask an investigative journalist not to investigate, it's like asking a rugby player... not to rugby."

"Not to rugby?" Denton tried to suppress a laugh.

"Oh, you know what I mean," Sydney punched back at him.

"I played rugby at college. I got a concussion in my first game. My mother wouldn't let me play after that. I played hockey instead. Then I dislocated my knee." Denton lifted his left leg and wiggled it. "Gives me all kinds of grief in winter."

"What the hell," Sydney threw her arms in the air, "are you talking about? I've been had up on some trumped up charge of corporate theft, I'm side-lined from my job..."

"But it'll go away," Denton replied calmly. "That's what I came to tell you, to reassure you. That I don't for a second think you've done anything wrong. No one does. But we have to follow procedure. As much to protect you as anything."

"What a load of bollocks," Sydney cried, "that's the kind of crappy corporate codswallop we're forced to swallow all the time."

"Codswallop?" Denton asked.

"It's a word!" Sydney assured him.

"You're the journalist," Denton said. He dared take a step closer to her.

"Stay right there," Sydney squeaked.

"Why?" Denton asked, taking another small step towards Sydney.

"I don't know," Sydney admitted.

Denton stayed put for a moment.

"I want you to know I didn't have anything to do with all this. The timing is, well, it could just be a coincidence. A glitch in the software. Haig spoke to Minnie. A guy named Randall she worked with knows you were asking questions. Haig thinks that's the problem. He thinks right now you're collateral damage in his," Denton paused, "his predicament."

Sydney blinked back the tears that threatened to fall. "That collateral damage means I can't do my job."

"So you've got a few days off. Take a holiday, some R&R?" Denton suggested.

"Why do people keep saying that?" Sydney crossed her arms and stomped her foot. Denton shuffled a little closer.

"Stop it," Sydney warned.

"You're not a fan of relaxation?" Denton was standing close enough now that he could reach out and touch her. But he didn't. He kept his hands in his pockets.

"Not that it's relevant, but I like to be busy. I've never understood the whole relaxation thing. I'm not very good at it." Sydney mumbled.

"You don't have a favourite activity?" Denton asked. "Something to pass the time?"

"Are you asking if I knit? Or maybe you think I'm a paid-up member of the local Scrabble club?" Sydney rolled her eyes. He couldn't help chuckling.

"I'm not a big fan of Scrabble," Denton told her. "But I could think of something a little more exciting. If you're interested?"

He watched Sydney tip her head to the side, and finally she met his gaze.

Denton closed the remaining gap between them. He gently trailed his fingers across Sydney's arms, where they were folded across her chest, grazing her nipples. They hardened beneath her t-shirt. Sydney saw the anticipation flash in his eyes and knew in an instant what was about to happen. She should probably move away.

"You're not going to start dirty dancing with me are you?" she quipped.

"Not a chance. The only dancing I can do is the drunken stumbling kind."

Sydney tried not to smile.

"I'm not happy with you, and I don't know if I believe you had nothing to do with this."

"I know," Denton murmured, lowering his head to the nape of her neck and gently dropping a kiss on Sydney's soft skin.

"If you like, I can sign an affidavit swearing I had nothing to do with it." When he traced his way from her neck to her mouth, Denton felt Sydney relax.

"This is against all my rules," she whispered, and Denton replied,

"I like it when you're naughty."

Her body instinctively took over. She let her hands press firmly down Denton's back, then dragged her fingernails back up the length of his spine. Denton groaned and she pressed into him, her breath shallow and ragged.

Sydney felt Denton lift her off the ground, and she wrapped her legs around him.

"You're incredible," Denton whispered. He dropped on to the couch, with Sydney straddled on top of him.

A sense of urgency saw shoes kicked off across the sitting room floor, and they both fumbled with buttons and shimmied out of restrictive clothing until a pair of boxer shorts, a black lace bra, and matching knickers were all that separated them.

"You look amazing in this lace," Denton murmured into Sydney's ear, sliding a hand under the cup of her bra, "but as lovely as it is, it needs to come off."

Sydney reached behind her back and unclasped.

"God you're beautiful," Denton growled as she slid her bra off, draping it over the side of the couch. His hands were rough and warm and she closed her eyes and relaxed into his touch.

Sydney felt incredible. She could feel the heat building at her core, firing hotter each time Denton touched her.

Denton felt wildly impatient. He knew what was trapped beneath those silky knickers. He touched the lace and felt a surge of adrenalin when Sydney moaned and arched her back. Denton slid his thumb away and let his hands glide smoothly up, over her hips. She rocked gently, her head thrown back as Denton caressed her body.

"Hold on Syd," Denton panted. "Condom. I've got one in my wallet." Denton held her close and rolled her beneath him. "Wait right there," he demanded.

Sydney grinned and watched as Denton crawled around on the floor, looking for his wallet.

"A-ha!" he smiled, pulling it from the back pocket of his jeans and holding it up. He opened the folded leather. Receipts, visa cards and a pile of coins were tossed on to the carpet.

Then he was back, the foil pouch between his lips.

He knelt on the floor beside the couch.

"Miss me?" he asked and kissed her as if he'd been gone a month. He fumbled with the condom packet and laughed when Sydney declared he was doing a fantastic job. Then they both looked down and a quiet anticipation hummed between them.

Denton slid inside her, thrusting deep and strong so that Sydney could do nothing to control the waves of pure ecstasy as they took over every inch of her body. With every exquisite thrust, Sydney climbed higher and higher. Denton groaned as she wrapped her legs around him and as she cried out, Denton felt a surge of pleasure, thrust once more and let himself go.

They lay there for a time, eyes closed, letting their heart rates slow. Eventually, Denton spoke, breaking the cocoon of silence.

"Sydney Stone, I'm desperate for a glass of water. Shall I get you one too?"

She watched him manoeuvre himself gently away from her and felt the chill air as he walked to the kitchen, completely naked.

Denton Cole is naked in my house.

She didn't know what to do. She felt light-headed when she sat up, and strangely self-conscious, considering what had just happened on her couch. She reached for her t-shirt and held it up across her chest when Denton returned.

"Oh no," he smiled down at Sydney. "You won't be needing that," Denton whispered, gently tugging the t-shirt away from Sydney. "We're nowhere near done yet. Here, drink this." Sydney accepted the glass and gulped back the cool water. Denton took the empty glass from her and put it on the coffee table.

"Come on," he insisted, pulling Sydney off the couch, "I want to see your bedroom." He led her by the hand, and as Sydney followed, she took in the smooth and taut form of his buttocks. It was all the encouragement she needed.

18

Sydney woke in the early hours of the morning. She stretched her legs and felt an unstoppable grin spread across her face. Denton murmured something she couldn't interpret and kissed her shoulder. She knew she had broken all the rules, multiple times, and there would be fall out. But she was keen to ignore any and all consequences for a little while longer.

Sydney lay still as long as she could, listening to Denton's slow, easy breathing until eventually she had to brave the cold air and make a trip to the bathroom. While she was in there she gave her teeth a quick brush and combed her hands through her hair.

She was almost at the bedroom door when the beeping and buzzing of a cell phone grabbed her attention. Sydney laughed at the mess of clothes and shoes and bits and pieces that Denton had tossed from his wallet in their rush the night before. She found her own phone under a cushion, but there were no missed calls. The room was quiet until the buzzing started again. Down on all fours, Sydney followed the sound to the pocket of Denton's coat.

"Got it!" she yelled, yanking the phone out and pressing the accept call button. Then somewhat belatedly, she engaged her brain. She'd answered Denton Cole's phone. She had no idea what time it was, definitely before breakfast. What if it were someone from the office? Hey Syd, why are you answering your bosses phone? The morning after you've been stood down from work? What if it was someone on the board? Sydney froze with the phone in mid-air. She was about to cancel the call, but the desperate sound of a man's voice made her put it to her ear.

"Damn it Denton, I know you said to give you some time, but they're on to me mate. They don't know what I've got, but they know I've got something. They called my kid, Denton. They called Arabella in Switzerland. They told her some shit story that there was some kind of work emergency and they needed to get hold of me urgently. She's not stupid, so she told them she'd take a name and number and have me call them back. They hung up on her, so she called me right away. But if they can get to her, Denton. It's only a matter of time. Denton… mate, are you there?

"It's not Denton," Sydney told him.

"Who the hell is this and why have you got his phone?"

"I'm Sydney. Stone. I work with, I'm, a friend. Of Denton's."

"You're Stone?"

"Yes."

"The Journalist."

"Yes."

"You're a woman?"

"I am Sydney Stone. I am a journalist, and yes, last time I checked, I am a woman. And you, I'm guessing, are Justin Haig?"

"I am. Now as great as it is to talk to you Sydney, as you can probably guess, I'm in the middle of a rather screwed up situation. I have to go. Tell Denton I'll call him when I've got another phone. And tell him to pack his sunblock and get his arse over here."

"Over where?" Sydney asked.

"Fiji. I have to go."

"Where in Fiji?" Sydney rushed.

"Just tell Denton Fiji. He'll find me." The line went dead and Sydney stared at the phone in her hand. When she raised her head, she was looking at Denton, standing in the doorway of her bedroom, buck naked, arms crossed and a resigned look on his face.

"I had hoped for an entirely different wakeup call." He sighed. "You make the coffee, I'll put some pants on?"

"Haig is in Fiji." Sydney held up the phone as some sort of proof. "He wants you to go to Fiji. He said you'd be able to find him."

"Pacific Ocean. Middle of nowhere. Smart."

"Why is Haig in Fiji?"

"Pants and Coffee," Denton repeated. "Then you get the full story."

"I thought it best to involve as few people as possible. At least to start with. I had no idea what Haig had. He's a systems man, software stuff mostly. I figured he'd stumbled on to something he should have left alone. Vanguard works with political parties. I was thinking the usual stuff - maybe they'd used public money to fly private charter flights full of politicians on ski trips to Switzerland. Maybe they had some kind of dossier on the Prime Minister. Caught shagging the nanny, or maybe Vanguard was involved in bribes or something. You know, stupid stuff these lobbiest *slash* image consultant firms always seem on the edge of. If stuff came out it would be embarrassing for them and their clients, but worse for Haig. He'd been in their computer system with no authority to remove files. He'd already told me it was a grey area. He'd signed some kind of non-disclosure form when he started working there. I could imagine the slick media machine of a political lobby group. It'd chew him up and spit him out. Tell the world Justin Haig is a thief. Have him arrested. Throw all the privacy laws at him."

"Hold on," Sydney held her hand up, "I'm confused. Go back to the start."

Denton took a sip of his coffee and sighed. "You're going all journalist on me."

"I am," Sydney confirmed. Denton leaned over and kissed her. She worked into the kiss, loving his rough day-old stubble rubbing against her chin. For a moment she forgot everything, but she dug deep and pushed him away.

"Stop," Sydney demanded. "I need to know what the hell is going on. Go back to the start. And remember, I've got all day. Unlike some of us, I have nowhere to go and nothing to do."

Denton sat back down.

"I'm going to need more coffee."

Sydney refilled Denton's coffee cup from the plunger on the kitchen bench.

"Who is Justin Haig?" she asked. "I mean, who is Haig to you?"

"He's sort of my brother."

"Sort of?" Sydney asked.

"We went to boarding school, in Switzerland. From the age of eleven, Justin Haig slept in the bed beside me. We ate meals together, did homework. I broke his nose. He gave me stitches. His Dad was a top barrister. Always came to sports day. Mine is a rich prick who never set foot in any of my schools. I got to know Haig's family and they kind of adopted me. Haig and I, we've been there for each other, for all the important stuff. We're closer than friends. We're brothers." Denton shrugged.

Sydney nodded and sipped her coffee and let him continue.

"A couple of weeks ago, a guy Haig used to work with called him up for a favour. He was working at the Conservative Party Head Quarters, and their systems analyst was stuck at the hospital, his kid broke an arm or something. Anyway, they were having issues with a database, and the party secretary was going mental about a big donor drive or something. The Conservatives and Vanguard are—"

"Thick as thieves," Sydney said, "Vanguard consulted on the last election and they galloped over Labour. Now the Conservatives look like they'll take the next election outright. The polls suggest they have the numbers."

"Right," Denton nodded. "So Haig did a bit of contract work at the Conservative's head office a while back, and his mate, middle management type, wondered if he'd mind coming and taking a look. Save them from a right bollocking. So Haig rocks up in his lunch break, his mate signs him in. Haig finds some simple error and reboots the system. Quick and easy fix. Only while he's in there, he stumbles on to something else."

"What?" Sydney asked.

"I don't know," Denton admitted. "He won't tell me."

"He won't tell you?" Sydney was confused. "You don't know what Haig has?"

"No," Denton confirmed.

"Okay," Sydney shook her head to clear it. "How did you get involved?"

"Haig took a copy of the stuff he found. More out of curiosity, and because he was due back at work so he didn't have time to look at the details right then. He didn't mention it to his mate, just said there might be some other stuff that needed sorting. His mate said not to worry. That Haig had got them out of a jam, and their regular systems analyst would be back the next day."

"But Haig still took the copy of whatever it is. And someone found out?"

"Right," Denton nodded. "The next morning, he arrived at Vanguard at 9 am and found two security guards and Oscar L. Randall tearing his desk apart."

"Randall," Sydney said, "who is this guy?"

"He's got some fancy job title. Information Capture and Communications Enhancement Consultant. In reality, he's a fixer."

"He went to Oxford," Sydney tried to remember any other details she'd learned about Minnie's boss.

"He almost flunked out of Oxford. Over-privileged, under talented. But money talks and his family have a lot of it."

"So do yours," Sydney pointed out.

"I don't trade on mine," Denton threw back.

"Touchy subject?" Sydney asked.

"Annoying assumption," Denton replied.

"Sorry. Do you know this Randall guy?" Sydney asked.

"No, I got the research department to pull me up some information on the down-low. I'm hungry. Should we make toast?

Sydney got the toaster out of the cupboard. Denton had gone to Research, he'd done exactly what she had wanted to do. It smarted.

"If you'd told me sooner, we could have worked this out together."

"I didn't know who I could trust." Denton shrugged.

"Carry on," she said and put the bread in the toaster. "Randall searched Haig's desk?"

"Yes. Haig asks Randall what he's doing. Randall says he's had an anonymous tip-off that someone may have stolen electronic data from another organisation."

"What did Haig do?"

"He played dumb. Sat through a grilling with Randall and some suit the Conservatives sent over. Haig told them how he'd fixed the code, that yeah, he'd been checking a couple of things that might have caused the error, but he didn't see anything obvious and his mate had told him their own guy would be back the next day. Said he was doing them a favour, he'd been in there for less than 10 minutes, and he'd only been there to help out a mate."

"But he did find something," Sydney said.

"Yeah. Nothing gets past Haig. Funny story. He was headhunted by MI6, straight out of college. But he was in love with this girl at the time, a hippie tree hugger. He wanted to smoke weed and save a bunch of native trees far more than he wanted to sit in a cubicle decrypting code."

"So what happened then? Did Randall believe him?" The toast popped.

"Stupid question," Sydney laughed at herself, "Of course he didn't." Sydney spread thick slabs of butter on the toast in a haphazard manner and plonked it down on the table.

Denton immediately went to work on a slice and they sat in silence while he chewed and swallowed.

"Haig spent the next few days acting normal. Created a few issues so he could stay late for a legit reason, and covered his tracks as best he could."

"But Randall was on to him?"

"Randall and others. About a week later they broke into his apartment. It's just a small one bedroom, and Haig's not stupid, so there was nothing for them to find. But he's got a camera. Saw them looking through his drawers."

"He's got Randall on tape?"

Denton shook his head and helped himself to another piece of toast.

"No. Those types don't do their own dirty work. But they left their own hidden camera behind. So Haig figured things were getting serious. That's when he met me for lunch."

"Bloody hell," Sydney cried. "Did he go to the police?"

"That's tricky. Legally, he's in a bit of a bind. He took data off a private secure server. They will say he stole it."

"But there are protections for whistleblowing," Sydney said.

"Yes, but the law insists you report it within your organisation or to the right authority."

"Serious Fraud Office?" Sydney asked. "If he's found something that's worthy of this level of drama, he should take it there."

"Pretty much," Denton nodded. "But Haig says he's only part way to figuring out what this thing is. He was worried enough to come to me, but scared enough that he hasn't given me any details."

"What did you tell him to do?" Sydney asked.

"I told him to go to the cops anyway. Offer up what he had and let them deal with it."

"But Haig didn't go for that?"

"Obviously not. He came to me to see if I thought he could leak it to the media."

"So you put him on to me?" Sydney asked. "I got a memory stick, anonymous drop. Was that memory stick from you?"

"No," Denton shook his head. "The first I knew you were on to Haig, was when I saw your notes on your desk pad."

"Then who sent the memory stick to me?"

"Haig thinks it was Randall. The night before you got that USB stick, he cornered him in the office, indirectly suggested to Haig that he was messing with the wrong people. To think about how sensitive the public were about their private data getting into the wrong hands. Haig might find himself rotting in prison, and wouldn't it be amusing if that scenario had already been set in motion."

"They were setting me up," Sydney realised. "They wanted me to out Haig. Not as a whistleblower, but as an opportunistic thief."

"They would've been watching that day I had lunch with Haig. Wouldn't have been hard to figure out who I was. I paid the restaurant bill with my credit card. From there, they would only have to Google me, and find out my connections to Passion Media."

"And even knowing they were trying to set him up, he still hasn't gone to the police?" Sydney asked.

"Haig would have to admit he stole something. And now there are people out there who've seen him meet with the new CEO of Passion Media, before going to the authorities. His name is linked with mine. Not exactly a sound platform for whistleblowing."

"True," Sydney agreed.

"So we decided on a different plan," Denton explained. "Get Haig somewhere quiet, where he'd have at least a couple of days to work out exactly what he'd found, piece all the parts together, and when he was ready, we'd take it to serious fraud and give you the story at the same time. I just had to keep you off the story for a couple of days."

"But you couldn't talk me around," Sydney couldn't help a sly smile.

"I could of," Denton grinned, "but I was too busy doing other things to you." He leaned across the toast crumbs, and the butter smudged table and kissed her.

They suspended their conversation and moved their meeting to the shower, where Denton wrapped his arms around Sydney and kissed her wet soapy neck. She ran her hands down her bosses back and marvelled at how easy it was to embrace the lawlessness of their current entanglement. She laughed as they slipped around each other, and groaned when Denton slipped his hands over her breasts and kissed her deeply, then laughed again when he swore loudly when the water suddenly turned cold.

"It's okay," Sydney giggled, jumping out and wrapping herself in a bath towel.

"This," Denton pulled her hips close to his own, so his firm arousal nestled between them, "is not alright." He took the towel from her body and threw it on the ground. Then he cleared the shelf under the sink of half a dozen of her best fluffy bath towels, shaking them out and throwing them on the floor.

"Condoms are in the top drawer," Sydney grinned.

Wet and slippery, they took their time exploring each other, until Denton whispered,

"Bloody hell, I'm sorry but I can't hold on any longer Syd."

"Neither can I," she laughed. He came immediately and like a domino she followed.

"That was," Denton paused. "Nope. Can't do words yet." He closed his eyes and listened to the hum of the bathroom fan.

"We should probably, you know," Sydney elbowed Denton.

"I know. We should. Give a few minutes, then we'll go again."

Dressed, with fresh mugs of coffee, and another plate of toast, Investigative Journalist Sydney dived back in.

"Haig said he's in Fiji."

"Right," Denton nodded. "How sturdy is this table?" He gave it a jiggle.

"You want to do it on the table?"

"Don't you?"

Sydney felt her heart rate pick up. Denton's hair was slicked back, still damp from the shower. He smelled delicious, thanks to the vanilla and shea butter soap he'd used to lather them up. She eyed up the table. She'd got it from Ikea. How hard had she screwed on those legs?

"Stop it!" She cried, for herself as much as Denton. "We have to concentrate."

"We do. I apologise. Where were we?"

"Haig. Fiji. You didn't know he was there?" Sydney asked.

"No," Denton shook his head. "We agreed the less I knew about his whereabouts the better."

"You thought they might come and shake you down?" Sydney asked.

Denton looked amused. "Shake me down?" he grinned, "Like in the movies."

"You know what I mean," Sydney rolled her eyes.

"No, I didn't think they would be that brazen. But I figured they'd be concerned about Haig leaking whatever he's got, and they might call the police to report it as theft. Better to be able to tell the truth, that I didn't know his location and hadn't spoken to him in a few days."

"But now he's called you," Sydney said. "He must have figured out what they've been up to."

"I assume so," Denton agreed. "But we won't know till we get there."

"We?" Sydney asked.

"Have you ever been to Fiji?" Denton asked.

"No," Sydney shook her head.

"Come with me. You can get the scoop."

"But I'm suspended. I've got no accreditation."

"We'll be incognito," Denton smiled. "Two beach babes in a bikini and board shorts."

"You'd look good in a bikini," Sydney mused.

"Thanks." Denton lifted up his t-shirt, "I've been working out." Sydney soaked in his well-formed six-pack, barely resisting the urge to climb up on his lap and give them both another reason to shower again. But the water would still be cold and it really wouldn't help the weird feeling Sydney had about flying to Fiji with Denton Cole by her side.

"If I get found out," Sydney reminded him. "I'd probably lose my job."

"It'll be alright," Denton winked, "I know your boss."

19

Sydney, a seasoned traveller, felt prickles of panic as she dug into the back of her wardrobe for her summer clothes.

Less than 24 hours ago, I hated the man. Now I'm going to Fiji with him?

Essential underwear and toiletries were always ready in her small trolley case. Sydney threw a pair of shorts, a couple of t-shirts and the only sundress she owned on top, then zipped it up. She paced the floor of her apartment, passport gripped in her hand. She'd looked up the visa requirements. A British passport holder did not need a pre-approved travel visa or documentation. She could pick up a visitor permit on arrival in Fiji.

Fiji. Sydney fought the urge to take her toothbrush, and her clean underwear and summer clothes out of her trolley case and put them all back in the wardrobe, then climb in the case herself and zip it up, turning out the lights on whatever this ridiculous and legally dubious thing was that she'd stumbled into.

She went to the bathroom and applied foundation with rough determination. She stared at herself in the mirror.

"You can stay home," she told her reflection. "Call Denton and say you can't go."

Am I really going to fly to the other side of the world with Denton Cole?

"It's the story of a lifetime," she blinked through her mascara wand. "Most journalists would give their first born child to get a break like this."

But was she willing to risk her career on the word of a man she had only just met? Whose personal attributes, in particular, his ability to weaken her knees and bring her to orgasm, may have skewed her judgement? A man whose friend held stolen information that had upset some very serious people, willing to break into his house to have it returned. Denton didn't even know what Haig had, or why it was important, but he was heading out on a blind belief in friendship, a brotherhood bond.

Sydney flicked off the bathroom light. She checked once more that she had her passport, her wallet, her cell phone and charger. It was already 2 pm. Was it really less than 24 hours ago she'd been left in a blind panic, suspended from the job she loved, trapped by the man who she couldn't resist. Who had spent the night between her sheets. He was her boss and she knew better. It was all ridiculous. She should call him, claim a family emergency. *I could tell him Cornflake had to have his appendix out.* That would be the sensible course of action. Because the alternative meant spending the next few days in close proximity to Denton Cole. A prospect that seemed both careless and climactic.

Time had run out.

Was she really going to risk it all to follow Denton Cole out into the unknown?

Yes. She was.

Because despite all the ifs and buts, Sydney Stone was an investigative journalist. She lived for the next big reveal, the thrill of the chase. Because the minute the intercom buzzed, and Denton's voice filled her apartment, telling her the car was ready, Sydney felt an undeniable sense of purpose. A date with Denton Cole was a date with destiny.

With shaking hands, Sydney locked her front door. She had very little time to decipher the rush of emotions when the elevator dipped down, coming to a gentle stop on the ground floor. The doors opened and Denton reached out and took Sydney's hand. Both a comfort and a catastrophe, all bound up in some unexplainable force that pulled her towards him.

Sydney Stone was a woman who had always protected herself when it came to romantic entanglements. She prided herself on keeping a firm grasp on her own future, carefully considered, and always following a predetermined map.

Sydney Stone did not need a man.

But she'd never thought about the consequences of wanting one.

Sydney followed Denton to the British Airways Club queue, watched him flash a gold executive card, to which the agent said,

"Thank you, Sir, let me expedite your check-in."

In record time, they were seated in the first-class lounge, glasses of champagne resting on a polished table before them.

She lifted her drink and sipped. She watched Denton over the rim of her glass.

"A last minute business trip isn't unusual so it won't seem strange," he'd told Sydney before he'd called his personal assistant, someone called Harvey. But she could tell he was careful not to say where he was going, and he insisted Harvey keep the trip confidential.

"Tell anyone who asks that I've gone bush." Denton paused. "It just means I've 'unplugged' for the weekend.

No Harvey, you can't tell them I'm doing naked yoga. Tell them I'm golfing and there's no cell coverage at the lodge we're, ah, I'm, staying at.

No. Just me. Right. Do not buy cushions. Harvey, listen to me. You do not have any authority to buy cushions, throw rugs or anything else at John Lewis. I have to go now. If anyone's looking for me, I want you to call me immediately."

"He thinks it's a hostile takeover," Denton explained when he'd ended the call. "I didn't correct him."

Denton made another call, this time to a club in Soho, cancelling dinner reservations. And another to his helicopter pilot cancelling a trip to St Andrew's.

"It was a golf tournament. They won't miss me, I'm quite shit."

I should call someone. But who?

Sydney thought about calling Alfie, but her neighbour wasn't on night shift so there was no need to worry about Cornflake. She really wanted to call Matilda, but the risk was too great. No way Matilda would be as easy as Denton's assistant. Matilda would want details. *Explicit* details! If Matilda knew she was leaving the country with Denton Cole… first she would want to know if he was any good in bed, and then she'd want to know why.

But Sydney didn't know why. For the first time in her life, she was flying blind. She decided she would call Matilda in a day or two. She needed to protect Matilda, to keep her out of the grey areas of her investigation. Definitely not because she couldn't admit to Matilda, let alone herself, that the pending flight to Fiji was a risk to both her professional and personal existence.

She looked around the lounge, taking in the smooth velvet furniture and shiny surfaces. The quiet hush was a little off-putting. If she hadn't just walked through Terminal 5, she would not have believed she was in an airport. She admired a pair of Jimmy Choo's on a woman walking past and tucked her H&M boots under her chair.

She'd worn her usual travel clothes. A pair of soft cotton leggings, black. Her favourite Zara kimono blouse, white with tiny strawberries embroidered all over it. And a creamy white angora wool, wrap-around cardigan, for when she got cold on the flight. But a few of the women had her reconsidering her comfortable label-less choices. She'd already clocked a Dolce and Gabbana tulip shift dress, and even the teenager sitting two seats opposite was wearing a Marc Jacob denim jacket.

Denton didn't seem the least bit concerned about a lack of labels. He'd changed into a pair of tan pants and a mint and white striped open neck shirt. His navy cotton bomber jacket was draped across the arm of his chair. Sydney felt ridiculously relieved that she didn't recognise any labels. But judging him by his Italian loafers and the fact he just cancelled a helicopter, she was pretty sure they'd be designer.

Sydney was used to travelling alone. Her usual airport routine involved scrambling for a socket to plug in her phone or laptop, the short length of her power cable meaning she often sat cross-legged on the airport carpet, catching up on research and calling in favours so she could get a jump on her latest investigation. But with no accreditation and her only source for her only story, holed up in Fiji, there was no point powering up her laptop. Sydney had nothing to do. She picked up her phone, and though her finger hovered over Matilda's name, she knew she couldn't.

Not yet, anyway. She scrolled to Mum instead and sent a short text.

Taking a couple of days off, spur of the moment mini-break!

Not an outright lie.

Will come see you soon.

That probably was a lie, but her mother's reply was almost instant.

Safe.Travels.Syd.Glad.You.Taking.Time.Off.You.Work.To.Hard.Please.Come.Would.Love.To.See.You.

So she was still using the old brick of a mobile she'd had since Tony Blair ran the country. And she still hadn't found the space key.

Sydney glanced across at Denton. Her mother would be so excited to see her with a man. And someone as successful and charming as Denton Cole – her mother would have her barefoot and pregnant in no time. Sydney felt her chest tighten.

"Are you all sorted?" Denton asked. "Phones off?"

Sydney nodded. She closed her mother down, held the power button, swiped right and watched the screen go black. That was better. She sat back in her chair and breathed out.

20

Sydney had never experienced the luxury of flying First Class, and after the previous sleepless night with Denton Cole doing wicked and wonderful things to her, she found it very easy to drop off to sleep.

They changed aircraft in Hong Kong, and for the better part of the flight onwards to Fiji, Sydney and Denton sat facing each other. Sydney's first class area was transformed by a pleasant attendant into their very own small restaurant booth in the sky. Cups of coffee and water glasses were refreshed on the small table by the same delightful attendant, and when Sydney commented to Denton that her joyfulness was suspicious, he'd laughed a lot. Which made Sydney laugh because she hadn't been joking.

"This feels like a first date." Denton said.

"But we've already, you know," Sydney murmured. "I mean, is that weird? We don't really know much about each other."

"I googled you," Denton admitted. "Is that weird?"

"Yes!" Sydney cried. She crunched on a handful of salted cashews. "I googled you too."

"I think we should fill in the gaps," Denton suggested. "I'll go first."

Denton lived a standard upper-class childhood, nannies and tutors shuttled him between the UK and New York. He did as he was told, worked hard at school, university, and for the family business, always under his father's eagle eye. At 59, his father had a routine check-up. They discovered advanced prostate cancer. His father had the works, surgery, radiotherapy, chemotherapy and hormone treatment. And when the cancer was finally gone, so was his desire to run the family empire. Denton's father wanted to enjoy what years he had left, so on the night before his 26th birthday, Denton Cole and his sister Darcy became owners of their very wealthy and prosperous family business. Or *businesses* really. The Cole Corporation.

Sydney explained her own success had come not because of her father, but in spite of him. Denton asked about her mother, and Sydney found herself recalling her early years growing up with a mother who always said yes.

"Only child guilt I think, but she would let me bring home all the neighbourhood kids, and would feed them all biscuits and juice. One time I hosted my very own animal show and I invited all the kids in our street and told them to bring their pets. It was chaos - cats and dogs everywhere. And rabbits. A goat, and I think there might have been a peacock there. My mother just laughed and handed out ice cream cones."

Sydney sat quietly staring at her cup of coffee. Her father's death had opened a deep divide between Sydney and her mother, a gap that suddenly seemed vast and intensely sad. She didn't mention any of that.

"It sounds like you had a good mum," Denton offered a thumb and wiped away a tear from Sydney's cheek.

"Sorry," Sydney sniffed, "I was somewhere else."

"Are your parents still together?" Denton asked, and saw the cloud of anger pass over Sydney's face.

"My father died a few years ago. Gosh, will you look at that. We'll be starting our descent any minute. I'll just go and freshen myself up while the bathroom is free."

Sydney braced herself against the bathroom door. There was a very good reason Sydney seldom thought about her Dad. She let the water run and splashed her face, before shaking herself back to reality. The first class bathroom came fully stocked. If she was going to make it through the next few days with Denton, her emotional armour would need to be much stronger. She channelled Sensible Sydney, and set about using the variety of little bottles of face cleanser and moisturiser and found a little toothbrush to scrub her teeth.

She left clean and fresh, with a steady smile, at least on the outside.

The crew were preparing the cabin for landing and Denton was back in his own seat.

Sydney gave him a bright smile, then took her own and tightened her seat belt. The aircraft tilted as it dropped below the clouds.

Calm and steady. It had been a mistake to joke around, pretending they were on a first date. As if there were potential for a real relationship. That was not going to happen. The attraction she felt for Denton was purely physical. That was okay. Better than okay, it was brilliant! There would be no messy emotions involved. Only weak women fell in love with handsome strangers. Usually in lame romantic movies.

It's like itching a scratch, isn't that what they say? She could enjoy her time with Denton without falling head over heels. Sydney liked having her feet firmly on the ground.

"Okay?" Denton asked, leaning across the aisle. "Ready for the Southern Hemisphere?"

"Bring it on!" Sydney gave him a thumbs up. She'd had her head in the clouds, but now it was time to get to work. Time for some old-style Sydney snooping.

She was ready to land.

21

Denton followed Sydney down the steps of the aircraft and on to the tarmac. The air was warm and humid and they both disrobed as they walked, cardigans and coats shrugged off as they shuffled into the terminal with the other passengers.

The air inside was cooler, and though it was early morning, three men with ukuleles played music for their captive audience.

"Everyone's smiling," Sydney noted.

"Including you," Denton laughed.

The queue was slow but steady. In due course, Denton's passport was stamped and Sydney was ushered through after him. They were legal visitors in Fiji for up to four months. Denton imagined what four months on a tropical island with Sydney would be like. A seaside bungalow, a hammock strung between two coconut trees.

"So how do we find Haig?" Sydney asked.

Denton shook off the island hideaway fantasy and focused on real life.

"First we check in to the hotel and get some rest. Then we can track down Haig."

Denton started walking, his leather carry-on bumping against his leg.

"There's the shuttle bus to the Hilton."

"It's the high season," Sydney reasoned, wheeling her bag along and trying to catch up. "Won't the Hilton be booked solid? And if we turn up without a pre-booking we'll pay the full rack-rate."

"I've got it covered," Denton assured Sydney. "I asked you to come with me, so I'll cover the costs."

"I'm not short of cash," Sydney explained, "but one night at the Hilton probably costs more than my last mortgage payment!" But Denton had already joined the line for the shuttle.

"Don't worry," Denton assured her, and pulled her gently into the queue. The others lining up were mostly older, slightly rounder versions of themselves, dragging larger amounts of luggage and fanning their faces with their passports.

At the entrance to the bus, the driver looked concerned.

"Sorry Sir, No booking, no bus."

Denton opened his wallet, pulled out a metallic card and handed it discreetly to the driver, whose demeanour changed in an instant. Denton liked the look of amusement on Sydney's face.

"Welcome Sir, come inside, come inside."

"I'm guessing that wasn't your Oyster Card," Sydney whispered as she accepted a beautiful frangipani lei. They were ushered up the steps.

They took two seats at the front of the air-conditioned bus, and were presented with a bottle of chilled water.

"No big deal, but I know the CEO," Denton shrugged.

"You've been here before?" Sydney asked.

"No, never been to Fiji before. But I've been to Tahiti, Hawaii and there's a small boutique hotel in Vanuatu."

"Ah," Sydney rolled her eyes.

"Problem?" Denton asked Sydney. "You don't approve of my travel destinations?"

"No," Sydney shrugged. "It's just all so, I don't know, cliché?"

"What is?"

"This," Sydney whispered, waving her hand around. "It's like Noah's ark for entitled rich folk. Look at him," Sydney's eyes followed an older gentleman as he boarded the bus, then held his hand out to a young blonde, sporting a pair of very large, very pert breasts, barely restrained in a spaghetti strap sundress.

"She could be his daughter," Denton suggested, then the old man cupped one of the woman's butt cheeks.

Sydney laughed, a free-floating sound he felt the urge to hear again and again. He'd touched a nerve earlier, asking about her family. He'd wanted to tell her he understood.

It's not like my family by birth are anything to brag about. But she'd taken her time in the bathroom and by the time she got back to her seat they were starting to descend.

The driver welcomed them aboard and eased the bus on to the road. Sydney had the window seat and Denton watched her take in the view of the island.

"You packed the wrong sunglasses. I told you these ones hurt my nose." Denton glanced back at the old man as he grumbled at his younger companion, who shrugged her shoulders and reapplied her lip gloss in a small compact mirror.

"Those glasses are like, really in right now darling. Give them a chance."

Sydney elbowed Denton and grinned.

"Retirement goals?" She winked. Then went back to her window.

"You know, I don't think I've ever seen real coconut trees."

"Is that how you think of me?" Denton asked.

"What do you mean?"

"Do you think of me like that man," he whispered, tilting his head across the aisle of the bus. "Entitled. Rich. You think I bring women to tropical islands, so they can stroke my—"

Sydney's eyes widened.

"Ego." Denton laughed.

"I don't know how I think of you yet," Sydney smiled. She very carefully unscrewed the cap from her water bottle and took a sip.

"Think about it now," he teased. "Am I a rich prick or am I one of the good guys?"

He watched her mull it over. Her brow creased and her lip sucked in between her teeth. Then a faint flush of pink in her cheeks, and that sparkle in her eyes.

"Okay, I'm leaning a little more towards good guy than rich prick. But I reserve the right to change my mind!" Sydney hurried.

"Good to know, having left my ego in my other pants. But if you're in the mood for stroking something, -" Denton raised his eyebrows.

Sydney rolled her eyes and elbowed him hard, and Denton threw his head back laughing.

But in the back of her mind, Sydney knew it bothered her. The idea of Denton being in Tahiti or Vanuatu with some floozy with perfectly manicured fingernails and a whole wardrobe of Louis Vuitton Cruise Wear. An image niggled on the edges of her memory. It had been a week after his heart attack. Her mother's watery eyes, her broken-hearted body leaned over the washing machine, with her dad's crumpled casual weekend pants in her hands, the last of his clothes that she would ever wash. As always, Sydney imagined a duplicate pair of pants, in a house across town, and her father's floozy stuffing them in her own washing machine with her un-entitled grief.

What did she really know about Denton, this man sitting next to her? She knew how he made her feel. The way her skin tingled when he touched her. The fuzzy cotton wool feeling that filled her head when he was near. Sydney knew the way her body responded to Denton. But that was all physics and chemistry. Pheromones and hormones and all that stuff.

Damn sure that's not the basis for anything more than a fling. Right?

As the bus drove them on to the hotel, Sydney reasoned another deal with herself.

Surely, in a different time zone, heading towards a luxury resort, on a tropical island, with a good-looking man, definitely stroke-worthy, I can park any misgivings in a temporary holding zone, and just live in the moment? Just this once.

.

22

"The honeymoon suite," Denton announced as he swung back the oversized door, its dark stained wood carved in intricate patterns. "I'll refrain from carrying you over the threshold."

Sydney stopped for a moment and breathed it all in.

"You know. I never really understood the whole big white wedding thing," she said, "but if this is the prize, I might have to rethink things!"

"Sydney Stone. You just described a honeymoon as a prize. Like you won the claw game and came away with a giant purple teddy bear."

"Yes."

"You hopeless romantic you," he laughed, emptying his pockets on to the small entrance table.

"I can 100% guarantee you that I've never been accused of that!"

Sydney dropped her bag and pulled at her boots, peeling her socks off and standing still for a moment, letting the marble tiles transfer their coolness through the soles of her feet and up through her body. She padded across the room, taking in the vases of fresh flowers and bowls of tropical fruit placed on every table, and she almost cried when she slipped through the white curtains at the back of the suite, and saw the beautiful private plunge pool, with delicate flower petals floating on the surface.

"Come on then." Denton appeared beside her completely naked. He stretched his arms up towards the morning sun, not the only salutation his body offered. He stepped down into the water.

"It's warm," he encouraged.

For once she didn't hesitate. She turned her face to the sun and quickly took her clothes off, leaving them in a pile on the marble floor.

The minute she stepped into the water, Sydney felt a tightness she hadn't even known existed, begin to slowly release. Denton was right about the warm water and she lay her head back and let herself float into his arms. Sydney closed her eyes and let her body respond to his touch.

"You're driving me crazy," Denton whispered, and Sydney smiled as he wrapped an arm around her hips and pulled her close.

London was yesterday, so far away in miles and in mind. Sydney felt sure she had travelled through a looking glass. She'd shifted through a vortex, and landed in some alternate universe. Fiji was most definitely in an entirely different dimension to the one she'd left behind.

Sydney felt nothing but pure light and joy when Denton lay beside her on the enormous cloud-like bed, their skin and hair still damp from the pool. She could smell frangipani and hibiscus and though she'd sworn she was good for nothing but sleep, Denton's fingers were moving in gentle, barely-there strokes across her nipples, and a slow warmth at her core was too delicious to ignore. She let it pulse and grow within her.

"Get a condom," she whispered. He disappeared, and the moments his hands weren't on her body seemed unbearable.

"Ready?"

"Oh hell yes."

He slid effortlessly inside her, and she groaned as his long controlled strokes took her right to the edge. Her breath grew ragged as he plunged deep inside her again and again until she cried out as wave after wave of pleasure coursed through her body.

Sydney wrapped her arms around Denton's neck and kissed him as he moaned in release and pulsed within her, then she opened her eyes and watched him fall back to earth on the bed beside her, warm and slick with sweat.

Her own body set adrift, Sydney closed her eyes again. Softened and spent, she felt Denton pull her into his arms. She drifted away into a deep hazy sleep.

Sydney was roused by the smell of strong coffee. The light outside was fading and heavy with sleep, she struggled to sit up.

"It's evening," Denton chuckled. "I set my alarm for three, but you looked so peaceful, I didn't have the heart to wake you. It's about five now," he said, checking the time on his phone.

"Yes, 5:05 pm."

Denton produced a cup of coffee, which Sydney drank in three quick gulps.

"More," she demanded.

"Your wish is my command," Denton said, taking the cup.

When the caffeine kicked in, Sydney shrugged into a white fluffy robe and drifted into the main room of their hotel suite. Denton, seated at the glass dining table, was pouring water from a tall silver carafe. He placed it back on the table beside a tray of cheese and crackers and an abundant selection of peeled and sliced tropical fruit.

Sydney's stomach rumbled. She folded herself into a chair and took a large piece of pineapple.

"I'm starving," Sydney told Denton.

"I've ordered sushi," Denton replied. "You said on the plane you loved sushi, but you can have whatever you like. They'll make you beans on toast if you ask."

"I do love sushi, and I do not want beans on toast," Sydney laughed. "Who would come here, to this tropical paradise, and ask for beans on toast?"

Denton looked sheepish.

"Tell me you didn't."

"I was starving," Denton laughed. "I had chips too."

"Shocking," Sydney admonished. "Although, now you've mentioned chips…"

It was early morning. Denton was breathing slow and steady and she lay for a while, contemplating kissing him awake. But she had no idea when he'd come to bed. She'd been ravenous when room service had knocked on the door the night before. The tempura battered sushi was delicious, she remembered that. But she'd crawled back to bed soon after and fallen straight back to sleep.

Sydney shrugged off the sheet and tiptoed across the room. She quietly unzipped her case. She slipped into her sundress, took a bottle of water from the mini-bar and made her way down the path to the beach, where the sun was just beginning to glow on the horizon.

It was better than she could have ever imagined, had she ever stopped to think about it. The sand was cool under her bare feet and the breeze made her shiver slightly, but it wasn't unpleasant. It was refreshing, and she took a deep breath of salty air.

Sydney loved her work and felt she had executed her life plan to perfection. But a feeling washed in with the tide, that maybe her determination to control her destiny had a downside.

What if I've been so focused on a successful career, I've accidentally trapped myself?

Was she living in a self-styled, corporate prison? Regardless of her pre-determined plans, Sydney was relishing every barefoot step of her new-found freedom. The soft white sand called her across to the water, and she stood on the edge of the tide.

I'm on the other side of the world, I'm upside down!

She had the beach to herself. So she did some twirling for a bit, then skipped along the water's edge. And as the morning sun crept slowly into the sky she stepped into the shallow water. It was warmer than she'd expected and she stood with her hands on her hips, watching it lap across her toes. She resisted an impromptu dip, knowing that the coral beyond could cut her feet and cause an infection that could land her in hospital.

It's one thing to be carefree, another entirely to be careless.

Still, Sydney marvelled at this person, standing on the edge of the beach in just a sundress. "I'm not even wearing any knickers!" she told the ocean.

Sydney had gripped on to a tight bundle of stress and consternation that had grown over the years as she built her career. She'd never thought of putting it down. Taking a break. She'd never opened her life up to the beauty of the world. She'd watched her friends go off on holiday, workmates with their photos of the Grand Canyon at sunrise and their Swiss Chalets. But Sydney had been too busy, too focused for fun.

She walked across the sand and had to admit that fun felt good. She hadn't felt this free in years, if ever, and that may, in part, have something to do with Denton Cole lying naked in her bed. But there was something else. Sydney could feel a part of herself unfurl. She contemplated other places she would like to visit. She could have a holiday alone. When this thing with Denton was over. She wasn't blind enough to think their shared holiday was more than a one-off.

But I could do this for myself. Maybe once a year? I could do one of those yoga meditation type trips. On top of a mountain somewhere. Or I could ride a camel in the desert. I wouldn't mind seeing the sun come up over the Grand Canyon.

Denton woke up alone. He was hard and horny and called out for Sydney. But there was no reply. He checked the bathroom and the sitting room, then he'd stood on the patio of their suite. He found her. A small figure down by the shoreline. He'd been about to yell out to her, wave her back to bed. But he watched instead, as she'd spun in circles and skipped along. She stopped, and stood with her hands on her hips, gazing down at the water, despite the magnificent sun, rising on the horizon. And Denton scrambled for his phone, adjusting the camera focus to capture the perfect moment.

When he lowered his phone and watched her without the filtered lens, he'd felt it. Deep within him. He wanted to make her happy. He hung on those moments when her face would light up. When she dropped that chip on her shoulder and let herself relax. He could do that for her. Over and over again. At the end of a long day at work, he wanted to be the one to pour her a glass of wine, and kiss her neck and make all her worries disappear. He wanted to visit every beautiful beach on every island in the Pacific and watch Sydney Stone in her pretty sundress, dancing with the waves. He wanted to steal these moments, watching her, knowing she would soon be in his arms.

Bloody hell, there's something deep there, he mused. He'd known Sydney less than a week, and here he was, thinking forever. He wasn't upset though, he just felt a little more critical examination was needed before he decided what to do.

His phone buzzed in the bedroom and Denton reluctantly went to find it.

"Your timing is impeccable," he told his old friend.

"Bula to you too. Let's get this party started."

23

We're meeting Haig tonight." Sydney felt the familiar surge of adrenalin. As much as she'd enjoyed the sunrise, and skipping a few pages of her rule book, she needed to remember this was first and foremost a work trip.

Granted, one with a sexy man who insisted he shower with her.

"I'm going to help you with those hard to reach places," he grinned.

"You've got a thing about bathrooms," Sydney mumbled through a mouthful of toothpaste.

"I've got a thing about you," Denton yelled over the shower.

Breakfast was served on the deck at Nuku restaurant within the grounds of the Hilton resort. They lingered over coffee and croissants, and Sydney listened as Denton relayed his conversation with Haig.

He was on an outer island, making arrangements to return to Nadi later in the day. He was purposefully vague, Denton assumed he would not want to arrange a time or a place over the phone.

Not for the first time, Sydney felt like she had stepped into a plot line from a Hollywood thriller.

"Is all the secrecy really necessary?" she asked. "I mean we're in the middle of nowhere. No one in London even knows we're here."

"Island Sydney is mellow." Denton let the waiter fill his coffee cup, then thanked him. When he had moved on to another table he said,

"It seems a bit of overkill to me too, but Haig is concerned. He's not a conspiracy theory nut job, in case you were wondering. If this thing has him jumpy, we should probably do what he says."

"I just wish we knew more of the story," Sydney grumbled. "I hate not knowing what's going on."

"Bring back Island Sydney," Denton advised. "We've got the rest of the day to relax. Then Journalist Sydney can come back out to play."

Sydney sipped her coffee and weighed it up. She had the whole day to do as she liked. She had no information, so there was nothing she could do but wait.

"Come on then." She stood and beckoned for Denton to follow her.

"If Haig isn't here till tonight, then for the rest of the day, Island Sydney is in charge." She marched along the path that led back to their villa. She called back to him,

"I want to feed some turtles, have a massage and lie in a hammock. But first," Sydney stopped walking and waited for Denton to catch up. She rose on her tiptoes and kissed him. She wrapped her arms around his neck and pressed her body into his, "there's something I need you to do for me."

24

They met Haig on a jetty at the rear of the hotel. He wasn't what Sydney expected. The photos she'd seen online didn't show how tall he was, nor the redness of his hair. And Justin Haig had not spent his time in Fiji catching any of the sun's rays. It was almost comical, to shake hands with the very pale lanky man, dressed in Bermuda shorts and a wrinkled linen shirt, a pair of Ray-Ban sunglasses perched on his head.

"I know what you're thinking," Haig nodded at Sydney. "Why would a tall skinny translucent man, such as myself, come to a place where his skin could crisp up faster than a prawn on a hot plate." Sydney smiled. Haig's British accent was mixed with something else. Australian?

"I'll have you know, I tan up quite nicely. It's a slow curing process, but by the end of summer, I'm far less opaque. Cole, tell her mate."

"Once, we went surfing in the rain. Haig got sunburnt."

"Once, Cole went surfing and a jellyfish stung him on his—"

"Thigh." Denton finished. Sydney grinned.

"Sure mate," Haig winked at Sydney. "Whatever you say."

"It's bloody great to see you mate," Denton threw an arm around his friend. "I've got to say, you're the master of suspense."

"I know," Haig agreed. "Very James Bond."

"I was thinking Austin Powers."

"You're a cruel man, Denton Cole."

The banter between the two continued as they strolled back to the hotel.

"I booked the suite next door to you and I've organised dinner to come to us. God I'm starving," Haig said. "Travelled all day on half a pineapple and a bag of M&M's."

They walked through the hotel grounds, the sun setting in pink and orange hues behind them. Haig dragged a small carry on suitcase, its wheels bumping and echoing loudly on the pebbled path.

"So, Sydney Stone. What's your story?"

"She's the journalist, Haig. She should be the one asking the questions."

"It's okay," Sydney told them both. "What would you like to know?"

"Are you shagging your boss or is this purely a business trip?"

"Bloody hell Haig, I know your mum taught you better manners than that."

"I've been an investigative journalist with Passion Media for the last eight years," Sydney offered. "I worked my way up. Intern, receptionist, then finding and filing stories. Mundane parking ticket quotas, went undercover as a receptionist in a brothel, that was for a story on people smugglers. I have not ever, nor will I ever, have sex with someone just to get a story, or to further my career. I didn't sleep my way up, but I do not judge those women who sometimes find themselves with limited ways and means of getting what they want from their careers."

"Right-o!" Haig nodded.

"But yes," Sydney shrugged, "I am shagging my boss."

"I like this one," Haig said after they collected his room key from the front desk. "She's normal."

"Normal as opposed to?" Sydney enquired.

"That woman you dated with the stick up her arse," Haig grinned.

"Oh god," Denton sighed. Haig put the room card in his door, then waited for the beep.

"Let's not have this conversation again, Haig."

"He can't drop a comment like that and leave me hanging," Sydney reasoned. "I want to know about the stick-girl!

"Two against one it seems," Haig winked at Sydney.

He stood with his hands on his hips and looked around at his suite.

"This place is top notch."

It was identical to Sydney and Denton's room next door. A waiter in a crisp white shirt and black linen shorts appeared from the balcony.

"Good evening. My name is Alon. I have laid the table outside, as per your request Mr Haig. Would you like a moment or shall I show you through?"

"Now's good," Haig quickly replied. "I'm starving."

The waiter turned out to be a fine bartender, the cocktails he styled with coconut and mango were easy to drink. Sydney took the flower from her place setting and tucked it behind her ear.

"Now Sydney. I believe you were enquiring after stick-girl, as you so eloquently called her."

Sydney grinned at Denton, who shook his head and laughed. In the fading light, his eyes matched the ocean behind him so perfectly. Sydney would have loved to snap the perfect photograph.

"She was a nightmare. Wouldn't eat anything that wasn't organic. Unless she was drunk. Then she'd get through a Big Mac like the cavewoman she descended from! Then she'd wake up in the morning and complain at us for hours for turning her into a cow murderer."

"I think *you* called her a cow murderer," Denton said.

"Probably. Sounds like me!" Haig rested a freckled arm on the back of his chair.

"Now. Sydney. I'm sure Cole has been on his best behaviour, and I hate to have to spoil his good boy image. But your boss, it turns out," Haig put a hand on Sydney's in consolation, "is a bit of a playboy."

"I am not a playboy," Denton shook his head.

"Really," Haig mused. "Do you think this warrants further investigation, Ms Stone?"

"Oh yes Mr Haig, I think it does."

"Denton was in a magazine," Haig told Sydney, taking a drink of his frothy cocktail from an oversized glass goblet.

"*Not* a business magazine."

"What kind of magazine?" Sydney encouraged.

"Definitely not a magazine his father could have put on display in the reception area of Cole Incorporated. Not a magazine his mother ever mentioned in the Cole Family Christmas newsletter."

"Your mother does the Christmas brag rag Haig, not mine."

"Ah, but my mum loved your magazine! For a long time, Denton's male modelling moment was pride of place on the coffee table in the lounge."

"That was all you Haig," Denton interjected, "he bought so many copies of the darn thing. Every time I took one away, there was a new copy in its place the next morning."

"Tell me!" Sydney demanded. And Haig did not disappoint.

"Denton Cole, aka *Titanium*, no last name, like Madonna. Denton *'Titanium'* Cole, was on the front cover of Teen Heat magazine. He took the number one spot of the top ten hotties in the Hottest Heart Throb Holiday Spots of Summer, June edition, 2002."

Sydney turned to Denton, her mouth wide open.

"You were a male model?"

"Briefly."

"And you were called Titanium?"

"How do you even remember all that?" Denton shook his head at Haig.

"I have a magnificent memory." Haig turned his attention back to Sydney.

"Our friend Denton was going through some emotional turmoil, a phase if you will," Haig leaned back in his chair.

"I was 19," Denton explained. "Gap year, existential crisis in regards to living off Daddy's money. I was feeling trapped. I wanted to do something different. Something that wasn't, - expected."

Sydney shifted her eyes back and forth between Denton and Haig.

"I have no words," she exclaimed. "A male model! I bet your parents didn't expect Titanium!"

"The name was spur of the moment. The woman from the magazine was a real flirt. She kept telling me how strong my biceps were. That type of corny stuff you lap up when you're a teenager. At the last minute, when she gave me the contract and legal release to sign, I realised I couldn't use my real name. My father would have killed me. And that magazine woman came past and said, 'Oh you're such a babe, your muscles are like,'"

"Titanium!" Sydney and Haig said at the same time.

"It was a bit of fun. I wasn't even sure they'd use my photos."

"Oh but they did!" Haig sat forward resting his elbows on the table and his chin in his hands. He plastered a dreamy look on his face. "It was magnificent! I will never forget the day Teen Heat came out. We were back in London. Blustery I remember, the squirrels were quite delightful in Hyde Park." Haig paused, took a delicate sip from his cocktail.

"Quite delightful."

Then he continued.

"I remember like it was yesterday. You could not shift the grin from my face. You see, Sydney Stone, I'd talked myself into a job as an intern for some tech start-up company. I stayed late, misused the office photocopier, then strolled home and covered our local bar with Titanium. Copies of his front page debut on every table, all over the bathroom walls – ladies and gents. He was a hit! And I'm only mildly ashamed to admit I used his buff bod to get some action of my own."

Sydney shook her head, taking it all in.

"Okay," Haig conceded, "I'm not ashamed at all. I carried a copy of Teen Heat around with me wherever I went. It was a wonderful conversation starter. I would casually flick to Titanium's page in the magazine, and when the object of my desire glanced across I would smile ruefully and explain how the dude in the photo with the mega-awesome abs was my best friend. That Titanium wasn't his real name (of course)."

"They'd take a look at Haig and assume he was lying," Denton interjected.

"They'd ask for proof, of course, so my best friend here would bring them around to our apartment, and make me lift up my shirt. To prove it was me."

"No way, he pimped you out?"

Denton nodded. "Don't be fooled by his charm. Justin Haig is the real playboy."

"And you never took advantage of your Titanium status?"

"Well, not as often as you did," Denton pointed to his mate.

"That's not my fault," Haig shrugged, "It was a public service. You understand Sydney, I simply offered a consolation prize. Cole here had ample opportunity, offers of marriage and babies. They looked so heartbroken when he turned them down. I made them feel better!"

"I think," Denton laid his hands on the table, "we can take a break from the teenage diaries of Justin Haig and Denton Cole."

"AKA *Titanium*." Haig grinned across the table.

"No one here had forgotten," Denton told his friend.

Sydney saw the relief on Denton's face when the waiter reappeared.

"It seems this kind gentleman would like to provide us with some sustenance!" Haig declared. "Let's eat!"

They chatted easily through dinner, enjoying the fresh air and watching the sunset across the water. Sydney would have loved to talk more about Denton – *aka Titanium,* and the marriage and baby proposals, but teenage romance stories were only entertaining when they were someone else's!

Would I want Denton and Haig to know about AJ, my first boyfriend, and the first time we met? How we were at the local pool, and AJ tripped on a pool noodle, fell towards the water and reached out for me to save him, only to drag us both, fully clothed, into the water. Sydney still blushed at the memory of their senior class rolling around laughing.

Denton had handled Haig's friendly ribbing well, so she'd spared him further questions about his Titanium days. She was happy to sit back and listen. The two men were catching up on each other's lives. Names of friends and colleagues Sydney had no connection to floated across the table. Some were married, one in a castle in France, another got married in Vegas, to a girl he'd met at a casino buffet. A smattering of babies had been born, and it turned out Haig had a daughter, Arabella, who was no longer in love with her daddy as she had been in her pre-teen days. Instead, Haig's 'baby,' with all her 15 years of life experience, liked to stomp into a room, roll her eyes, then arch her eyebrow and say "Really?"

"Did she get the tickets I sent her for the Little Mix concert?" Denton asked.

"You're a bastard, Cole," Haig sighed across the table. "I'm quoting your god-daughter here,

'You are so boring, Dad. Why can't you be like Uncle D.'" Haig pushed his chair back and gave an excellent demonstration of the walk, pause, eye roll, eyebrow lift.

Denton seemed quite pleased with his role as popular uncle.

"I can't help it if I'm awesome," Denton laughed.

"It's okay." Haig slipped back into his chair. "I told Arabella I'd get her a copy of Teen Heat. One look at Uncle Titanium in a speedo with his bleached hair and Arabella might change her mind."

"Speedo?" Sydney had to ask. "And bleached?"

"I'll hook you up when we get back home," Haig winked.

But the mention of home gave a note of sobriety to the table. With their meal finished, Denton thanked their waiter and asked for a pot of strong black coffee in the sitting room.

When Sydney returned from the bathroom, the balcony table was clear, and a tray with coffee, sugar and cream was waiting on the small glass coffee table. Haig tipped the waiter well, and Sydney watched him nod in appreciation and leave the suite, quietly clicking the door closed behind him.

It was time to continue their evening undisturbed.

"Shall we?" Sydney asked.

25

Haig took a thin computer tablet from his bag and placed it on the coffee table, then took a seat beside Denton on the small sofa. Sydney tucked herself into one of the comfortable occasional chairs opposite the pair.

They were such opposites to look at. Haig was tall and thin and topped with a rich bronze crop of hair. Denton, on the other hand, was average in height, but his athletic body was muscular and strong. Sydney almost matched Denton in height, but she felt small beside them both. Not a physical observation, more a reflection of the life experiences the two men had shared. Sydney's own life felt very safe and seemingly innocuous. No Vegas weddings or career swerves in her past.

Not until Denton Cole walked into my office.

Haig looked from Denton to Sydney.

"After I tell you what we're facing, I can't undo it. So if either of you have any doubts you need to speak up now. I will happily shake your hand, Cole, and kiss you goodbye Sydney, in an overly familiar way for a man you've just met. You can walk out the door and fly back to old Blighty, to your everyday lives and careers. You're not locked in to this. Yet."

"I'm on gardening leave, who knows if I even have a job to go back to," Sydney shrugged, "and I didn't come all this way to chicken out seconds before I find out what the hell is going on." Sydney looked at Denton who nodded in agreement.

"Whatever it is Haig, it's too big for you to handle alone. So get on with it."

"Here we go then." Haig opened an application on the tablet and a script of computer dialogue appeared.

"This is what I got off the server at The Conservative Party Head Quarters, and what I subsequently found on Vanguard's server."

Sydney and Denton leaned over the coffee table and watched the long lines of code fill the screen.

"I'll keep this as simple as I can," Haig said. "They've been using covert software."

"They?" Sydney asked.

"Vanguard, or someone they know created
it. Conservatives have run with it. They call it Badger."

"What does it do?" Sydney asked.

"It burrows into unsuspecting computer systems. Searches for information from usually restricted sources. From what I've seen, Badger's purpose right now, is to locate the private information of Conservative Party members. They're focused on what they call 'donor viability.' Badger finds information they can exploit to increase member's financial input into the party."

"They're targeting their own people?" Sydney clarified with Haig.

"Yes. Elections are won by the biggest wallet. It's not an original concept. It's their version of phishing. They know they're in the right area, their members have already given their support. But now they can drop the net deeper, and haul up all kinds of information. Stuff that
will encourage generosity."

"Blackmail," Denton stated.

"Exactly. Badger can gain access to email accounts, data logs and reports, electronic calendars and location information, and photo storage applications. Here's an example you'll want to see. This is an email I stumbled upon, somewhat *not – legally*."

Sydney lifted the tablet from the coffee table and read out loud from the screen.

"Badger testing going well. Further to this morning's discussion, consider this.

'John and Sally' haven't donated in a while, and are not responding to the usual party donation requests. Badger gives us John's email and his photo storage files suggests he's playing away from home. With Sally's cousin. Perhaps John's developed an online gambling habit. Poor John. Someone might suggest he gets some help, because it would be awful if that information made it out to the public. John is so grateful to the party for their continued discretion, his donations double this year."

Haig took the tablet back from Sydney and closed the email, then tapped at the screen. The internal web-server system for Passion Media appeared.

"Is that our system?" Denton asked.

"Sure is. It was one of the easier trails to follow." Cole put the tablet back on the table so they could all see. "It looks like Badger was pushed into Passion Media through a backdoor in a recently installed software programme."

Sydney's head snapped up.

"The accounting upgrade. That thing was rushed in. We all told them it was too quick, but two of the board members were adamant we needed it."

"Were you in any of those meetings Cole?" Haig asked.

"No. It was all signed off before I got there. They were installing it the day I arrived. Who was the project lead?" Denton asked Sydney.

"Vernon Berry. He insisted. Said it was an integral part of the network so it needed a director as project lead. And he's the Chief Financial Officer. So it made sense."

"Doesn't look good, but don't assume this Berry guy is directly involved," Haig told them. "This is something someone has gone to a lot of trouble to hide. Remember, I only found it by chance. It took me a week to figure out it came from Vanguard, and a couple more days to follow it to Passion. It was a complete fluke I stumbled over it when I did. Since then I've been using some stuff only a few people would know about or be able to track. Whoever designed this is good. Just not as good as me."

"So we can't be sure Berry's involved," Denton said, "But you know what Haig, he's got shifty eyes."

"Damn it Cole," Haig sighed. "Not the shifty eyes."

"It's a thing." Denton insisted.

"Ever since he was, oh, about 11 years old," Haig told Sydney, "Cole has been able to judge a person by the shiftiness of their eyes." Haig rolled his own.

"It's a thing. Berry has shifty eyes."

"Denton Cole. Business Magnate turned psychic. Don't tell me our profit and loss position, I can determine wealth by the arch of your eyebrow."

"Just get on with it, Haig. Or I'll tell her about the time you tried to walk on water."

"It was ice. So yes, technically water, and I did walk on it."

"Technically, you crawled on it."

"I was really drunk."

"So was I, but I didn't ask my mother to call the Pope."

"I wanted it in The Guinness Book of World records. Mum was really good about it."

"She was worried you'd get hypothermia."

"No chance. My blood was diluted with vodka."

"And Kahlua."

"Was that the coffee liquor stuff?"

"The bottle I got your mother to say thanks for having me."

"To be fair, you were pouring the drinks."

"You were sculling it straight from the bottle."

"Yes, I was doing that. But only because you left your post to chat up Amy Dinklee."

"Amy was chatting *me* up, actually. And if we're going down that road, let's talk about Belinda Trundle."

"Ah yes, *a fundle with Trundle*."

Sydney snorted with laughter. She liked this side of Denton. Animated, and somehow softer. Haig brought out his playful side and Sydney could only imagine the hearts they broke with their good looks and boyish charm in their teenage years. But she soon realised that Denton and Haig had so much history, they would carry on all night.

"Boys, as much as you're amusing me, and offering great insight into your misspent youth, I think we'd better get back to the main issue."

They all leaned forward and Haig went back to tapping things on the screen.

Haig said, "From what I can see, they've only run a couple of live tests. For example, there are only two hits on Passion Media. They looked at two items on your calendar Cole, a golf game you've got scheduled with the leader of Young Labour.-"

"They'll not get much out of that," Denton shrugged. "*Young* is the key word there. She's the daughter of someone vaguely important. Felicity someone-hyphenated-something.
My assistant Harvey set it up. He owed her Dad a favour."

"The other is a lunch date you had at The Ivy." Haig pointed to the screen. "Couple of days ago. Morris James and Alex Coleman."

Sydney assumed the look of shock on her face reflected Denton's.

"Who are they?" Haig asked.

"The heads of The British Daily News, and The Sunday Star," Denton answered.

"The big boys!" Sydney whistled. "How on earth did you get them in the same room?"

"Closed dining room. Different entrances and exits. Utmost privacy. Or so I thought," Denton sighed. "There's a lot of restructuring and change happening across the Media industry at the moment. I'm aware you've been pushing for quite a while for Passion Media to get better at online news and reporting," Denton told Sydney. "But we're seen as small fry. We have a reputation for the magazine stuff, rather than hard hitting journalism. But I like what Passion are doing in news and current affairs. So I thought I'd scope out the opposition. Get the lay of the land. See if they even consider us players."

"And?" Sydney asked.

"Everyone and everything is a threat to those guys. They were quite clear. Step on to the news highway and they'll squash us. Like bugs on a windscreen."

"Arseholes," Sydney grumbled. "They're all celebrity gossip anyway. I'll show them some squashed bugs." Sydney got up to close the doors to the patio and retrieve her cardigan from the back of the chair. The night had closed in around them. She shrugged into her cardigan and turned on a lamp.

"So you've got proof they've hacked into Passion. And with all the whistleblowing in the last few years, Assange with Wikileaks and Manning in the States, I'm wondering Haig, and please don't take this the wrong way," Sydney asked, "but why didn't you report it straight away? Just knowing they are capable of using this software, and that it's sitting there on their servers. I have to say as a journalist, I would have made a pretty strong story out of it. And you'd have been protected by the whistleblower legislation."

"What I have is small scale right now," Haig replied. "I'm not saying I didn't consider blowing it out of the water straight away, but I'd have lost before the story even went to print. The Conservative Party would

claim unlawful access. They'd say they had been hacked and had no idea Badger was on their servers. Which might be true. Or it might not.

Vanguard would scramble to clean up before anyone got near them. And if they weren't able to, they'd make themselves victims as well. *Poor us, we've been hacked too.* Then they'd go after me. They'd say I've got all the skills to create such a hack, that I had illegally accessed both computer systems, and then they'd show timelines and data archives and mention the fact that I protested student fee increases in an article I wrote for the university paper years ago, while the Conservatives were in Government. And suddenly I'm at best a liberal leftie, at worst a digital terrorist. My fingerprints were already all over it. They would say I invented Badger and planted it. They'd say I was blackmailing *them.*"

"But you have proof now," Sydney tried again.

"They're still a step ahead Sydney. Believe me, I'm even more exposed now. In fact, I'll make the story worse, shall I? I came out here to Fiji and hid away. I threatened to reveal all and I demanded money in a Swiss bank account, yes I have a few of those. When they wouldn't cooperate, I called in my mate Denton and his 'lady friend' at Passion Media, who jumped on a plane, and came out here to join me in taking down the big bad Conservatives, using stolen information from inside their organisation."

"But that's all conjecture," Sydney pointed out.

"That's all it ever is in politics. It took me half a sleepless night to come up with that scenario," Haig pointed out. "And I've got others. There's the one where they plant a whole lot of stolen files in my apartment and lock me up for fraud and theft. Or the one where they don't even bother framing me and just tie up loose ends with a quick car accident or home invasion. How long do you think a party full of spin doctors would take to come up with similar scenarios?"

"He's right," Denton said. "And us all here, with stolen information. Frolicking on the sand and having a slap-up dinner. Waiters and hotel staff would corroborate the story. Wouldn't be too hard to make it look bad."

Sydney sunk back into her chair. The only noise came from a gecko chirping on the patio.

"How about this," Sydney offered. "Haig still has a shot under The Protected Disclosure Act." Sydney stood up and started pacing, "It would be pretty tough. We'd have to find someone we trust in police, or maybe a Member of Parliament, someone sympathetic to hearing about this, and willing to believe it. But even then, the law protects the business first. What Haig said is right. The Conservatives could say they were unaware of Badger, that they were the victims of Haig's malicious intent to injure their party. And a judge would have to consider why Haig didn't first take the information to the party president. Hell, he didn't even tell his friend who asked him for help in the first place, or someone in the HR department. You can't take information from an organisation unless it's in the public interest."

"But it is," Denton argued, "surely the public are interested when people's private information is being stolen?"

"And therein lies our problem," Haig sighed. "Right now, a nameless, faceless person or organisation may have seen your private information. But they haven't taken anything. There's definitely scope there for it to be stolen."

"But they've been in Passion Media's systems," Denton pointed out.

"A dummy run. Easy enough to fob off as some glitch in Badger beyond their control, that they had no idea was happening. They say the programme was operating without human involvement. Again. Something, or someone, outside their control."

"You're not giving us much to go forward with here mate," Denton complained.

"There is something," Haig rolled his shoulders a couple of times, held his hands over the tablet screen like a pianist waiting for the conductor's cue.

26

Haig's fingers worked their way across the touch screen, opening and moving files at high speed. Sydney perched on the edge of the couch beside Denton, waiting for Haig.

"Best if you never saw me do this," Haig told them both.

"Is that Vanguard?" Sydney asked. "You're in their system!"

"It took a bit of work. No frolicking on the beach for me these last few days."

"How?" Denton asked.

"He turned the worm," Sydney grinned.

"I did," Haig smiled. "I found the back arse of the badger and I climbed up in there."

"That's disgusting." Sydney laughed.

"But bloody brilliant," Denton slapped his friend on the back.

"Don't get too excited. I'm only as good as the next computer genius. I've thrown all I've got at it, as well as the expertise of an underground hacker in Amsterdam."

"So now we can spy on them?" Denton asked.

"Yes." Haig nodded. "But that means all grey areas are gone. We are breaking the law."

"Only a little bit," Sydney offered.

"And they did do it first," Haig smiled and shrugged.

"What's your plan?" Denton asked Haig.

"This, my friends, is the Conservatives 'update your membership' page on their new mobile application. Set to go live in 24 hours. Designed and built in collaboration with Vanguard. They're embarking on a huge refresher campaign to prepare for the election next year. And would you believe it, they're in an unprecedented position to advertise across all media outlets, thanks to a very generous donation from an anonymous source."

"How anonymous?" Sydney asked.

"Name not mentioned at all in their system. Even their emails are clean."

"How hard did you check?" Sydney asked. The investigative journalist in her wanted to push Haig aside and search through the system herself.

"I turned them inside out."

"Damn," Denton sighed.

"Ah, don't be a defeatist!" Haig smiled. "You forgot I climbed up the backside of their badger." He reached forward and a few screens later, he brought up a list of electronic banking transactions.

"Not exactly legal, but..."

Sydney skimmed the names.

"Randall's there, no surprise. Vernon Berry!" Sydney exclaimed.

"And will you look at that," Denton pointed to the screen. "Morris James, CEO of The British Daily News."

"Does Morris James have shifty eyes?" Sydney inquired.

Denton gave a quick nod.

"Face like a ferret."

"Let me get this right," Denton said. "Conservative Party supporters will get this app on their phones and tablets. Then they'll submit their membership renewal through the app and hand the party the keys to their private information."

"But not only their own information." Sydney got up and started pacing again. "Those people will email and communicate with other people online, and they could all be susceptible too."

"Exactly," Haig nodded. "But here's the good bit."

Haig tapped away at the keyboard and a screen of scrolling code appeared. A series of characters and numbers, a language foreign to Sydney and Denton, but to Haig, probably easier to read and understand than English.

"Basically," Haig began, "in terms mere mortals such as yourselves can understand, I've inserted a mirror. Whatever information they filter through Badger and extract, will be duplicated, then the data will bounce out."

"Where will it bounce out to?" Denton asked.

"I don't know," Haig admitted. "I thought it was safest to jump it around. Could be in Hong Kong one minute, then Switzerland the next. Maybe Australia, Finland, or Germany. I've avoided the United States. I don't want to end up in a prison cell with Kim Dot Com."

"He's avoided extradition so far," Denton tried reassuring Haig. "Living the good life in Aotearoa."

"He's a millionaire, with lots of lawyers," Haig told him. "I've got a flat in Hackney and a guy who I paid a few hundred quid to finalise my mortgage."

"Good point," Denton acceded.

"So, let me get this straight. We've got 24 hours till their app goes live and Badger with it? That doesn't give us much time."

"No," Haig shook his head, "They go live, then it'll take another day or so for Badger to collect the data, and only then will we get anything worthwhile to bust these bozos."

"48 hours," Denton nodded. "It's ambitious."

"I know," Haig told his friend. "But it's all about risk and return. We could wait a week, or a month, and dig up all kinds of dirt. But we're working on the cusp of the law here. And if we stockpile information, it makes us just as bad as them. And just as liable as them."

"We get in, we catch them with their fingers in the cookie jar, then we get out." Denton ran a hand through his hair.

Sydney checked Google from her phone. It was 9:30 pm Sunday night in Fiji. That made it 10:30 am on Sunday morning in London.

"They're a whole day behind us," Sydney shared.

"If Badger goes live when work starts in London tomorrow, Monday morning, then we've only got a few hours to get organised. We need a plan. How does the information bounce to us when we need it, and what are we going to do with it?" Denton asked.

They all looked at each other for a moment.

"We need someone connected."

Sydney jumped up. She grabbed the notepad and pen from the writing desk and dragged the hard-backed chair across the room. She sat up straight, pen and paper ready.

"I need some law enforcement contacts we can trust." She paused her pen above the paper and looked to Denton and Haig. "Who do you know?"

Denton was unsurprisingly well connected, and with three possible names on the list, Sydney turned the page over and started making notes.

"If we work with the authorities, and if our proof is good enough to get a deal so Haig won't be prosecuted, then I say we break the story online. And not just anywhere online. www.passionnewsinternational.com ."

Denton looked confused.

"Sydney, there's no such thing as Passion News International," Denton stated.

"Not yet," Sydney smiled. "But there's this guy in IT. Sam. He's good with websites. We had this idea a few months ago, for a dedicated news presence. Fits in with what you were saying earlier," Sydney pitched to Denton, "about Passion being good at news and current affairs. What a way to stamp our mark. We'd attract a lot of attention with a kick-ass exclusive story involving fraud and online espionage."

"I'm not sure Sydney. We go to some guy called Sam and say hey, build us a website? "

"He's already built it. And Sam does this stuff in his sleep. I trust him completely. I guarantee you he can have PNI ready to go in the next 48 hours."

"PNI?"

"Passion News International. We've kind of been working on it for a few months."

"I've got concerns," Denton admitted. "Can Passion Media cope with this level of scrutiny? And Vernon Berry's name keeps coming up. His connection is hugely compromising for the company."

"That's why we get in first. Make the story work for us, rather than against us."

"I like the idea of keeping this in-house," Haig looked at Denton. "If we let it out to the mainstream media, we can't guarantee what direction this goes in. If we feed the story through Passion, we have a better chance of it coming out like we want."

"We control the narrative," Sydney explained. "What do you think Denton?"

"I want to see this PNI website before it goes up. And now we know Passion Media has been compromised, we host PNI on a completely different server. It needs to happen quickly and quietly. Completely off the grid. I want total sign off."

"Of course," Sydney agreed. "I can call Sam in a couple of hours. He'll be in church right now. Doesn't miss a Sunday. But I'll try and catch him before his afternoon support group. He teaches web building to a bunch of guys who've been released from jail."

"Sounds like a saint," Denton muttered.

"What?" Sydney looked up from the notes she was scribbling.

"Nothing," Denton shook his head. But Haig was grinning from ear to ear.

"Question for you Haig. Do you want to be directly quoted? Do you want people to know who you are?"

"It might come out eventually," Denton put in. "But we could give you a bit of time. Refer to you as an IT Consultant."

Haig shuddered.

"Am I the new Edward Snowdon? I feel like I should be researching countries that don't have extradition treaties."

"Let's keep your name out of it as long as we can," Sydney offered. "We can make the tabloids work for it, then we'll scoop 'em, just when they're about to reveal your identity." Sydney grinned.

"Your woman's gone all Katie Couric on us."

"She's gone all Sydney Stone on us," Denton corrected.

"We're all sorted then," Haig agreed. "Let's meet back here for breakfast. Don't use your cellphones. Sydney, call your website guy from the hotel lobby, okay? Other than that, no emails, no phone calls, no texts."

"We get it," Denton stood and stretched.

"I'm not sure how crazy this thing is going to get. I suggest you both go frolic somewhere for a few hours and let me get this thing tied up tight." Haig poured himself a cup of fresh coffee from the pot they'd largely ignored on the table.

"I don't frolic," Denton told his friend.

"Did I say frolic? I'm terrible with F words. I meant fu-" Haig stopped and smiled.

Denton ushered Sydney to the door.

"You are lucky you're in the midst of a conspiracy mate."

"You gonna beat me up behind the bike sheds?" Haig laughed.

"No," Denton smiled. "I'll get Sydney to do it."

27

"A walk?" Denton suggested. Sydney nodded and they followed the path, through the sleepy resort garden, until their feet touched the sand. He reached for Sydney's hand. They'd left the lights of the resort behind them, and they stood side by side, waiting while their eyes adjusted to the darkness.

"Can I ask you a question?" she asked, letting Denton wrap an arm around her waist and pull her close.

"Yes, I've got a condom in my pocket," he whispered in her ear.

"That's some classy organisational skills," Sydney laughed, "but not in fact my question." She closed her eyes and Denton could think of nothing but her warm body in his arms.

"Let's talk before we get, you know, carried away," Sydney suggested.

"Too late, that's not my pocket calculator pressing up against you," he murmured between kisses.

Sydney pulled back.

"This, situation, Denton I just want to check you know what you're doing."

Denton tilted his head back. Then he slid his hands around her waist and linked his fingers together at the small of her waist.

"Sydney. I absolutely know what I'm doing. I'm not sure I've ever told you this." Denton paused and stared deeply into her eyes. "I know what I'm doing because, and I'm sorry to have to break this to you, but I'm not a virgin." He grinned at her confused expression, then willingly took the hefty push she gave him, staggering backward, then steadying his feet and stepping back to wrap her in his arms.

"I was talking about Badger," Sydney cried. "Get your brain out of your pants."

"I was thinking about badgers too," Denton laughed. "One in particular. No wait, I was thinking about a beaver."

"Denton," Sydney grinned. "Can we be serious for just one second? This scandal is going to be huge. And I want you to know it would be okay if you decided to walk away."

"Walk away?" Denton's brow creased.

"I want you to know how much you're risking by taking part in this."

She had a studied evenness to her voice that he didn't like. He released her and stepped back on the sand, putting a little distance between them, both literally and emotionally.

"That's my best friend back there," Denton told her, his voice tense with suppressed anger. "You think I should turn my back on him?"

"No I don't. But that doesn't mean you have to be front and centre in this. I can cover for you. It's my job."

"You're suspended if I remember correctly."

"I still have a level of protection," Sydney said. "This blurring of lines, in a way it's kind of expected of me. It's my job to investigate. People expect me to be here."

"But not me?"

"It's just, you're the Chief Executive Officer and majority shareholder of a media organisation. You have a reputation and a career to protect."

"Let me guess, you're an investigative journalist and a management consultant too now?" Denton bit back.

"No."

"Oh right, sorry, you're just an expert on public relations?"

"No Denton, if you'd drop the sarcasm for a moment, and that chip on your shoulder, you'd see there's a level of truth to what I'm saying."

"Ha! You're one to talk. You had more than a chip when I met you. A bloody brick."

Why had she started this? What she was saying wasn't unreasonable in a business sense. But Haig was family, and he really thought she'd understand that.

"You think the board will appreciate Passion Media being dragged through the mud by the guy who tumbled in last week with his millions of dollars."

"You think that's all I brought with me?"

"Of course not. But it's not about what I think," Sydney sighed. "It's about how things look. You're a big boy Denton. You've played this game before."

"What's that supposed to mean?"

Sydney glared at Denton.

"Look, I assumed we could have an open and honest conversation about this. I thought you'd have the same concerns I do, and that maybe we would be able to work through them. Together. But you're being an idiot."

"You want open and honest, what do you mean I've played this game before?"

"Fine. Butler Walsh Wells. 2012."

"You investigated me."

"It's my job. But I didn't go digging. And you googled me too."

"Fine. Say what you want to say Sydney."

"In 2012 you were on the board of Butler Walsh and Wells when you found out Jacob Wells had employed some creative accounting methods. You reported him to the board. He was stood down."

"And it turned out it wasn't Jacob Wells. It was one of his Senior Associates. Get to the point Sydney."

"Butler Walsh *Wells*," Sydney repeated. Denton stood with his hands on his hips and waited.

"What's their name now Denton?"

"What's that got to do with—"

"What's their name," Sydney yelled.

"Butler Walsh. They're Butler Walsh."

"And you know why?" Sydney asked.

"I've got a feeling you're going to tell me."

"Mud sticks Denton. Wells did nothing wrong. He was fully exonerated. But it was too late by then."

"Thanks for reminding me of the most awful damn mistakes I've ever made in my career. But here's the thing Sydney. I'm not Wells." Denton glanced down the beach. He had an aching desire to get away from Sydney Stone. Far, far away.

"You're not Wells *yet*." Sydney quipped.

"You got one thing right Sydney. I am a big boy. I've been around the block a few times, and believe me when I tell you, I can manage my own business affairs without your help. As you'll know because you've obviously swatted up. My millions did not fall off the back of my Daddy's truck. Nor did they come by while I cowered in a corner and let someone else make decisions for me. You can Google me as much as you like," Denton pointed his finger at Sydney, "But you do not get to tell me how to act, and you definitely do not get an opinion on how I conduct my business."

"I was not swatting up. I looked you up after our first meeting, I had no idea who you were—"

"Save it," Denton held his hand up. "I've heard enough." Then he turned away.

Sydney watched him stalk down the beach. When he disappeared in the darkness, she sunk into the sand and let out the breath she'd been holding. She tried to get a grip on her ragged breathing but it quickly turning into sobs of pure pain and anguish.

I was trying to protect him, I was trying to...

What was she trying to do? And more importantly, why?

Sydney stared out at the inky ocean. She hugged her knees beneath her chin and let her tears flow. In the darkness, Sydney tried to pretend she didn't know the real reason she had started that conversation with Denton Cole.

Until now, she had been quite successful in pretending her feelings for Denton did not go beyond satisfying their mutual physical needs. She'd even felt proud of herself, not getting emotionally attached. But she'd just stuck herself smack bang in the centre of Denton's world. Right where his professional and personal lives intersected. And he was right to question her motives. Why were her feelings for Denton so hard to control? She was madly attracted to him, convincing herself it all stopped there. But tonight, she'd been worried about him. She'd wanted to protect him.

But she wasn't falling in love.

Wait, where the hell did that come from? Love and Denton Cole in the same sentence? Was she losing her mind? She couldn't be. Love lead to places Sydney had never been weak enough to go. Her barriers were there for a reason. To protect her.

But with Denton, it was taking all Sydney had to ignore the reality that those walls she'd lived behind had holes. They were weak and flimsy.

Sydney needed those walls. They were her only protection.

She grabbed fistfuls of sand and let it fall through her shaking hands, desperate with the fear that deep down she knew her walls were crumbling, and she didn't know how to fix them.

28

A muffled knock drew Sydney from a restless sleep. She listened to Denton making small talk with a room service attendant. She heard the door close and a few moments later he appeared, carrying a tray laden with pastries and a large flask of coffee. He placed it down gently on the end of the bed.

Sydney rubbed her tired eyes. She'd let herself into their room the night before and found no trace of Denton. After a long shower, she had hoped he'd be there when she emerged from the bathroom. When he wasn't, she waited for him, through a series of late-night news bulletins, but gave up in the early hours, falling asleep with the bedroom television playing reruns of Friends.

She hadn't heard him come back. But here he was, pouring coffee into small white mugs.

"Is it a one sugar morning, or two?"

"Two," Sydney whispered. She sat up in bed, shifting the pillows to make herself more comfortable.

"Peace offering?" he enquired, holding out one of the mugs.

"Where did you go?" Sydney asked. She took the mug and sipped her coffee. She worked her face to look calm though her chest was tight with a tangle of feelings. She was so relieved to have him sitting there on the edge of the bed. She had fallen asleep thinking maybe, whatever it was that she had shared with Denton had come to an end.

"Look, Sydney. About last night. I'm sorry I got so wound up."

"It's okay," she shook her head. "I overstepped."

"I needed some time, so I walked around and thought it through. And I don't think you overstepped. You were concerned about me. I'm just an idiot who's really not used to people standing up to me. Or standing up *for me*, if I'm honest. I've always got things done on my own, and I think you might have bruised my ego."

"I could have handled it better."

"No, it was me." Denton paused, then took her coffee mug and put it on the bedside table beside his own. "You're incredible Sydney Stone. I hope you know that." He kissed her, and Sydney felt her eyes fill with tears. Three times in one week. She'd be crying at bank commercials on the telly next!

"I hate that I've made you sad," Denton said, brushing his thumb across her cheek. She let herself relax in his arms, powerless to resist as he explored the contours of her body, kissing his way from her mouth, along the length of her neck and lower still. She felt hot and tingly and pushed away the bed sheets, pulling Denton down on top of her. She closed her eyes and thought of nothing but the feeling of his lips and the softness of his touch. When he pulled away she was breathless, her head a fuzzy mess of lingering desire.

Denton grinned above her and she tried to pull him down again.

"Hold on Syd, I'm going to get back to that in a moment," he laughed, and Sydney groaned.

"Hang on, I've got to say this. You need to know how grateful I am. You're sticking your neck out with this whole thing. And I'm sorry I walked away last night. You didn't deserve that. You said exactly what I would have said to anyone else in my position. I respect that you've got my back, Sydney. But please, I want you to understand that Haig is family. And I don't believe in running away just because a situation gets a little bit complicated."

"Okay," Sydney nodded.

"You were doing your job, Sydney. I respect that. I shouldn't have left you there. I was wrong. You are an amazing journalist Sydney. And the fact you were willing to put my career before your own. That's incredible."

"It's my job." Sydney's voice was barely audible and she felt a sudden urge to throw herself across the bed and cry. Denton respected her for her job performance, her commercial loyalty. And with an alarming jolt of reality, Sydney realised it was most definitely not in her job description to fall in love with Denton Cole.

"You, your opinion, Sydney, it means a lot to me. More than a lot,"

Denton watched Sydney. The colour had drained from her face.

"Are you alright?" he asked. She nodded and smiled.

"I wanted you to know how I felt before anything else happened."

Sydney nodded again. There were no words. It seemed impossible she'd ever be able to describe the state of confusion she was feeling. Alarm bells were screaming. Sydney Stone was doing her job. But she was also doing her boss, and that broke too many rules.

Sydney knew exactly what she should do, what she *had* to do. She could feel every nerve ending twitch from muscle memory, willing her to scramble out of bed, out of the hotel room, out of Fiji, and as far away from any romantic involvement with Denton Cole as she could possibly get.

Sydney realised it was time to acknowledge what she'd known in her head all along. Without a shadow of a doubt, there was no future with Denton Cole.

"Sydney I really want you to understand. You, your opinion, it means a lot to me, but I'm still not saying it right, what I need to say. What I mean to say, god this isn't easy."

When he'd been walking around in the dark, early hours of the morning, Denton hadn't considered how nervous he would be, telling Sydney how much he cared about her. But he'd never had to proclaim his love for anyone before. Because before he met Sydney, he'd never really felt it.

But Sydney wasn't really listening. She was surer than ever, that regardless of how happy she'd been spending time with Denton if she didn't call time now, it would ultimately end with her beaten down and broken.

Sydney knew how to survive. She knew what she needed to do. She took a deep breath,

"Denton, I think we need to stop—"

It wasn't a knock on the door. It was three heavy hammering thuds. A brief pause, then the sound of a fist crashing into the door three more times.

Denton held his finger to his lips and they both waited.

"Mr Cole. Open this god damn door or I'll break it down."

"One moment," Denton called out. "It's okay," he told Sydney. Though the sick feeling in her stomach told her it was not. Sydney slid from the bed and pulled on the robe Denton threw at her.

When Denton opened the door he was pushed back into the room by a man wearing a suit befitting a Monday morning on Wall Street rather than a Fijian spa resort, where the morning temperature was already over 27 degrees Celsius.

"Let me guess, you're going scuba diving today and you'd like to know if we'll join you?" Denton asked, tucking Sydney in behind him. "Unfortunately, Sydney and I have other plans. A spot of tennis, a few laps of the pool."

The suited man was much larger than Denton, and his bald head was covered in beads of sweat.

"You think being a smart arse is wise right now? Take a seat."

"I think we'll stand," Denton replied.

The suited man grunted.

"Get in here Mr Haig."

Sydney gasped. Haig's bottom lip was split and swollen. He was holding a hand over his ribs on the same side.

"Haig," Denton nodded to his friend who gave a small shrug. "I see our friends wanted you for a spot of scuba diving too."

"A swim with the fishes?" Haig attempted a laugh, but his eyes creased in pain.

"Take it easy mate," Denton made a step towards Haig but the strong arm of the bald suited man put a large paw on his chest.

"You've been a bit reckless, Mr Cole."

Their eyes all turned to the man standing behind Haig.

"Morris James." Denton glared.

"Ferret-face," Sydney murmured.

"It's a pleasure to meet you too Miss Stone." Morris James held his hand out. Sydney raised her eyebrows and crossed her arms over her chest.

"I'm guessing you're the reason he looks like that?" Sydney motioned towards Haig.

"I have no idea what you're talking about. Mr Haig can tell you exactly what happened to him. Go ahead, Mr Haig."

Sydney looked at Denton. She saw a shadow of anger pass over his face.

"I was out surfing. I over-estimated my abilities." Haig turned to face Morris James. "Apparently I've got a reputation for pushing reasonable limits." Haig was panting with the exertion of talking. "Did I get your story right?"

"The limelight is all yours today Mr Haig. Why don't you tell Mr Cole your other news." Morris James was the picture of a man who had the whole cake and was about to shove it down their throats. He put his hands in the pockets of his tan pants and rocked back and forth in a pair of brand new boat shoes. His salmon coloured shirt was neatly ironed with creases along the short sleeves, and bone dry, in direct contrast to his henchman who wiped at his forehead with a hotel napkin.

"I've decided to return to the United Kingdom with these gentlemen. They have a private jet waiting at Nadi airport. They've kindly agreed to look after me for a couple of days. While I think through my employment options."

Sydney could feel the anger emanate from Denton's body.

"Mr Cole, I'm sure you understand the sensitivity of the situation," Morris James smiled. "There's a very important press conference on Wednesday, and I don't need to tell you how much trouble Mr Haig could face if any of Vanguard's private and confidential information were to find its way into the media. Or the private and confidential information of its clients." He paused for a moment, trading glares with Denton.

"I'll take it from your silence that you understand."

James Morris took his hands from his pockets and checked the chunky silver watch attached to his skinny wrist. Sydney longed to tell him he looked like a schoolboy playing dress up. That his oversized pink linen shirt looked ridiculous on his tiny body. But one look at Haig reminded her what was at stake. She held her tongue.

"I think we'll head out to the airport now," Morris jovially said. Sydney wanted to break a vase over his head. "I've assured Mr Haig we have some excellent painkillers onboard. I broke a rib playing polo once. Dreadfully painful."

"Are you really okay?" Sydney asked Haig.

"Box of fluffy ducks," he winced.

"One last word of advice Mr Cole. You too Miss Stone. On behalf of Vanguard, and their clients, I highly recommend you take a step back from this damaging and fruitless investigation. We would hate the nature of your organisations part in this *situation*, to be made public. It really wouldn't look good for Passion Media if their lead investigative journalist knew about a possible leak of Government information, and a probable illegal software hacking ring, and rather than report it, she used that information for her own personal gain. If someone discovered she'd actually worked with Mr Haig here while she was under investigation for fraud. Well, she may never work again."

Sydney closed her eyes. Everything she had worked so hard for was hanging on the edge of oblivion. She saw Denton move forward but quickly reached out and put a hand on his back. "Stop," she whispered. "You'll make it worse."

"Listen to your girlfriend Mr Cole. Imagine what it would look like if it were to emerge that Miss Stone here was sleeping with her boss. Trading secrets under the covers? Or perhaps you and Haig were sharing something else?"

"That's enough," Haig yelled, now bent almost in half.

"Denton. Call my mother. Tell her I'm sorry I won't be at dinner tomorrow night. And Morris. You leave them out of it. I got us into this mess, and I told you I'd get us out."

"Of course," Morris smiled. "But in my line of work, it's important to always have a plan B."

The bald suit man ushered Haig out of the room, and Morris James followed behind.

"You're a nasty piece of work," Denton called after him.

"I'll take that as a compliment," James replied. "Remember what I told you, Mr Cole. Stay off the road. I've been swatting bugs like you for a very long time."

Sydney and Denton stared at the door for a long time after it closed. The silence pressed in around them. Sydney let a small sob escape but Denton shook his head.

"No." He wrapped her in a fierce embrace. "We can't do that. That's exactly what he wants."

Sydney took a shaky breath, pulling her emotions back from the brink.

"Damn it Denton. Morris James is the head of the British Daily News. This Badger thing just jumped the shark. We have no idea how many people are involved in this. They've got Haig. How do we, I mean, what do we, do we call the police?" Sydney asked.

Denton shook his head,

"Which police? The Fijian police department wouldn't know where to start. I'm guessing it would take us a while to explain what's going on, and Morris would be long gone before they get anywhere near his private plane. And if we have the British police meet the plane in London, who do you think they'll go after?"

"Haig." Sydney sat down heavily on the edge of the sofa. "I have no idea where we go from here."

"New Zealand," Denton replied. He grabbed his cell phone from the coffee table.

"Stop," Sydney cried. "Haig said no technology. Anything you type could end up in Badger."

"Concierge then." Sydney followed Denton into the bedroom and watched him digging in his bag.

"Where the hell are my pants?"

"New Zealand?" Sydney asked. She started pulling clothes from her own bag. "Why did you say New Zealand?"

"Haig said to call his mother about missing dinner. His mother lives in New Zealand."

"You think he was giving you some kind of message?"

"I know he was. He said call my mother. Mrs Haig doesn't like talking on the phone. She likes letters. Or she likes you right there in person." Denton stripped off his t-shirt and replaced it with a clean, checkered shirt. His fingers worked quickly through the buttons. "She says people who send text messages are lazy. And she didn't raise lazy sons."

Sydney stopped sorting through her underwear and met Denton's gaze.

"So when you said Haig is family…"

Denton ran a hand through his hair.

"Yes, I really meant it. I'll fill you in later. Throw me your passport, we need to get moving."

29

They got lucky. The morning flight was delayed and they'd scrambled two middle seats which neither were bothered about.

They landed in Auckland just after lunch and chose at random a rental car kiosk. They were rewarded with the only vehicle available on the spot, – a two-door Holden Barina.

"It's no bigger than a shopping cart," Denton grumbled as he folded himself into the driver's seat and wedged it back as far as it would go.

He stole a glance at Sydney and thought about the conversation he'd been trying to have with her when Morris James and his muscle man had interrupted.

Her seatbelt clicked and she looked up at him.

"Ready when you are."

Out of the city, heading east across the North Island, Denton felt nervous. He was about to take Sydney Stone to Pauanui, a small town on the Coromandel Coast, and the only place he'd ever truly felt at home. Would Flo and Ed love Sydney as much as he hoped?

"You okay?" Sydney asked. "You keep looking at me funny."

If it wasn't for Haig, he'd have never sought out Sydney Stone, and it was doubtful they'd ever have made it this far.

"I'm okay. Just thinking about Haig."

And how he brought you to me.

Denton made a mental note to never mention that to Haig. He'd never hear the end of it.

"Are you hungry?" Sydney asked. "I wouldn't mind a drink."

Denton pulled in at a petrol station, and took control of the snacks. He insisted they buy Burger Rings and Deep Spring fizz, which they consumed while they listened to a radio station where the hosts spoke with a muddy mix of vowel sounds.

"Chups!" Denton grinned.

"Burga Rungs," Sydney tried.

"You're a natural," Denton grinned. "And look at that, we're almost home!"

The short drive through the New Zealand countryside had Sydney glued to her window.

"It's been so long since I've seen paddocks from anywhere other than a plane window," Sydney sighed. So many shades of green, from stretches of farmland to the deep dusky hues of the hills in the distance. It reminded Sydney of her old life. Her family home on the outskirts of Cambridge, where a small three bedroom bungalow had housed her carefree childhood. She'd lived there worry free and full of confidence.

"It's weird isn't it," Denton said, turning the sound down on the radio. "I've lived in cities all my life. Washington, London, New York, Hong Kong, back to London. A short stint in Paris that was truly awful."

"Because you can't speak French?"

"Non, j'ai eu une appendicite. Deux semaines à l'hôpital."

"No fun." Sydney patted Denton's thigh. He put a hand over hers.

"I don't really give much thought to the countryside," he admitted. "But every time I come here, I get in the car and I'm driving out to Pauanui and then it hits me how much I've missed it. But it's odd because I haven't really thought about it since the last time, so I can't have missed it that much. But I know I have. I'm not sure if that even makes sense."

"I get it," Sydney nodded. "I was kind of thinking the same thing. I mean all this green grass, it reminds me of my family home. I grew up in the countryside, as you so cutely put it," Sydney smiled. "It's all so lush."

"You're lush, and if you don't move your hand I'm going to have to park us up on the side of the road in a hurry."

Sydney grinned, let her hand linger a while longer then moved it back to her side of the vehicle.

"Now I'm not sure if I should thank you or curse you, Miss Stone."

"You're welcome," Sydney blew Denton a kiss, then reached into the bag for another Burger Ring.

"Where did you grow up?" Denton asked.

"Just outside of Cambridge. I've been sitting here trying to work out when I was last there."

"You don't get back home much? Does your family still live there?"

Sydney felt a wave of discomfort at Denton's questions and took her time deciding how to reply.

"No brothers or sisters. My mother still lives there. Not in our old family home. She's in Cambridge now. Near the university." She braced herself for the next question Denton would ask. Where was her father? It seemed like the natural progression of the conversation, but Denton hit a passing lane, indicated right and sped up to pass a car towing a caravan. When he settled back into the left-hand lane, Sydney was relieved that Denton took a different track.

"We went on holiday once to the English countryside. I'm ashamed to say I don't know where. My father rented us a house for three months while he worked. I want to say it was in Oxfordshire, but maybe it was Yorkshire? Anyway, my mother cried the whole time. Then one morning we woke up and she'd taken herself off back to London on urgent business."

"She just left?"

"We had a nanny. Her name was Mandy. She took my sister and me on these amazing long walks. Adventures really. We'd hunt for eels in the stream. Build forts in the forest. I don't think it really was a forest," Denton mused. "More like a dozen trees planted in the back of a field."

"We had a forest like that! We called it the woods. Mum and I would look for fairies," Sydney laughed. "and build them houses out of leaves and twigs."

"I cried for a week after my father came to get us. Damn it, I just can't remember which county it was." Denton eased the car around a bend. "But I do remember I was happy. You know, really happy. Jump out of bed in the morning, run around the yard in your pyjamas chasing ducks type happy."

Sydney nodded,

"Rolling down grassy hills, gumboots in muddy puddles, jam and real butter sandwiches happy." She said. "Did you really cry for a whole week?" Sydney asked.

"I did. We'd flown to New York. It was the week I turned eight and I refused to have a birthday party. That's when I received my first Cole family father-son talk. I was ushered into his library and told I was born to do great things. I was a very lucky child, to have the greatness of two countries, England and America, and my father, and his father, had worked hard to provide every opportunity I was refusing to engage in."

"Ouch," Sydney grimaced. "That's a lot of pressure."

"Cole men don't bow down to pressure," Denton explained in a very posh and loud voice that was obviously his father's. "They rise up."

"Is that what you did?" Sydney asked. "You rose up?"

"No choice back then. I did what was expected of me."

Sydney looked across at Denton and was surprised by the emptiness in his eyes. She was going to ask him how he really felt, but Denton spoke before her thoughts became words.

"So I was forcibly removed from the countryside. What's your excuse?"

Sydney could have told Denton the truth. She considered it, briefly, but the story she had been telling since she was seventeen years old was tried, if not really true.

"I went off to university, discovered a passion for journalism, and was seduced by the bright lights and big stories in the city of London."

"Was it hard? Leaving your family behind?"

"I missed my mum," Sydney replied. "I missed the pubs. I'd been so eager to escape, but I forgot how much comfort there is in walking into a room where everyone knows you and will buy you a beer if you forgot your wallet. Oh, but when I got to London! It was like putting on a favourite coat. It made me feel like anything was possible. There's always something to do in London. Shows and museums and restaurants and people, so many people. Like opening a new book every day."

"You make it sound so romantic," Denton smiled. "I almost feel homesick."

Sydney went back to gazing out the window. She thought about the stuff she'd left out. How her departure from Cambridge came hot on the heels of her father's deceit. A decade-old affair with a woman half his age that only came out after the self-serving lousy pig had keeled over and died at a bank meeting, where he'd been trying to secure a second mortgage on their family home, so he could purchase his mistress an apartment.

To this day, she still couldn't believe that while her mother had waited at home, making his meals and ironing his shirts, her father had been taking trips to Paris and Prague and Venice with his floozy.

She wanted to tell Denton the whole story. The real version. But she'd only ever talked to one person about it, and it had not gone well.

After her father's funeral, and in the days that followed, Sydney had begged her mother to face what had been going on behind her back. She wanted to confront the other woman. She needed her father's mistress to see the misery she had caused. And she really needed her mother to be as angry as she was.

But Sydney's mother flatly refused. Despite her best attempts to get her mother to see through her grief, to see the man she'd actually been married to, her mother wasn't moved.

"Stop searching Syd, stop bringing me bank statements, because I won't look. I don't want to see your receipts and timelines and ticket stubs. I'm sorry. I know it's a lot to deal with and it's not fair on you. But all you will find is another version of a life I spent years creating. We have memories, we have good times. I don't need another version of what happened. Just leave it alone Sydney. Leave me with my memories."

And so Sydney left. She kissed her mother goodbye, and went back to university. She sat on the train cradling a lukewarm cup of tea, and she planned her strategy. She would leave the lies and the falsehoods of her childhood behind. But she would never forget. And she would never let a man have that kind of power over her. The power to make her feel foolish and sad and small. She loved her mother, but she vowed she would never be like her. Sydney would never let a man lie to her. She would never be tricked into believing something was beautiful and pure when it was really the opposite. Because Sydney knew that when it came to love, it was a fairytale that simply didn't exist.

Happily-ever-afters were for fools.

"Pauanui," Denton broke through her thoughts. Sydney saw that houses now lined the side of the road. They passed a busy shopping village. A wine bar and a pizza restaurant appeared to be popular with the locals, judging by the full car park and busy outside tables.

Denton took a right, drove down toward the ocean, then followed the road as it eased left.

He parked in front of a modern, two-story house. Sydney could see a woman through a large bay window. Unmistakably Haig's mother, even through the window Sydney could see she was tall with a head of ginger curls. She watched Haig's mother pick up a tea towel and dry her hands, then glance up and out towards them. She tipped her head as if trying to place the car. Perhaps thinking they were a couple of lost tourists.

Denton leaned over and kissed Sydney on the cheek. "Ready?"

30

Sydney was with Denton on the front path when Florence Haig looked up and out of the kitchen window, grasped her chest and shrieked. A moment later the front door was flung open and she'd tripped down the front steps and pulled Denton into a hug.

"You're ruining my mascara," she cried, holding Denton back so she could look him over, then she pulled him in for another hug. "What the hell are you doing here?" she asked.

"And you brought a friend!" Florence smiled at Sydney but didn't give them time to answer. She took Denton's hand and pulled him up the path.

"Come in, come in, I'll put the jug on. Ed, get in here," she yelled, "you'll never guess who's here!"

Sydney followed Florence and Denton inside. Through the front door, they stood in a hallway the walls of which were lined with photos of babies in christening gowns and toddlers on tricycles. They led on to the first day of school photographs, football trophies and dress up costumes. Sydney grinned when she found Denton as a young teenager, standing shirtless beside Haig, hands on hips, with what looked like a public swimming pool in the background.

"They were lifeguards."

Sydney jumped, she hadn't realised Florence was beside her. "We were living in Wellington then. Ed was working on some government project, I forget what it was now. Those two worked their summer at McKenzie Baths."

"It was Justin's idea. He thought it would be like Baywatch." Denton shook his head. "It was not."

"Go on, the girls loved you." Florence ushered Sydney through the hall and into an open plan kitchen-dining area.

"Flo, those girls were mostly aged three to seven. The only rescues we made were retrieving beach balls and swim rings from the deep end."

Sydney watched Denton's face light up when Edward Haig appeared in the hallway.

"What are you doing here son," Edward cried, "trying to give an old man a stroke?"

Edward Haig didn't look like a man about to keel over. He sported a thick spread of dark brown hair and a matching moustache. His skin was deeply tanned, weathered from a life outdoors. Sydney would be surprised if a lick of SPF30 had ever touched the man's cheeks.

"It's good to see you lad. Who's your lady friend?"

"This is Sydney. She's our chief investigative journalist at Passion Media."

"That's your latest business?" Edward asked. "I knew it was media something or other."

He took the hand Sydney offered and kissed it.

"Pleasure to meet you. First time we've had one of your ladies here son." Edward winked at his wife and Sydney could have sworn Denton blushed.

"Come see this view, Sydney." Denton ushered her over to the large patio doors.

"You've embarrassed him. Leave the boy alone," Florence told her husband. "Come help me cut the cake."

Florence moved into the open plan kitchen, keeping up a steady stream of chatter. "I made a carrot cake just this morning. It's supposed to be for the school. They've got a twilight gala tomorrow night. But I can make another one."

"Why don't we just put those biscuits out?" Edward asked his wife. "Save you the effort of making another one."

"No, Ed! It's no effort. Denton and his, ah, *friend*, have come all the way from England. The least we can do is give them a piece of cake. You do eat cake?" Florence looked stricken for a moment.

"I love carrot cake," Sydney assured her. "It's my favourite."

"Thank the Lord! Justin's baby mama won't eat cake. Something about the refined sugar in it. I told her the carrots are healthy. Surely they cancel out the sugar. But no. She preferred to eat some weird lumpy white stuff."

"Cottage cheese." Denton winked at Sydney.

"I prefer my cheese normal, yellow and sliced. Or grated. Now, where did I put the fancy cake slice?"

Sydney stood beside Denton, staring out at the ocean.

"I like them," Sydney whispered. Denton put his hands in his pockets and rocked gently on the spot.

"You're getting carrot cake, so I'd say they like you too," he replied.

"Come on you two," Florence called. "Grab a seat and you can tell us what on earth you're doing here!"

Sydney wasn't sure the explanation they gave Florence and Edward was sufficient. She had seen a look pass between them. An unspoken understanding that something fishy was going on.

"I spoke to Justin, must have been the night before last." Edward was rolling the side of his moustache between the finger and thumb of his right hand. "He said you'd been helping him with a small problem."

"He's been working for a firm called Vanguard. They're a political lobby group, they run campaigns and marketing strategy. That kind of thing." Denton sipped his coffee and kept what he hoped was a bland look on his face.

"You boys getting involved in politics?" Edward laughed.

"Not exactly Ed. Haig was doing his computer thing. He came across an issue and called me looking for some business advice."

"Did you two get the problem solved then?" Ed asked, taking a sip from his mug of tea.

"Almost."

"And this problem of Justin's, it wouldn't have anything to do with your impromptu visit? And your lady friend here, and her journalistic investigations?"

Sydney coughed and tried to swallow the bit of carrot cake wedged in her throat. But Denton's determined eyes came to life. He sat up straight.

"I take the fifth. So does my client."

"You're not in America now Mr Bigshot," Edward grinned. "And since when did Sydney need legal representation?"

Denton made a show of looking at his wrist.

"Since we arrived approximately 28 minutes ago."

Ed leaned forward and tapped Sydney on the shoulder then pointed at Denton.

"You do know he's not a real lawyer," Ed whispered loudly. "I, on the other hand..."

"Don't listen to him Sydney." Denton put his hand on Sydney's. "His last case was over 30 years ago."

"True," Ed nodded. "But I won it. Ester versus Green. Shared driveway dispute. It was 1988, It had been a very wet summer. The weeds were knee high..."

Later in the evening, while Ed and Denton argued over the barbeque, Sydney walked barefoot along Pauanui Beach. Despite the seriousness of the situation, the afternoon with the Haig's had lifted her. She'd forgotten the comfort of having people to sit around a table with. To be part of conversations that rolled over and into each other. The gentle ribbing she'd received about her love of reality television. Being pulled into tales of Haig and Denton's teenage years. She heard those stories for the first time, but knew they'd been retold time and again with varying degrees of accuracy. But the retelling itself was more important than the accuracy. It didn't matter if they had the exact date or place or person present when the event happened.

Denton swore he did not steal Ed's car, though he may have 'borrowed' it for a late night McDonald's run. Ed swore he was not disappointed when neither Denton and Justin went to law school. Or medical school. And promised again, that he did not yell *that* loudly, or for *that* long when Justin was kicked off the swim team for missing practice four times in a row.

"He was in love with her." Denton threw his arms up in the air. "He was in pursuit of something greater than swimming."

"She was a trollop." Florence waved the cake fork at Denton. "He's always attracted to the loose ones."

"She's a lawyer now," Denton rebutted.

"Civil or criminal?" Ed asked. "Prosecution or defence?"

"Criminal. Defence."

"Case closed!" Ed declared.

She felt comfortable with the Haig family. She'd searched out Denton's hand and held it through the afternoon. He'd draped an arm across her shoulder as they watched the sun edge down in the sky until Ed had declared it time to light the barbeque.

But just beneath the surface was something else. She stopped walking and scrunched sand between her toes. Beneath the comfort, clouds were looming.

I won't think about it. I can't.

But without warning, she felt tears roll quietly down her cheeks. She stared out at the ocean taking shallow, steadying breaths.

"Jet lag. I'm just tired. Too tired to think," Sydney said softly into the ebb and flow of the tide. She walked across the soft sand. Cool water rolled over her toes before an invisible force pulled it away again.

Sydney and Denton were put on dishes duty.

"You okay?" Denton asked, leaning into the dishwasher and rearranging the plates so he could fit more in. "You seem a bit distracted."

"Just tired," Sydney smiled.

Denton pushed the dishwasher tray in and closed the door.

"It's been a crazy few days." He leaned an elbow on the bench while Sydney used a dishcloth to wipe down the drain board and the taps. "I'm glad we've got a moment alone. I wanted to talk to you."

"About Haig? Did you find something?" Sydney asked. Denton had snuck away earlier in the evening, on a search for anything Haig may have left with his parents, any clue as to why he would mention his mother before he left Fiji with Morris James.

"Nothing," he sighed. "I thought Haig wanted us to come here, but maybe I got it wrong."

"You were so sure," Sydney pointed out.

"I know. But being here I've kind of realised how insane this whole thing is. I'm not sure I know what I'm doing," he admitted. "Not just with Haig. I've been thinking about why I brought you here Sydney."

"For Haig," she replied. "For the story." She took four mugs from the cupboard and lined them up on the bench beside Denton's elbow. "You couldn't exactly leave me in Fiji. Do you know where the teabags live?" Sydney asked.

"Yes, we're here for Haig, for the story. But there's something else."

"Florence said something about after dinner biscuits. Do you know what they are? And where they would be?"

Denton sighed. He took a jar down from the top shelf in the pantry.

"The teabags are in that wooden box over there. Now stop for a moment and listen to me. I want to talk about us."

Sydney wasn't sure she was ready. She had decided Denton could go one of two ways. He'd tell her he made a mistake getting involved with her and thought it best she leave. Or he might say he'd felt a strong connection building between them, and was thinking about where their future lay when they returned home.

Both options filled Sydney with fear. Both felt to Sydney like she was losing control. She had worked so hard to avoid this situation. To avoid giving so much power to a man, that he could manipulate her into putting her own needs aside, willing to forgive anything he did so long as he didn't leave her.

"Stop," Sydney whispered.

"But I want to tell you this Sydney."

"Please stop talking."

"I want to be honest with you."

"I'm a bit stuck son." Edward wandered into the kitchen holding an old laptop, and Sydney busied herself cramming teabags into the teapot.

"It says I need to update the windows. But last time I did that, it crashed. Justin had to reboot something. Do you think you could take a look?"

"No, he can't!" Florence yelled from the couch. "Justin told him it wasn't worth it. It's too old now."

Florence came into the kitchen with her hands on her hips.

"Good try Ed, but if you want to look up the golf, then you'd better get out to the garage and unwrap that fancy computer thing that came this morning."

"A computer came this morning?" Sydney asked.

"Where from?" Denton demanded.

"Justin," Ed grumbled. "No help that boy. *Just get a new one Dad!.* And he calls himself a computer wizard."

"No he doesn't," Florence laughed. "You call him that."

"Not anymore. I don't need a fancy machine that plays holograms or whatever they do these days. I just want this one!" He shook the old laptop in the air.

"Let's take a look at the new one anyway," Denton said, heading down the hallway. Sydney was right behind him.

Denton flicked the light switch in the garage. In the fluorescent glow he scanned the room until his eyes settled on a red and yellow courier box on a shelf, balanced on a stack of old tennis rackets.

"How did he know?" Sydney asked. "He must have sent it before we even got to Fiji."

"He's a boy scout," Denton said, "always prepared."

He ripped the courier box open revealing the laptop box inside. "Bloody marvellous."

"I was getting worried," Sydney admitted.

"I was mildly concerned," Denton agreed.

"I don't want it," Ed called from within the house.

"Ignore him!" Florence cried out after him.

Sydney got the giggles and Denton pulled her into his arms.

"Those two!" he exclaimed, rolling his eyes. For a moment he just stood there staring at her. Then he kissed her with an urgency and passion that Sydney couldn't resist. She felt a rush of pleasure. She wrapped her arms around Denton's neck and moaned as his hand caressed her breast. He pulled her closer, and Sydney was awash in a sea of Denton. She could form no coherent thought patterns, let alone communicate them to the man who was simultaneously pleasuring her and probably ruining her life. It was Denton who pulled away first, breathing heavily, pressing his forehead against her own.

"Send it back!" Ed's voice carried to the garage.

"Sorry," Denton puffed, then kissed her again, softly this time. "We better get into this."

"Of course," Sydney nodded. She took a step back and let Denton smooth her t-shirt back into place. "Later," he whispered, "we can finish what we started."

Sydney tried to make sense of her feelings. In the kitchen she'd been desperate to escape, and yet the moment Denton's lips connected with her own, all sensibility deserted her.

This can't go on. She touched her fingers to her lips. How easy it was, to let Denton push past her defences. *I'm losing my mind, I'd have probably let him take me - right there on the workbench, if he hadn't pulled away.*

"Syd," Denton pressed into her thoughts, dragging her back to reality. "Are you coming? We really need to do this."

Sydney turned and followed him out of the garage.

She switched off the light and closed the door.

31

The laptop wasn't new. Justin Haig, or someone he knew, had configured it in advance. It lit up when Denton powered it up, and he quickly navigated through the password screen.

"How did you know the password was Titanium?" Sydney asked.

"Predictable bastard. Same as his Netflix password. He never gets tired of it."

They had the laptop on the dining room table, and Edward and Florence hovered in the background, waiting to see what all the fuss was about.

The home screen had three icons on it. But only one labelled Badger.

"Not exactly rocket science," Sydney mused. "He's not hiding this thing. What if someone got to this before us?"

"Hey Flo, if we hadn't been here, how long would this laptop have sat on the shelf in the garage?" Denton asked.

"As long as Ed here was living and breathing. Or until Justin came home."

"That's because I don't need a new computer," Ed said firmly.

"You're saying this laptop isn't for Ed. And Justin knew no one would look here?" Flo asked.

"Exactly," Denton nodded. Sydney admired Haig's planning.

"He's a smart boy my Justin," Florence agreed. "Can't find a decent wife, but good with all the other stuff."

"Florence, isn't that sexist?"

"Never mind Ed, Sydney knows I'm off the record. That's what I'm supposed to say dear, isn't it?"

Sydney nodded.

"I think it's best if we all stay off the record."

Denton double clicked the badger icon, and when prompted, he clicked the yes button and agreed to run the programme. The screen filled with scrolling layers of code that neither Denton nor Sydney understood. They watched until a message appeared across the screen.

"Badger operational. Stand by for data retrieval." Sydney read off the screen.

"What's Badger?" Florence asked.

"It's a computer system. Of sorts. Best not go into too much detail," Denton shrugged in apology.

"What do we do now?" Sydney asked.

"Now," Denton took in a deep breath, then let it out slowly, "we wait."

"Just how legal is this data retrieval thing?" Ed asked after they'd stared at the unchanged screen for a minute or so. Denton and Sydney looked at each other, then back at Ed.

"There may be some grey areas," Sydney offered, "but it's not our fault."

"There's stuff we can't say Ed. You and Flo wouldn't be in any trouble. But if you want us to go, we can find a motel or something," Denton offered.

"Don't be ridiculous," Ed said, pulling up a chair. "This is like the time we found a floppy disk on the floor of the Deputy Prime Ministers car." He paused and smiled. "Don't ask me what we were doing in the Deputy Prime

Minister's car, and I won't ask you what data you're retrieving. Or who you're retrieving it from."

"Politics!" Florence shook her head. "So much excitement and it's already past my bedtime. I'll make a pot of coffee."

"Justin is on the right side of this," Sydney offered.

They sat and watched the screen again.

The second cup made Sydney a bit jittery. She tried to soak up some of the caffeine with the after dinner biscuits. Florence had tired of watching the blinking cursor on the laptop screen and returned to the television, where Sydney could see her dozing in a recliner chair, a lemon coloured mohair blanket draped across her lap.

Ed was still at the table, playing solitaire with an old pack of cards, letting Denton offer suggestions as long as he didn't try to touch the deck. There had been a tense stand-off 75 minutes earlier when Denton had attempted to move the Queen of Hearts on to a King that Ed had been saving for a different row of cards.

Ed gave up just after eleven. He shook a sleepy Flo awake and they said good night. Despite the caffeine pumping through her body making her leg bounce under the table, Sydney's eyes felt heavy.

The quiet roll of waves outside was repetitive, almost hypnotic, so that when Justin Haig's laptop finally pinged to life at 12:02 am, she all but jumped out of her skin.

It pinged again.

And again.

35 minutes later, at 12:37 am, a grey box appeared on the screen.

"It says there is sufficient data to collate." Denton clicked the *Okay* button and his smile slowly grew. When he looked at Sydney, there was a sparkle in his eyes that told her everything she needed to know.

"We got 'em." she stated.

"We do," Denton agreed. "And look at this." He double clicked a line item that displayed an internal conversation sent between two computers at Vanguard. "They're talking about Badger. They've already singled out two targets. Listen to this." Denton read aloud,

"'Mary Multiple Affairs Aldridge will be increasing her contribution in the coming months,' and then someone replies,

'I knew that bitch was sleeping with Brunning. See what you can find on him. We'll take 'em both.'"

Denton couldn't believe it.

"They're really going after their own."

"Well, technically Mary Aldridge is a Conservative Party Member. She probably doesn't even know who Vanguard are."

Denton closed out of the message.

"How often do you think political campaigns come down to money?" he asked.

"It's always an issue. But this scheme seems counter intuitive," Sydney said. "Surely they risk losing their support base?"

"They're only going after the big fish," Denton replied. "People like this Mary Aldridge won't know where the information came from. But you can be damn sure they'll want to avoid a scandal."

"*Lady* Mary Aldridge. I just googled her. Brunning is a horse breeder."

"You think Lady Mary is going to come forward and let the whole of Britain know she's been cheating on her husband with the man who breeds her show ponies?"

"No," Sydney shook her head. "She'll pay up and keep quiet."

"Exactly. Now I think we need to print." Denton stated.

"Two copies," Sydney agreed. "We take one with us. The other we leave here with Ed."

"There's a safe in the spare bedroom."

They worked quickly and quietly, finding the printer in Ed's office, downloading the drivers on to the laptop and waiting patiently for the seemingly endless pages of data to print in black and white.

They took them back to the dining room table, where they made two large piles.

Sydney used Haig's laptop to book flights back to London, leaving in the afternoon. Denton cleared the biscuit crumbs and coffee mugs.

Sydney barely had the energy to slide between the cool sheets of the single bed in the spare room before her eyes closed, and she dropped into a deep dreamless sleep.

Denton's hand on her shoulder pulled her awake. He was kneeling beside her bed.

"What's the time? What's wrong?" Sydney asked, struggling to sit up.

"Nothing," Denton whispered, "It's early. But we started something earlier, and I can't sleep with a half-finished project."

"You make it sound like you've got a history paper due," Sydney whispered.

"I never studied history," Denton said, sliding a hand under the blankets and tiptoeing his fingers up her thigh, tantalisingly close to her already pulsing core. His hand lingered for a moment. "But I did take advanced business entrepreneurship, and there's something new I'm keen to explore."

In the darkness, she reached out for Denton Cole, and in doing so let her last shred of control dissolve.

32

Sydney listened to a lawn mower somewhere beyond her window. A jet lagged fuzziness engulfed her. She'd been awake for over an hour, trying to stop the cascade of feelings she felt for a man she'd only met a week ago.

One bloody week. May as well be a life time.

She rested her forehead against Denton's shoulder.

She felt flimsy. Waking up squashed in a tiny bed with Denton made her happy, but when she tried to imagine a real relationship, it seemed so abstract, so unbelievable. She'd prided herself on being happy on her own. And yet here she was, once again lost in the possibility that Denton Cole could fit in her life on a more permanent basis.

Who said he even wants that?

"Morning," Denton whispered, "time to get up?"

"No, it's still early," Sydney assured him. "But I've got an angle on Haig for my article. I should get up and start writing."

Her attempt to leave the bed was met with sleepy protests from Denton, who pulled her back into the curve of his body and kissed the nape of her neck.

"Stay," he murmured. "Rest. That's an order."

"Just a few minutes then," she agreed and watched him sleep for as long as she could until the need for the bathroom was overwhelming.

She washed her hands and dried them on a peach hand towel, then stared at herself in the mirror. Her lips were chaffed from the countless kisses she had shared with Denton just a few hours earlier. Under the covers, he'd explored without restraint and Sydney's face flushed at the memory. She was still smiling as she crept back down the hallway.

"I'm usually the only one up this early." Sydney turned to see Florence in the hallway.

"Do you want to join me? I've just made a pot of tea." And though Sydney felt a real desire to climb back into bed with Denton, she was craving some kind of guidance. She had neither her own mother, nor any girlfriends near, but Florence knew Denton, maybe better than he knew himself. That much Sydney had realised within a few minutes of meeting her.

Florence carried the teapot and a small jug of milk into the sitting room. Sydney followed with two white mugs and a box of breakfast biscuits, from a different container in the pantry.

"I had no idea they were a thing," she told Florence.

"You must think I live on biscuits! I know they're a total joke." Florence screwed her nose up at the box. "But once in a while, I'm a willing participant in the magic of marketing, especially if it means I can pretend that eating biscuits for breakfast is a healthy alternative to a spinach and tomato omelette or a bowl of porridge." Florence took a biscuit and dunked it into her cup of tea.

"Go on, they're good for you. Says so on the box!"

Sydney took the box Florence offered. Apparently the apricot coconut fusion biscuits inside had the same energy and fibre of two Weetabix and milk. She took one for herself and followed Florence's lead, dunking it in her mug.

"Let's talk about you and Denton. Have you been together long?" Florence asked.

"Oh," Sydney swallowed a hot sip of tea. She had wanted to talk about Denton but expected she would ease into the conversation. Florence's direct approach caught her off guard.

"Sorry," Florence patted Sydney on the knee. "I don't mean to pry."

"It's okay," Sydney said. She took another sip and thought about how to answer.

"We met, a couple of weeks ago." Sydney considered how little time they had actually been in each other's lives.

"Wow. So much has happened in the last few days. It feels so long ago, that day he walked into Passion Media."

"He makes a very good first impression," Florence smiled. She crossed her legs, laying the flap of her dressing gown over her lap.

"You know, when Denton came into our family he was only 15. So uptight! Like a middle-aged man trapped in a teenage body, with nothing but tradition and history and a family name to live up to."

Sydney nodded.

"I know his family name precedes him," Sydney offered, "though to be honest I'd never heard of them before I met him. But he obviously takes it quite seriously."

"Far too serious if you ask me." Florence reached for another biscuit, giving the box back to Sydney before she settled back on the couch.

"Justin found him at boarding school. I wasn't keen at first, but Ed's job had us bouncing around Europe at that point, and there was talk of Dubai. So Louis Academy for Boys seemed a sensible option. And Justin loved it, so it all worked out. But Denton Cole, well he was at Louis Academy for a purpose. Family obligations and his father being able to hold his head up high in public. This stuffy little lad arrived on our doorstep one summer and I don't know how, but we managed to hold on to him!" Florence paused. "I like to think we've balanced out all that rich prick, stick up the arse stuff."

Sydney giggled.

"I don't have time for that nonsense. Ed was always telling me to go easy on Denton, said it was the world he was raised in. But I wouldn't have it. You know the first time we had a BBQ for tea he asked for a knife and fork. Had to show him how to wrap the bread around the sausage and shove it in his gob."

"He's so relaxed here," Sydney said.

"It took a couple of years. First Christmas, Justin had to drag him away from his textbooks. The boy could dressage a pony but he'd never learned to ride a bike or mow the lawns."

"City boys," Sydney rolled her eyes. They clinked their mugs of tea.

"The boy couldn't surf. But Ed sorted him out. This uptight ball of future-focused tension and pressure pulled on a wetsuit and the first time out there he was hooked. You should have seen it! Like he unravelled right there in front of our eyes, and out came this charming, funny lad who liked to bake apple crumble, played cricket on the beach, and read the whole series of Sweet Valley High School books from the library. But don't you tell him I told you that."

Sydney smiled and sipped her tea. She thought about Denton and the way he'd snapped when she had suggested he step away from Badger. She still believed she was right, to warn him. That it wasn't wise for him to get involved in such a messy political scandal. But being with the

Haig's, she could see why Denton was determined to help. That asking him to step away from Badger was asking him to step away from his family. Not the one he was born to, but the family who had helped him find his childhood. They were far more important than any career aspirations or his reputation.

"He likes you," Florence winked at Sydney.

"Ed said he'd never brought anyone, you know, a girlfriend, here."

"No. He's always tried to keep a low profile when it comes to romance. I've never seen him with anyone real." Florence paused. "Justin, well he's always falling in love, calling to tell me he's met *the one*. He throws us the odd story, but Denton's always been a bit of a closed book."

Sydney nodded. She wasn't sure what to say, so she stayed quiet.

"I've always looked at all those pretty young things as a sort of accessory. A part of the Cole Family image, you know?"

Sydney nodded again, but she didn't know. Who were these pretty young things?

"Arm candy!" Florence declared. Sydney watched her uncross her legs, then re-cross them and pat her dressing gown into place. "It says something, that he never brought them here. Never brought them home. They were just a bit of fun on the side."

Sydney couldn't help it. The feeling of possibility she had woken with was slowly seeping away.

"Listen to me!" Florence self-admonished. "You don't need to hear tales of girlfriends past. How very rude of me. What I was trying to tell you, is I think you and Denton are on to something. I've got a sixth sense when it comes to affairs of the heart."

Sydney forced her mouth into a smile.

"He's not a pushover," Florence said, "but I'd say he's on a very definite lean in your direction."

Florence stood and stretched.

"Come on love, let's see if we've got enough eggs for a real breakfast."

33

Sydney stepped out of the shower. She could hear laughter from down the hallway. Denton was helping clear the breakfast dishes. They were working and laughing together with the familial ease that came from years of repeating the same tasks. Sydney imagined Justin Haig joining in with his irreverent humour and boyish charm. His daughter Arabella would be there sometimes too. A happy family.

But Sydney wasn't happy. She was tired.

On the ride back to Auckland Airport, Sydney tried hard to match Denton's excitement. He stopped at a café and got them double shot lattes. She could see he was a good man.

But aren't they all in the beginning?

"Syd, did you hear me?"

Sydney blinked and shook her head.

"Miles away sorry."

"You're on another planet."

"Jet lag. And nervous, I guess. About writing this story. It has to be good." Sydney gave a weak smile and let him take her hand in his own. Watched as he raised it to his lips and dropped a gentle kiss on the back of her hand.

"You will write the article and it will be incredible, and we will get you back to work," Denton stated. A weaker Sydney would be left with no doubts.

"I'm going to look after you."

It only made Sydney more anxious.

She opened her mouth. She wanted to tell him. She wanted to lay it all out before him, the words rolled before her eyes as if queued on a teleprompter.

I am falling in love with you Denton Cole, and though you might think that is a good thing, the very core of me knows what a huge mistake I've made.

Because you are a man of infinite means. You have women that come and go from your life, with their limited expectations of distraction and display. But I have spent my whole life trying to avoid this very situation. I am scared that my feelings for you will blind me. I'm slowly forgetting the me before you, and if I don't stop this now, I'm opening myself up to the shame and humiliation, which will surely come when you get tired of me. When there is no exciting story to chase, when you are away on business in Hong Kong or Amsterdam or New York, and there are beautiful women who won't complain about your absence. Who will demand nothing of you but your money and status. Women who will offer themselves without fear or concern for the future.

Sydney's mouth was open and dry. The words waited patiently to be said.

"God I'm looking forward to seeing Haig. I can't wait to get back to London," Denton said, and she clamped her mouth shut. She focused on the white lines dividing one side of the road from the other and tried to ignore the sense of trepidation growing inside her.

Sydney may have been new to business class travel but was more grateful for her pod seat than even the flight attendant expected.

"It's exactly what I need," she told him and quickly established a routine that she mastered over the following eleven hours from Auckland to their Los Angeles stopover point. When Sydney wasn't pretending to nap, with an eye mask secured across her watery eyes, she used her laptop as a barrier. Despite her guilty conscience, Sydney felt too fragile for any meaningful conversation with Denton, so she worked on her Badger story. She cross-checked details and reread the notes she had taken in Fiji, perfecting the timeline from the mysterious delivery of the USB stick to when Haig revealed Badger and what it was capable of. She wrote thousands of words, then went back and deleted whole sections and rewrote them. With each word Sydney typed, sentences formed, paragraphs emerged and Sydney quietly pulled the Badger story together. She was back doing what she loved, and Sydney felt strength and safety in the familiar.

Sydney Stone was an investigative journalist. That's who she'd always wanted to be. All she'd ever needed to be.

The layover in Los Angeles wasn't a long one. The immigration queues were long and slow and by the time they'd had their finger prints taken and their eyes scanned, they returned to the transit lounge and were advised reboarding wasn't far off.

Sydney took her time in the bathroom.

"Jet lag's got me good," she lied when she joined Denton for Business Class pre-boarding. "I hope I can get some sleep on this flight."

"It's brutal," Denton agreed. "But before we land, there are things we need to talk about. To straighten out."

"Agreed," Sydney nodded. "We're so close to taking down Badger, we don't want to stuff it up. Do you think Haig is alright?

"I hope so. But there's something else Sydney. Something I've been trying to tell you."

"Miss Stone. Mr Cole. Welcome aboard, let me show you to your seats. I'm so sorry we weren't able to seat you closer together. It's a full flight this evening. You're here Mr Cole, and Miss Stone, if you follow me..."

Sydney gave Denton an apologetic shrug and shuffled down the aisle to take her seat.

Once again they climbed into the sky, homeward bound, and Sydney felt immense relief.

Home to London, where I will get my life back on track.

She asked for a cup of tea and a tray of cheese and crackers from the flight attendant and relaxed back in her chair. Sydney would land on her feet when the aircraft touched down. The old Sydney, the woman she had moulded herself into over years of careful planning, would reappear when her feet touched the ground. The Sydney from Fiji and New Zealand would fade into the past. And though she felt broken now, it was a pain she could manage.

I can tidy this interlude with Denton away, just as I have the other short-lived relationships I tried in the past.

Sydney sipped her tea and for a brief moment, her heart felt unbearably heavy. She blinked to keep the tears at bay. Sydney knew she had never felt love for the other men in her life, nothing close to what she was feeling for Denton. But just as quickly, Sydney shook it off.

Who really knows what love is anyway? Sydney reasoned. This Badger story was one of the biggest she had ever investigated or written. The emotions and drama a story like this evoked had likely crossed over into Sydney and Denton's personal life. An easy mistake to make in the heat of the moment. But now that the story was ready to break, it was an error easily rectified.

Sydney sat forward and stared hard at the back of Denton's seat. He'd used the airline's seat message system at the start of their flight, told her he was going to sleep for a few hours. She'd agreed it was a good idea.

Sydney forced her body back into her own chair, flipped her screen on and re-read Denton's last message.

I know you're worried, but we've got this. We make a great team, you and I. xx

She took a shaky breath and pressed the button to turn the screen black.

She pushed the cheese and crackers aside. She would read through her article again. The second to last paragraph wasn't quite right.

34

Denton Cole and Sydney Stone were barely through the aircraft door when a woman in a beige overcoat and an orange woollen hat came galloping down the air bridge towards them.

Detective Tabitha Lynch flipped her police identification with seasoned practice.

"Mr Cole, Ms Stone. Follow me."

They were the first and only words she spoke, before marching them through a side door, down a flight of stairs, and through a series of beige, unmemorable corridors. They popped out through a side door and found themselves in the arrivals hall, where a customs official ushered them to a closed customs booth.

They were quickly accepted back into the United Kingdom.

The detective nodded her approval at the customs official, then paused for a moment. She scratched beneath her woolly orange hat, looked both ways, then started walking again.

"She's a bit odd. Are we sure we can trust her?" Sydney whispered to Denton. She juggled her laptop and handbag and tried to keep up with both Denton and the detective.

"She's a friend of a friend at Scotland Yard. And right now, we don't have much choice."

They hurried the length of another corridor that eventually opened out to a wide semicircle of offices. The central reception desk was empty. Sydney guessed it was abandoned sometime in the late 80's, judging by the dusty push-button telephone and the chunky beige stapler. Behind the reception desk were four doors, B10 through B13.

Detective Lynch opened the door labelled B12 and ushered them inside a windowless room.

"Wait here," she nodded, then disappeared.

"I guess it's a good thing she didn't lock us in here." Sydney scanned their surroundings. A large rectangular desk filled most of the room. It held two items. A beige telephone with large white buttons, and a desk pad, its white paper still pristine in the cellophane wrapping from the office stationery supply store.

There were three chairs. Denton skirted around the desk and sat in the swivel chair, meant for the office's owner. He adjusted its height to his liking. Sydney took one of the padded visitor chairs. She felt claustrophobic after hours in an aeroplane. Both her mind and body were thoroughly confused. She had expected a lengthy trudge through immigration, then transport away from the airport. Usually, she'd take the Tube. She thought of that moment when the train would come up from underground. She liked how daylight flashed between brick buildings.

Confinement in a beige square was not the post-flight pattern she'd unconsciously prepped for.

Something entirely different was going to happen today. She sat quietly across from Denton, one leg jiggling with nervous energy. They waited for Detective Tabitha Lynch to return.

"Do you think she got lost?" Sydney eventually asked Denton. She put it at 22 minutes since they'd been left in B12. "This better not be like one of those horror movies. We hear screams from B13 but when I go check it out, no one's there?"

"Then the power shuts off and when you try to get back in here, the door is locked."

"You think there are skeletal remains of people like us, in long forgotten rooms all over Heathrow?" Sydney asked, then jumped when the detective's orange hat appeared around the door, her head following behind.

"Sorry about the wait," she grinned. "Scotland Yard thought you might like to see this before you head back to the office." The detective placed a laptop bag on the desk between them. "We weren't sure you'd land in time." The computer she removed from the bag was like nothing Sydney had seen before. A bulky unit, it took the detective a few minutes to set it up.

"I know a guy in tech," the detective explained while she plugged things in and pushed buttons. "He gets me all the good stuff."

She finally stood and said,

"You'll want to come around this side Mr Cole, so you get a good view. I think it might just make your day!"

Denton and Sydney sat side by side with the laptop screen glowing on the desk between them. The detective hovered at their shoulders.

"Live feed," she explained. They watched as a media conference assembled before their eyes.

A number of chairs had been organised in rows before a fancy mahogany lectern, where a couple of reporters Sydney recognised from television, were setting up their microphones.

A woman to the right of the screen was obviously doing a piece to camera.

"Hold on," the detective said, leaning between Sydney and Denton, adjusting the sound on the laptop. The reporter's voice jumped to life in B12.

'An unexpected, and somewhat unusual press conference is due to begin any moment here at the Grand Hills Hotel. The Chief Executive of Vanguard, a lobby group well known in political circles, along with the Deputy Board Chairman of the Conservative Party, are both said to be just behind these doors. This mutual press conference is thought to have something to do with rumours that broke yesterday suggesting both organisations may have been subjected to some form of cyber-attack.'

"They're going to twist the story," Sydney said flatly.

"Maybe," Detective Tabitha Lynch offered, "or maybe not." She rocked back and forth on a pair of shiny black shoes.

"Welcome to my parlour said the spider to the fly."

Sydney turned back to the screen.

'Information from inside the Conservative Party has suggested today's announcement could be the first in a series of measures to firm up the Conservative Party's privacy and security systems, in particular, the way they store membership information. They want this done now so that any issues can be ironed out before next year's election. Sydney felt her stomach clench. She sat on her hands to stop them shaking. She watched the reporter give a thumbs up to her cameraman.

When all the microphones were ready on the podium, a woman in a navy-blue trouser suit asked that members of the media please take their seats. The reporter they'd just listened to scrambled past other members of the press to claim a front row seat. Sydney glanced at Denton but his face gave nothing away. He stared intently at the screen, his eyes flicking from side to side, searching the parts of the room they could see on the illuminated screen.

"Can you see Haig?" he asked. Sydney shook her head.

The men who were ushered on to the podium stood side by side. Sydney looked from the screen to Denton, then back at the screen.

"Is that?"

"I think so."

"Quiet please," the woman in the trouser suit asked, then after a long pause, demanded.

"We won't start until there's quiet." She stood like a school matron, arms crossed, nose in the air, waiting for the last whispers from the room to fade away.

"Let me start by introducing Mr Oscar L. Randall from Vanguard. Mr Randall is a long-term supporter of the Conservative Party and will be standing in the by-election for Finsbury." She held a hand out towards Oscar Randall, who produced a smug smile that filled his whole face, the edges of his mouth curling up so they almost touched his oversized tortoiseshell glasses.

The woman nodded towards Randall, then moved her hand slightly over, to acknowledge the other man.

"This is Mr Vernon Berry."

"What the hell is he doing there?" Sydney asked Denton.

"We obviously overlooked something." The last time he'd seen Vernon Berry was in the boardroom at Passion Media. As Chief Financial Officer, Vernon Berry had overseen the upgrade of the accounting system, and it was Vernon Berry who had insisted Sydney be put on leave. He thought back to Fiji. They knew he was tied up with Badger, but it was becoming apparent they'd underestimated his involvement.

"Mr Berry was just yesterday appointed Chief Executive and Treasurer of the Conservative Party."

"It's insane," Sydney shook her head. Denton gritted his teeth.

"He's way more involved than we thought."

The media at the press conference had grown loud, and the pant-suited women shushed the room once again.

"Please, we need to press on. Gentlemen," she took a step back and waited.

Sydney leaned forward and watched the screen. Randall dipped his head in subservience to the new Chief Executive of the Conservative Party, and Vernon Berry stepped towards the microphone.

"Thank you all for coming today. I will read out a statement, as will Mr Randall. There will be a short question and answer session afterward, where we will both attempt to answer your questions to the best of our abilities. But let me be clear. Oscar Randall has been instrumental in bringing this very serious situation to the attention of both Vanguard and the Conservative Party, and without his attention to detail and quick actions, things could have been much worse." Vernon Berry stopped to clear his throat. The room appeared to move forward an inch, the bevy of journalists hoping for something they could lead the front page and the mid-day news with. Sydney had been in the middle of that pack on many occasions. She gripped the sides of her chair.

"Sometime in the last month, an attempt, *or attempts*, have been made to hack into the computer systems of both Vanguard and the Conservative Party. They have used, what in simple terms amounts to a type of worm. A worm that can move between software systems and carry back information to the hackers."

A murmur travelled through the room.

"It is no secret the Conservative Party have a close working relationship with Vanguard, and we work together in a number of areas from campaign financing to advertising and marketing."

"We believe this hack is politically motivated, and Mr Randall and I have taken all the information we have to the police and we are working together to uncover the perpetrators."

"Bullshit," Denton shook his head.

"Look," Sydney grabbed Denton's arm. She pointed to a spot on the screen, where Justin Haig had appeared in a doorway to the left of the podium. But he was leaning casually up against a doorframe and didn't appear to be in pain. The image was too far away to see his split lip or make out any bruising.

"He looks okay," Denton patted Sydney's hand where it still gripped the sleeve of his shirt.

"His tie is crooked," Sydney said, blinking back tears. It was the relief at seeing him unharmed after his enforced departure from Fiji.

"But if Haig's there at the press conference, where's Morris James?"

Something was happening on the screen. A group of suited men approached Randall and Berry at the lectern. One of them held up his identification and murmured something the microphones could not pick up. The journalists in the room perked up, heads bobbing up and down like meerkats, trying to get a glimpse of what was occurring. A couple of camera flashes made Randall blink.

"Stop this nonsense," he demanded. "We're in the middle of a press conference. If you could please stand aside." His voice was picked up clearly by the microphones, and this time the man with the identification in his hand spoke loud and clear so he was also able to be heard by all present.

"Mr Randall. Mr Berry. As I just said, I'm from the fraud squad at Scotland Yard. We'd appreciate it if you could step outside the room with us, please." The man put his identification back in the inside pocket of his suit jacket. He motioned towards the door where Haig was leaning. Haig smiled and casually moved a small step over. A handful of uniformed police officers were visible in the room on the other side of the door.

"This is ridiculous," Vernon Berry blustered. "Can we not get through this press conference first? It is important the public know what has happened."

"I agree completely. That's why Detective Inspector Wells will be making a statement in just a moment."

The noise in the room grew as the two men reluctantly shuffled away from the microphones. Their anger was evident. Randall, in particular, looked nervous. He'd swapped his confident stance for a number of jerky hand gestures and nervous shuffling of feet. The flash of cameras and loudly shouted questions from reporters continued until both men had been led out of the room. Haig only moved away when both men had passed by, then he stepped fully into the room and the door shut firmly behind him.

The woman in the pant suit was back at the lectern, looking a little confused.

"Ladies and Gentlemen. There appears to be a slight change to this morning's proceedings."

"Understatement of the year," Denton laughed, squeezing Sydney's hand.

"Detective Inspector Wells has advised me that he will read out a statement and that he will not be taking any questions today. More information will be given as and when appropriate." The woman stepped back, then dithered for a moment, and looked a little lost as she wandered away from the podium.

In contrast, Inspector Wells walked quickly across to the microphones, unfolded a white A4 piece of paper, cleared his throat and began talking in a very loud, very fast voice.

"At 10:15 am this morning, search warrants were issued for both Vanguard and the Conservative Party Head Quarters and computer equipment is in the process of being impounded. An investigation into fraud, computer hacking and theft has been launched. At this stage, we are speaking with a very small number of high-level staff, who are helping us with enquiries. The President of Vanguard and the Leader of the Conservative Party are not among those under investigation and have been 100% open and honest with the information they can and have provided. They are co-operating willingly and are as concerned as we are. It appears they are as much a victim as anyone else.

Our investigation has been launched based on information that came to us from a concerned staff member, and that is all we will be saying, at this stage, regarding the identification of this individual.

A list of those arrested and or charged will be made available in due course.

The investigation is a shared operation between Scotland Yard and the Parliamentary Security Services. I would like to reiterate, the board members of Vanguard and The Conservative Party are not under investigation, and at this stage, we believe no sitting Member of Parliament is involved in this situation. Thank you for your time."

With that, the room erupted. Journalists jumped to life, seats were knocked over as they raced for the doors, phones pressed to ears.

"Can you find out if your tech buddy has Passion News International ready to launch?" Denton asked.

"Already did. Flick of a switch and we'll be live." Sydney grinned. "He's just waiting for your approval."

"Do it." Denton nodded.

"You want to read what I've written first?" Sydney asked.

"I trust you." Denton hugged Sydney hard, then turned to a very cheerful Detective Tabitha Lynch.

"This was so much fun!" she reached out and shook Denton's hand. "I came off maternity leave for this. Got the call this morning. Didn't even have time to wash my hair." She lifted the orange woolly hat and revealed a birds nest of blond curls.

"Sorry I couldn't get you to the press conference in time. We'd have never made it through the traffic. But I thought this would be the next best thing!"

"You have no idea how grateful we are," Sydney shook the detective's hand. "Now, how the hell do we get out of here?"

"I've got a car waiting for you. Follow me."

Sydney made the phone call as they wove their way to the pick-up zone at Heathrow.

"Mr Cole says put it up," she told Sam. "We're on our way to the office," Sydney puffed. "He wants it up now?" Sam clarified.

"Right now."

35

A state of heightened excitement had spread through Passion Media, and Sydney was struck by the almost party-like atmosphere as the lift opened and she entered the reception area with Denton by her side. It had taken almost two hours to get through the city, London traffic having no respect for Passion Media scooping the biggest political scandal of the year.

But it seemed from the cheers and applause, the staff at Passion Media didn't mind the delay.

The champagne was already on ice, no doubt Matilda's effort, and the large flat screen television was blaring from the main conference room. Denton was immediately surrounded by a small group of lawyers and board members. He gave a helpless shrug in Sydney's direction and mouthed 'see you soon,' before being swallowed up by the mob of suits.

"You're going to be famous," Matilda said, hugging her tightly, "and the IT department hates Sam. And you. The server crashed. So they copied your article to the Facebook page and twitter's going off. The phone hasn't stopped ringing. They all want to interview you."

Sydney held on to Matilda's hug. She couldn't let go.

"You okay?" Matilda asked.

No. I just broke the biggest story of my career, I haven't slept for days, oh and I fell in love with my boss who it turns out has a thing for bimbos, and now it's all a huge mess.

She swallowed it all down. Now was not the time to fall apart.

"Bloody jet lag." Sydney took a step back from Matilda and forced her lips to smile. "I'll dump my bag in my office then I can start answering questions."

"Excellent," Matilda nodded. "But can I recommend we make a quick trip to the ladies? You'll want to do something about those bags under your eyes."

Matilda produced an industrial size makeup bag and made a miraculous job of hiding Sydney's lack of sleep.

"Anything you want to talk about?" she smiled as she dabbed concealer under Sydney's eyes.

"Later," Sydney squeezed her friend's arm. "Let me get through all this first."

"Okay Babe," Matilda took out a MAC pallet of eye shadows. "Close your eyes."

She sent an intern out to Zara for a pantsuit and shirt,

"So Sydney Stone isn't remembered as a wrinkly bag lady."

Then she found another intern wandering the hall drinking champagne from a cat mug.

"You. Go and get Ms Stone a large caramel latte from the good deli on the corner. Double shot. And keep doing it every hour on the hour until I tell you to stop. Got it?"

The young boy nodded and scurried away.

Matilda guarded her boss and mentor with a fierce determination that would see her go far if she ever wanted to join a diplomatic protection squad. As the afternoon progressed, no one got any of Sydney's precious time without approval from Matilda. The Royal Family would be lucky to have her.

"She's unavailable at this moment. You may email me a request, outlining the reasons you wish to speak with Ms Stone, and I will either place your request in priority order, or I will place it in the rubbish bin. Depending on its validity."

Sydney dragged her into the office, embarrassed by the fuss. But Matilda was unapologetic.

"You're bigger than Kim Kardashian right now." She'd explained.

"I don't want to be," Sydney exclaimed. "The story is the story."

"Ah, but the story is made even more exciting by an incredibly intelligent female investigative journalist, uncovering the scandalous behaviour of an old boys' network of political cronies."

Sydney stared at Matilda, then repeated,

"I'm not the story."

"Sure thing boss. You are not the story."

But Matilda didn't leave. She worked from Sydney's desk, taking calls and prioritising.

"I don't want to be the story," Sydney tried to impress on Matilda again.

"I will make sure that message is conveyed to your fandom," Matilda assured her boss.

Sydney rolled her eyes, then for just a moment let them close. She let her body rest into the blissful darkness.

"No!" Matilda yelled. Sydney's head flew up, her eyes blinking with fright.

"You've got two minutes before Sam will be here to walk you through the new dashboard they've added to the Passion News International website. They've done something in the cloud so it's stopped crashing. Look - coffee and a muffin!"

"Thank you so much," Sydney thanked the intern who half bowed as he exited her office.

Another intern, the one who'd gone to get the suit from Zara, stuck her head around the door. "Ms Stone, your story is great. I'm a journalism major and I'd love to talk with you when you've got some spare time?"

"Definitely," Sydney agreed. She yawned and let her eyes close again.

"NO!" Matilda screamed again. The intern scarpered.

"Just two minutes," Sydney begged. "Let me nap."

"I obviously can't leave you here, you'll fall into a coma. You must keep moving," Matilda demanded. "Bring your coffee and come with me."

And so Sydney followed Matilda through the office. She spoke with the board members and co-workers with the most urgent need for attention, as per Matilda's evaluation, and accepted the calls Matilda transferred to her from other media organisations and news networks.

She stood and talked for three live television news interviews, under the Passion Media sign at reception, with Matilda beside her just off camera, to make sure Sydney neither drooled or slurred her words.

When Sydney finally sat back down at her desk, she'd lost track of all time. The dark sky and twinkling lights of the city stretched out before her. She was truly exhausted. But still the adrenalin pumped through her body.

That'll be the 10 litres of coffee, Sydney mused.

She dragged her gaze inward from the window and found herself looking at the neat row of sticky notes Matilda had stretched across her desk, in order from most important to least. The letters and numbers blurred before her.

Sydney stood up and stretched. She shrugged into her coat and thought about the Passion Media staff at a champagne bar down the road that she'd never heard of. Sydney had insisted Matilda go. She deserved more than a glass of champagne for all her hard work.

Sydney checked the time on her phone. 7:16 pm. The party would be in full swing. She thought about Denton. Since arriving back at the office, they had shared a meeting with the lawyers for 45 minutes, Sydney had passed him in the hallway twice, and received a text about an hour ago, telling her he was stuck with the board in a closed-door meeting and had no idea when he would see daylight again. If she wanted to go home, he'd call her when he was done and meet her there.

Sydney shuffled back over to the window and stared out at the city lights again.

The office was quiet. The whole of Passion Media had been a hive of noisy drama all day, and it was a relief to hear nothing but the odd electronic blip, and the hum of abandoned computers. A cleaner, probably Carmen, was vacuuming the office next door.

He would call her. That's what Denton had said. It didn't matter when. Tonight. In the Morning. Tomorrow afternoon.

Denton Cole would call Sydney Stone.

She held down the button on the side of her phone and swiped right. The screen went black. She opened the top drawer of her desk and placed it inside with the paper clips and the stapler and the mini Mars bars.

Sydney closed the drawer.

She ignored the bag she had shuttled from one side of the world to the other, and then back again. She took her handbag from the hook on the back of the door, slid it over the sleeve of the new Zara suit jacket that held no associations with anything or anyone before.

She shivered outside on the footpath, but it took less than a minute to flag down a black cab.

"Kings Cross Station please."

36

"You were on the news!" Sydney's mother's face was flush with excitement. She was wearing what appeared to be a bunny onesie, the hood was up over her head with two pink and grey ears flopping when she moved.

Sydney nodded.

"I was on the news."

"You've been in Fiji and New Zealand! Did you meet a hobbit?"

Sydney had hit what she assumed was her maximum level of sleep deprivation. Each time her eyes closed on the train ride from London to Cambridge, the lady two seats over would strike up another loud conversation, her laugh was a squeal so evil, Sydney began to believe it was travelling down through the woman, across the floor of the train, and up through the seats until it found a host to feast on, in this case, Sydney. She imagined the sound as it burrowed into her brain causing all kinds of pain and infecting her with an evil so powerful she spent a long time clinging to the seat so that she did not give in to the desire to rise up and bash the woman over the head with her shoe.

"Syd, did you hear me love? Come inside. It's 3 am. The neighbour's curtains will be twitching."

Sydney did as she was told, following her mother down a short corridor to a small sitting room.

"You're on the fold out couch." Her mother sat on the edge of the mattress and bounced a bit. "I've only had it a few weeks. But you're not the first. Auntie Jane's friend Samantha came and stayed last week. She was a strange woman. She didn't eat anything from animals, starts with a V. But not the vegetarians. The other one."

"Vegan?" Sydney offered. Now that she was standing in front of a bed, her body was giving up. She vaguely considered bursting into tears but she didn't have the energy.

"Syd, open your eyes!"

Sydney did as she was told.

"I asked if you've had anything to eat."

"Not hungry."

"I didn't ask if you were hungry. I asked if you've eaten."

"I had a cup of tea on the train. And a scone thing." She was lying about the scone.

"You're telling tales," her mother shook her head. "The day you eat a scone is the day I eat a mushroom. Wait here."

She returned a moment later with a banana, already peeled.

"I don't know what it is about scones that you don't like."

"Stodgy," Sydney stated and took a bite of banana.

"I'll be up early tomorrow morning," Sydney's mother went on. "I'm helping Auntie Jane sell jam at the markets. You don't have to come. I'll close the door so I don't wake you up. You look like the walking dead, so I dare say you'll need a big sleep."

Sydney swallowed the last of the banana, shrugged off her shoes and coat and climbed between the sheets. She smiled as her mum helped pull the fluffy warm duvet up to her chest. She hugged it tightly.

"There's an extra blanket at the end of the bed, just in case. I'm so glad you called. I've missed you so much. See you in the morning love."

Sydney closed her eyes and her mother switched off the light. She gave no resistance as the darkness pulled her under.

37

Sydney's brain offered limited functionality. Her mouth felt fuzzy, and she needed to use the bathroom. The house was quiet and she fought the need to open her eyes until she was absolutely busting, then reluctantly stumbled out of bed and staggered through the house, opening the door to the linen cupboard and next the garage, before she gave up looking for a downstairs loo and dragged her body up the stairs.

Her mother's bathroom made her smile. It was set up like a day spa. A magnificent bath, easily big enough to fit two people, and the walls were tiled in polished white marble with rose gold accents. There were groups of candles on glass shelves matching an oversized glass bowl sink.

The room smelled like vanilla, and when Sydney peaked inside a tall thin cupboard she found a selection of toothbrushes and a stack of lavender scented face clothes and hand towels.

It was a relief to scrub her face clean with hot water. It would feel wonderful to stand under a hot shower, but a cursory look didn't unveil one. She contemplated the bath, but she knew she'd either fall asleep before it was full or fall asleep once she climbed in. It wasn't worth the effort.

She padded downstairs and climbed back into her fold out bed.

What's the time? There's definitely daylight behind the curtains. Do I care enough to go look for a clock? She would usually check her phone. She felt sad when she visualised it lying abandoned in the drawer at Passion Media.

But she'd had no choice.

Sydney lay in bed and contemplated the darkened room.

The last time she'd been here, in her mother's home, she had been appalled that her mother intended to buy it. The room Sydney was now lying in had been painted aubergine.The tatty curtains were poo brown crushed velvet. The kitchen wasn't a kitchen, unless you counted a concrete tub in the corner of a mouldy room and a dirty wooden benchtop. Open shelves had been slapped on the wall by some previous owner, and Sydney remembered the thick layer of grime that covered them all. There had been one power socket, that an oven, straight out of a 1970's sitcom, was plugged into, it's frayed cord clearly not meeting any electrical safety standards. A fridge in the back porch used an extension cord hooked like dirty flagless bunting across the roof, to share the socket with the oven.

Back then, in the aftermath of her father's death and the revelations of his cheating, Sydney's mother had shown her daughter the house with a fierce optimism. She encouraged Sydney to squeeze past the fridge and have a look at the backyard, but Sydney had politely declined the invitation.

She had made her exit as quickly as possible, and since then had come up with countless excuses as to why she couldn't make it home for Christmas, or how it would be better for her mother to visit London, so Sydney could take her to the ballet, or the latest West End musical, or the National Gallery.

But here she was. And the house her mother had insisted on buying held no resemblance to its original state.

"Just like me."

The sitting room where Sydney now lay was painted a soft biscuit brown, and the thick curtains were an even softer caramel colour. The fireplace, once a dirty hole in the wall, was now encased in stone, with a large wooden mantel. An oversized candle, it's diameter large enough to hold three wicks, sat on a round of slate on the pale wooden coffee table, that had been moved under the window to make room for the fold out couch.

The light fixture that hung over Sydney was an oversized paper orb, its surface a series of cut-out circles.

She emptied the glass of water her mother had put on a small table beside her bed. She saw a muesli bar and three copies of Woman's Own. Sydney ate her snack while reading an article on how to cut your hair at home. Her eyes grew heavy. She got halfway through a recipe for a ginger and plum cheesecake.

It was pitch black in the sitting room when she came to once again. She lay still, listening to her mother pottering around in the kitchen. The glorious smell of roast chicken eventually pulled her up and out of bed. She was still wearing the Zara shirt and pants from the day before. She thought of her small bag, standing idly behind the door in her office, but then she didn't feel like remembering. She wrapped herself in the spare blanket from the end of the bed, then padded down the hall and into the kitchen.

"She rises!" her mother laughed. "I've been in twice, just to check you were still breathing." Sydney watched her mother dump a bag of spinach leaves into a wooden bowl.

"It's bamboo." Sydney's mother held the bowl aloft to show her. "Supposed to be good for the environment." She watched her mother add a chopped orange, a diced capsicum and slices of cucumber to the spinach in the bowl. She wiped her hands on her apron and stood with her hands on her hips.

"You didn't bring a suitcase."

"No," Sydney shook her head. "It was an impromptu decision to come, I just..."

"Needed to get away from all the attention?" Her mother asked. She took a bottle of wine from the fridge and unscrewed the top.

"Sit down at the table love. Chicken's ready in three minutes." Sydney's mother had always been precise when it came to meal times. Sydney sank into her chair and her mother's reliability.

The small dining table in the corner of the kitchen was just big enough for two settings. She draped the blanket over the back of the chair, ignoring the crinkled state of the clothes she had slept in.

"It must be strange to be the news when you're usually reporting it," her mother said, carrying over two wine glasses and taking a seat opposite Sydney. "You were on every channel last night! I can't believe how far you had to travel to get the story. I've never been to New Zealand. Did you get to look around or was it all work? Oh Syd, I was glad you called. I know it's not easy for you coming home. But I also know you never liked being the centre of attention, and if you don't want to talk about those politicians and their naughty lies, that's okay with me. You're very smart to take a few days away from the drama. But if you need to contact your office or get some work done, there's a little alcove up on the landing. I've got a laptop and there's wifi. But I'm not on a very big plan."

Sydney took a sip of wine. She didn't want to give her mother the real reason she'd come home. On the train ride to Cambridge she had planned on saying she'd been involved with someone at work, and that it hadn't worked out. Simple.

But the oven timer chimed, and her mother gave her a quick hug before she got busy dishing out roast potatoes and slices of roast chicken and telling Sydney to serve her own salad. And her mother had provided the perfect reason for her visit.

It was much easier to stay quiet, to leave the past where it was. At least for the time being.

"Thank you, Mum." Sydney smiled. "This is just what I need."

38

Denton ordered an Americano and chose a table at the back of the bakery.

It was warm and quiet, and when the bacon arrived, crispy and delicious on a warm buttery bap, it went some of the way to easing the irritation that had been building inside since Sydney disappeared. He'd turned up at her apartment as soon as he'd got away from the office. He'd knocked until his knuckles hurt, then assumed the jet lag had caught up with her, and she was fast asleep, just beyond his reach. He'd reluctantly returned to his own apartment and set his alarm, which dutifully woke him nine hours later. He'd crawled to the kitchen for water and painkillers. Then he'd called Sydney. Her cell phone went straight to message. He'd hung up and sent her a text saying he'd see her at the office soon. No reply. He'd called again after his shower. Again after he'd mainlined two cups of coffee and again when he got to work and realised she wasn't there. Still no reply.

He'd gone back to her apartment then. His knuckles once again took to hammering, but the only person he roused was Sydney's next door neighbour Alfie.

"I haven't seen her," he'd yawned. "Hold on though, I've got a key to her place. Even if she's taken a sleeping pill and is fast asleep in her unicorn onesie, we can check her vitals and sneak out."

Cornflake wove between Denton's legs while he waited for Alfie to find the key. He desperately wanted to see Sydney in her unicorn onesie. But when they opened her front door it was cold and empty. Denton let Alfie check the bedroom, but he knew Sydney wasn't there. Alfie shrugged when he returned.

"Bed's not been slept in. Doesn't look like she's been home at all."

Denton's phone chimed in his pocket. It was Matilda and the news wasn't good.

"I'm in her office. Her cell phone is in the top drawer of her desk. Her bag is still here too."

"Right," Denton said.

"I got her next of kin details from Human Resources. She's gone home, Mr Cole. I talked to her mum. She says Sydney turned up in the middle of the night, and has pretty much been asleep since then. She hasn't said much, but her mum thinks she's struggling with her face being all over the news."

"What do you think?" Denton asked.

Matilda was quiet.

"I'm not sure what's going on Mr Cole, but Sydney hasn't missed a day of work in the whole time I've known her."

"She's fine, Alfie. Gone home to her mum's for a bit."

"She could have bloody told us," Alfie laughed. He locked Sydney's front door and offered Denton a cup of coffee.

"Not today Alfie, maybe next time."

Would there be a next time?

The next 24 hours were somewhat blurry.

Matilda intercepted all Sydney related calls and emails, passing him the most important ones, therefore mitigating any immediate concern, or even knowledge of her absence.

He napped on his couch between visits from Sam, who was scrambling to build up Passion News International, relying on an already overstretched editorial team, but always with a smile on his face. But did Denton know when Sydney was coming back?

No. He didn't.

Standing ovation for your disappearing act Miss Stone!

If he'd been a magician, he'd have reached into his magic hat and pulled Sydney Stone out by her fuzzy little bunny ears.

"Can I bring you a sandwich Mr Cole?"

"No thanks Matilda. I'm out for lunch. Yes you can close your mouth. I've been told nothing bad will happen if I leave the building for an hour."

His workload just kept growing. Denton was paying an expert in cybersecurity, recommended by Haig. She'd been tasked with clearing any and all trace of Badger from Passion Media, and then she was going to improve security. She'd turned up and immediately pissed off most of the IT department insisting they change nearly every process they currently followed.

He'd found the perfect replacement for Vernon Berry as Chief Financial Officer, and spent most of the previous afternoon convincing the board she was worth every zero she'd requested on her paycheck. Scotland Yard's people at Serious Fraud were keen for further interviews, which he'd so far managed to push out till early the next week, letting Passion Media's lawyers handle the logistics on his and Sydney's behalf.

And if she doesn't like that, she'll have to come back and tell me!

A number of times he came close to asking Matilda to give him Sydney's mum's number. But his feelings were raw, and he flip-flopped constantly about what would he say.

'Hey Syd, when we were in Fiji I fell in love with you, I just never got around to telling you. But better late than never, yeah?'

But then his bruised ego would push in,

'Hey Syd, you know how we travelled to the other side of the world together, and I introduced you to my family, and we nailed a bunch of cyber crooks but then you disappeared and left me to tidy up the mess? Yeah, I'm just calling to say thanks darling. You're a real keeper.'

He was pissed off and tired and really bloody confused. So he'd taken a leaf out of the Sydney Stone playbook, and he'd done a bunk. The office wouldn't burn down if he took a couple of hours off.

Justin Haig took one look at his friend and shook his head.

"What happened to you?" he asked, "You look like you got some fashion advice from a three year old, then got dressed in the dark."

Denton ran a hand through his peacock tail hair. He hadn't bothered shaving and his shirt was not living up to its price tag, mostly because it had fallen off the hanger while he'd showered and he hadn't been bothered enough to iron out the creases.

"You can talk, that fat lip you got courtesy of Morris James is beginning to look more like a giant cold sore, and that tie, mate, really? Maroon and yellow. You look like a tall skinny Ron Weasley."

They grinned and hugged.

"I'm glad you're okay Haig. I was worried."

"Bloody hell mate, I was packing it."

A scream from behind the counter drew their attention and a young woman came running at Haig.

"Mr Haig!" She cried and threw her arms around his neck. "It was you, wasn't it," she whispered. "They said there was a whistleblower and I know it's you. I've got your papers, the ones I accidentally printed off. I was supposed to give them to that kick-ass journalist, Sydney Stone. I've got them in my bag. Been carrying them around for days and days. I didn't know what to do with them when I couldn't get hold of Sydney."

"You've got printouts? I think Serious Fraud are going to want to talk to you."

"They already called. Should I give the stuff to them?"

"Yes!" Haig and Cole both said at the same time.

"Okay, okay." she laughed. "I just wanted to check with Sydney first. Is she okay?"

"Sure," Denton half shrugged.

"Jim!" Haig called across the café, and a man in a black apron waved back, then continued serving his customers.

"You guys hooked up yet?" Haig grinned. "I told you he was keen. He was always disappointed when I did the coffee run for you."

"Shut up," Minnie shoved Haig. "Introduce me to your friend."

"Denton Cole." Denton held out his hand, and Minnie took it in her own.

"Oh I know you. You've been in all the papers and on the telly. You look kind of different."

"The camera adds ten pounds," Haig told Minnie. "And he's eating his feelings."

"You could use a few bacon sandwiches yourself, Ron Weasley," Denton threw back at Haig.

Minnie snorted in laughter,

"It's funny 'cause it's true. Go find a table and I'll come take your order."

Haig took a seat beside Denton and stared out the window.

"I can't stop looking at it," he grinned pointing across the road to where a line of yellow police tape stretched across the front of Vanguard. A bored looking police officer was standing guard. "This whole Badger thing. I want to say thank you. I really appreciate it man. Without you I'd have been in a whole world of pain. I owe you a lot Cole, despite the busted lip and a lack of employment options you've left me with."

"You're my brother," Denton replied. "You'd do the same for me."

"I would," Haig agreed.

"Right boys, what will it be?" Minnie had a notepad and pencil ready.

"I'm keen for that bacon sandwich," Denton said, "and a double shot latte."

"The usual for me Minnie," Haig said, "and someone else is joining us. She wants," Haig lifted his phone and read, "a cappuccino. Absolutely no cinnamon is to land anywhere near it, and do you have any plain cheese scones?"

"I think we've got a couple of scones left, I'll make sure to remove any shred of parsley."

Minnie went back behind the counter. Denton waited while Haig adjusted his chair and smoothed his Hogwarts tie.

"So are you going to tell me who's joining us?" Denton finally asked.

"I'd prefer to wait till she gets here."

"Why?" Denton asked. "I'm really not in the mood for any more secrets or surprises."

"Well this could be a bit of an awkward situation then."

"How very surprising," Denton said sarcastically. "Awkward Situation should have been your hyphenated middle name."

"I'll let you have that one," Haig nodded, "what with the serious fraud investigation. You helped me out, I'm returning the favour."

"Everything's fine," Denton explained. "That security expert you recommended is pissing everyone off, but damn she's good."

"I'm not talking about work. This is personal."

"We're here to talk about you and Sydney."

Both men looked up at a smiling Matilda.

"Denton Cole, this is an intervention."

39

"There's a reporter from one of the daily sleaze rags. She's got a source. Someone from the hotel in Fiji saw you and Sydney eating breakfast. And frolicking on the beach. Her words, definitely not mine." Matilda took a large bite from her cheese scone.

Haig weighed in,

"I don't know if you and Sydney were just hooking up, having a bit of fun, but I talked to Mum last night and she's adamant you and Sydney should get married as soon as possible, build a house next door to them and start giving her some grandbabies. Before they die."

"Not at all dramatic," Denton noted.

"I thought we weren't going to put pressure on him?" Matilda grumbled through a mouth full of scone.

"Right," Haig nodded. "No pressure. Take a year or two before you create an heir to the Cole dynasty." Denton shook his head and sipped his coffee.

"Look Mr Cole. Sydney kicks arse at work but when it comes to relationships, she's a big chicken. I don't know why or what happened, she's never told me. All she'll say is she doesn't have time to date, and she doesn't need a man who will end up making her miserable. As all men eventually do. Apparently."

"Have you talked to Sydney at all?" Haig asked Denton. "Have you tried calling her at her mum's?"

"No," Denton admitted. "Before we came home, I tried talking to her. But there was so much going on and she was distracted writing her story. I didn't want to put more pressure on her. Then she disappeared, and left me covering everything. Short of getting a psychic reading, how on earth am I supposed to know what she wants?"

"Do you know what *you* want?" Matilda asked. "I mean, we don't really know each other but from a quick Google search, I'd say you're not exactly a one-woman man. From the photographs I'd say you're more of a 'date a lot of different women who share the same taste in super high heels and expensive jewellery' kind of guy. I mean I have to say Mr Cole, I'm not going to sit here all sweet and cute if you've whisked Sydney away, swept her off her feet, made her fall in love with you, and all along it's been a pump and dump."

"Pump and dump?" Haig snorted.

"What? It's a thing." Matilda glared back.

"You might need to work on your sweet and cute." Haig grinned at Matilda who stuck her tongue out in reply.

"Oh I take it back, you're a delight," Haig smiled.

"Thank you," Matilda nodded. "But you can stop flirting. I have a boyfriend. He's a DJ."

"I wasn't flirting," Haig pushed back. "And a DJ?" he said, "probably really popular on the 16th birthday circuit."

"Sure you weren't flirting," Matilda waved him away. "Let's get back to Mr Cole and Sydney."

Haig opened his mouth to defend himself against the outrageous flirting allegations. Sure, Matilda looked fun and spunky. He'd enjoyed chatting with her when she'd called the night before, and maybe he'd been waiting for the phone to ring this morning. So what if he'd kind of been checking her out since she'd arrived at the cafe? She wasn't his type. Too chatty and bouncy. Definitely friend-zone.

"It's not what it looks like," Denton waded in. "Those women I took to events are friends of my assistant Harvey. I hate that red carpet crowd, but Harvey has a one in five rule. Every fifth invite, he finds me an event girl. Someone he knows won't bore me to sleep at the table, but who knows I'm not looking to start a love affair at the Business Leaders Awards Dinner or searching for a wife at the opening of a bowel cancer wing at the local hospital."

"You're not exactly painting a pretty picture Mr Cole. Is there a reason you get your secretary to set you up on dates?"

"Matilda, you have to stop calling me Mr Cole. And I know it looks terrible, but a few years ago I met this woman at the opening of an art gallery. She seemed normal enough, she was a friend of the artist I think. Anyway, she seemed fun so we went on a few dates. Ambrosia loved the red carpet events, couldn't contain her glee when our photo ended up in the entertainment sections of a couple of newspapers. Then we went to an event, a fashion thing one of her friends was promoting. That's when things got weird. More paparazzi than ever before. Back then I wasn't as private, I got out and about. But I wasn't even close to A list. More like D or E list when it was a quiet week in entertainment. Like, 'oh yes, and the guy behind James Cordon is eligible bachelor and business magnate Denton Cole.' That type of attention came my way. But we were outside this fashion thing in the middle of nowhere, and they're asking is Ambrosia my soul mate and was it true she'd shifted in with me. I mean she'd been sleeping over a fair bit, but I was travelling a lot. I didn't even know her middle name or what she liked doing on the weekends. She told me she was a professional travel blogger. I didn't even know that was a thing!

Anyway, when we got home I sat her down, and we talked and I gently let her know my feelings for her weren't the kind that were going to result in a wedding at The Ritz and a honeymoon in St Tropez. She *really* didn't take it well. She yelled a lot about how I'd led her on. And she locked herself in the bathroom and wouldn't leave. I was due in Switzerland for a conference, so I left her there. I figured she'd get hungry and eventually she'd have to leave."

"You left the bunny boiling unattended?" Haig shook his head.

"I was late for my flight," Denton shrugged.

"So what happened?" Matilda asked.

"She destroyed the apartment I'd been renting. Threw all my clothes down the rubbish chute. Smashed all the plates and glasses in the kitchen. Chopped the cords off all the kitchen appliances, and the television. Mixed pickle juice with mustard powder and rubbed it into the carpets."

"Full crae crae," Matilda shook her head.

"It didn't end there. She tried to sell a story to the tabloids, telling some ridiculous tale of how I was into weird kinky sex and how I liked to make her dress up in 80's shoulder pads and power suits, and could only get off to her reading my business profit and loss statements."

"Two things," Haig said.

"Her name was Ambrosia. Like the dessert? That was your first warning mate. And second, how come you never told me this till now?"

"You know exactly why," Denton answered. "You'd have laughed. A lot. And told everyone we know."

"True," Haig nodded.

"I got lucky, this all happened when you were working that contract in Abu Dhabi."

"I agree with Haig," Matilda interrupted. "Ambrosia is a ridiculous name."

"I'm usually right. I'm glad you can see that."

Matilda rolled her eyes at the grin on Haig's face.

 "You know what they say, Big ego, small—"

"Settle down children. Let me finish my story," Denton said. "It's actually how I met Dave Lloyd, my predecessor at Passion Media. When I got back from Switzerland I went straight to a friends cookbook launch. Dave came and found me and introduced himself. Said his staff had been talking about the story in the Daily Mail. Bloody embarrassing, but I said I thought Ambrosia would go away when she'd had her five minutes in the limelight. He's a good guy. We ate a lot of mini quiches, drank a lot of whiskey and talked about football. Then as we were leaving, Dave brought Ambrosia up again. He suggested I engage my lawyers. He was friends with some American soap star who'd been through a similar thing with her ex-husband. He offered to use his contacts, put the word out that Ambrosia wasn't a stable source. When I got home and saw the apartment, I called Dave and agreed. My lawyers got to work, threatened her with defamation and arrest for wilful damage of property."

"What did she say?" Matilda asked. "I love everything about this story."

"I never heard from her again."

"She just disappeared?" Haig asked.

Denton nodded.

"I paid for the damage to the apartment and I never heard from Ambrosia again. But it really made me nervous. It's not just my reputation at stake. It's my whole family who would suffer if someone like Ambrosia was determined to destroy my reputation. So I quit dating. And that's the reason for the event girls."

"You quit?" Haig asked, "like you went cold turkey?" Haig looked incredulous.

"I haven't been celibate if that's what you're concerned about. I've had the odd," Denton Cole looked at Matilda and tried to find the right words.

"Dalliance? Romantic interlude? Overnight liaison?" Matilda offered.

"Exactly. But I've been very careful to keep things simple." Denton explained.

"Cautiously casual." Matilda stated.

"Right," Denton nodded. "But then I arrived at Passion and Sydney was at the front desk and she looked all flustered and I tried to be charming and she had no time for me at all. And from that moment, nothing has been simple."

Haig yawned loudly.

"Blah, blah, blah, the world stopped spinning, your heart skipped a beat. You love her more than life itself."

Denton's face reddened.

"Bloody hell Cole, you do love her!" Haig exclaimed.

"It's so hard to understand why you're still single Haig. It's just beyond me that a beautiful, intelligent woman hasn't fallen for your charms," Matilda said drolly.

"As much as I'd love to stay and hear how your DJ boyfriend played at Brian McFadden's daughters sweet 16th birthday party, I've got an appointment at Scotland Yard this afternoon." Haig put his elbow on the table and rested his chin in his hand. "But do tell me Denton. Tell me how you and Sydney are meant to be together forever and how she makes the sun shine on even the rainiest of days."

Denton pushed his hand into Haig's elbow causing it to slip off the table. Haig wobbled for a moment, at the sudden imbalance.

Matilda grinned and winked at Haig.

"Nice. So we've determined that Haig is a dumbass and Mr Cole, sorry - Denton," Matilda corrected herself, "is in love with my best friend Sydney Stone."

Denton's cheeks flushed red.

"Well then," Haig banged both hands down on the table. "It's probably time you did something about it!"

40

Three days had passed since Sydney landed back on British soil. She lay like a starfish beneath the blankets on the fold out bed in her mother's sitting room. It was hard to comprehend she'd spent three whole days sleeping, reading trashy magazines and eating when and whatever her mother said she should.

An anxious feeling grew in the pit of her stomach every time she thought about using her mother's computer to check her emails or check the Passion International News website. She hadn't even found the nerve to turn on the television news. Sydney assumed her mother was not sharing her media embargo, but she had not mentioned Badger, or asked about what happened in Fiji or New Zealand, or commented on any of the political fallout that Sydney assumed was leading the news and keeping the political correspondents very busy.

Sydney felt guilty. She'd mislead her mother, letting her believe it was the pressure of breaking such a huge story and the need to escape the limelight that had brought her home. But she still couldn't bring herself to reveal the real reason.

Sydney propped herself up on a pile of pillows and flicked through the pages of a home and gardening magazine. Maybe she'd have a shower.

Being clean seemed an easier proposition than coming clean. She wanted to tell her mother about Denton Cole, but it was taking all Sydney's effort to keep at bay all thoughts of Denton, and how he might be feeling since she had walked away without explanation.

Sydney found her mother in the kitchen making scones.

"I think I might have a shower."

Her mother said,

"Good girl. You were about to be the recipient of a hospital-style bed bath!"

The hot water fell hard against her skin. Denton would be busy. He had an organisation to run. No doubt there would be internal investigations and reports. Denton Cole would be busy securing his financial future, and that of Passion Media. And he had other businesses to run. Shareholders to calm. He'd be putting out fires behind the scenes and hopefully taking advantage of the publicity and interest in the Badger story. Was Passion News International a success? She hoped so. She'd believed in Sam's idea. He was a good guy.

Whatever she'd shared with Denton over there, on the other side of the world, Sydney was sure he'd already forgotten. Beach life had been replaced with the reality that Denton Cole was a man of transactions in both his personal and professional life. Mutually exclusive agreements, with no long-term commitments to either.

Your version of events is based on a series of assumptions. But then Sydney closed her eyes and saw the photos of the beautiful women and their perfect hair. And that woman's tell all in The Daily Mail. It was wholly believable that Denton Cole had been a temporary slip. A fling that had finally been flung. She stuck her face under the water and washed away her tears. It was over. And no one was there to contradict her story.

When she emerged from the bathroom, her mother was in the kitchen, surrounded by brown paper bags overflowing with fresh produce.

"Want to help me make a vegetable quiche?" her mother asked.

It seemed to Sydney a lovely way to pass a winter's afternoon.

"I loved doing this when I was little. Making pastry with you in the warm kitchen." Sydney let her mum slip the apron over her head.

"Turn around, I'll tie you up."

Sydney pressed her still damp curls behind her ears.

"I remember standing on the kitchen stool, beating the eggs with the cream, and you'd grate the cheese, but you'd still be crying from chopping onions."

But her mother didn't join her in reminiscing. She rattled two teacups on to the bench and flicked the switch on the kettle.

"Sit down," she told Sydney. A demand, not a request.

"What's up?" Sydney asked, sliding into one of the chairs beside the small dining table. Her mother carried the cups over then went back for the teapot.

"Before we make quiche, I think we should probably have a wee chat about exactly what's up."

Sydney pulled one of the teacups over to her side of the table. She lifted the teapot.

"Wait," her mum put a hand on her arm. "Let it steep for a moment."

She put the teapot down and tried hard to remind herself that she was a fully grown adult now, but her mother's concern made her stomach twist.

Her mother sighed. "Sydney. I've just been accosted by a reporter from one of those daily newspapers, asking if you're hiding out here because your boss broke up with you."

"Oh god," Sydney covered her mouth with her hands.

"Saying nothing is not an option now Sydney, it's time to talk."

"Did you tell him I was here?" Sydney squeaked.

"It was a her," Sydney's mother replied, "and of course not. I'm not stupid."

Sydney couldn't speak. She was gripped with fear. Had Denton broken up with her in a newspaper? Had he leaked some story to the press in retaliation for her disappearing? An affair with her boss. It made it sound so sleazy.

"I think you owe me an explanation Sydney. Have you really been in a relationship with Denton Cole?"

"You know his name?" Sydney cringed, unwilling to meet her mother's eyes.

"Sydney. You may have been locked in a newsless bunker these past few days, but the rest of England, and probably other parts of the world, have been bombarded with stories about that newspaper boss and those politicians you exposed and how you and Denton Cole, and another man they aren't naming, brought them to their knees. So yes, of course I know who Denton Cole is. His face, and yours, have been on every newspaper and television news channel this week. What I want to know, is who Denton Cole is *to you*?"

Sydney could feel the tears forming but took a slow steadying breath. She tried hard to hold the door shut on the emotions she had been keeping locked away.

"It's not a story," Sydney tried. "Not worthy of some sleazy hack coming all the way here to find me, and bothering you..."

"She seemed to think her 'source' was quite reliable. But I'd like to get the story straight from the horse's mouth. Talk to me Pinkie-Pie."

The silence lingered while Sydney tried to find her words. She closed her eyes and imagined writing down her feelings. Cut and paste. Delete a few sentences. Arrow forward…

"Stop it," her mother begged. "Open your eyes Sydney. I'm right here. I don't need a perfect narrative. I'm not here to judge you or critique your life. I'm here. You don't need to do anything but open your mouth and start talking."

Sydney opened her eyes, blinking through tears, and heard her voice fill the room.

She told her mother about Denton. How she'd met him on his first day at Passion Media, and she'd hated him. But how he'd worked his way into her life. How closely they had worked on the investigation, and how it had led to a more personal relationship. How she had met his best friend Justin Haig, and the Haig family Denton Cole had practically grown up with in New Zealand. And that maybe the thought had crossed her mind, that she had fallen a little bit in love with him.

"But he's not the relationship type," Sydney declared.

"He told you this?" Her mother asked.

"He didn't need to. Florence, Justin Haig's mum, said he'd never been in a serious relationship, and one quick Google search confirmed it."

"Google?" Her mother looked confused. "You're an investigative journalist and you're making relationship decisions based on Google? No, worse than that, you're taking relationship advice from Google!"

"It's not just that, Mum." Sydney raised her voice. "It's me too. I'm not the relationship type!"

"Says who?"

"I say so," Sydney cried. "I've spent the last ten years building my own career. I've got my own flat, my own life. I don't need some man whose only intention is to trample all over my heart and leave me. Why would I do that? Why would I be that woman?"

"When you say 'why would I be that woman,'" Sydney's mother said in a quiet voice, "what you are really saying is why would you be like *me*."

"I didn't mean it to sound like that. I can see you're happy now," Sydney told her mother. "But what Dad did. He died, and you lost your husband, and then we found out he was living a lie, and everything we had as a family, all those memories crumbled away. And you never said anything. That woman was at his funeral and you never said a thing. I tried to tell you, to open your eyes, and you didn't want to know."

Sydney watched a single small tear glide gently down her mother's cheek.

"I don't want to judge you, Mum. You had to do things your way. But so did I. I decided on a different path," Sydney tried to explain. "Back then, I made a commitment to myself, that I would never let any man do that to me. I made a choice to live my life for me."

"That's a very lonely existence Sydney. One I'm very sorry to have had a hand in creating."

They sat in the quiet kitchen, the only sound came from the vegetables, the odd squeak and crumple of paper as gravity resettled them in their brown paper bags.

"Pudding!" Sydney's mother rose from her chair. "The quiche can wait. This is more of an ice cream conversation."

41

The date sponge came from little plastic containers, microwaved for a minute, then turned upside down on a plate so the gooey toffee sauce dribbled down the sides. The vanilla ice cream melted and pooled in a creamy moat around the little pudding hill.

"Love is messy." Sydney's mother took a bite of the sponge and encouraged Sydney to do the same. "I thought you coped so well with your father's death. But I was so busy working through my own feelings. You looked happy, and I never questioned that. I never thought to ask you. I thought, what doesn't kill you makes you stronger, and you are so strong Sydney. I loved coming to London and staying in your beautiful apartment and going out to shows and seeing where you work. You are a wonderful woman, with so much determination and drive and I love that about you. But all of that distracted me from the talk we never had."

Sydney used her spoon to shave off thin slivers of pudding. She didn't trust herself to talk.

"But we can talk now, don't you think? Better late than never?"

Her mother set about demolishing her pudding in three large bites then pushed the empty plate into the middle of the table. This gave her room to lean forward, her elbow on the table, her chin in her hand.

"Sydney. When your father died, and then his other woman arrived on my doorstep, you know what my first instinct was?"

"To slap her?" Sydney smiled.

"No!" her mother laughed, "I wanted to console her."

"What?" Sydney cried. "That women, all she ever wanted was Dad's money. More fool her, when she found out there wasn't any."

"The thing is Syd, she gave him her heart, knowing he wouldn't have that much to give in return. He had a family. He had a home. He had a life with us. But the honest truth is that our marriage wasn't exciting enough for him, *or me.* There was no challenge in our marriage."

"But Mum—"

"No Syd, you have to hear this. Your father and I, we were good friends, best friends. And I loved him, but we never really had a connection. And I know you'll tell me I sound like Dr Phil or whichever daytime telly person we're watching these days. But it's true. I've thought about this a lot over the years, about why we got together and why we got married. And I'm ashamed to admit, it was mostly convenience. We were sort of thrown together because our group of friends had paired off, and it was a comfortable arrangement, to have someone to talk to, to hold hands with at the movies. To pick me up and take me to the school dance. I'm not saying we didn't have fun. We had a great time! But then our friends started getting engaged, and we were going to weddings every few months and each time they'd ask your Dad, when was he going to pop the question, and my girlfriends would nudge me and show off their diamond engagement rings and I was green with envy, Sydney."

Sydney forgot her pudding. She was intrigued by this story of her parent's union, so different from the high school sweethearts who only loved each other version, that she had heard as a child.

"So I lay down a few hints, and I think your Dad got sick of all the nagging, and so one night, while we were watching Happy Days, and Chachi asked Joanie to marry him, your Dad said, I guess I'd better get the gang off my back, and make an honest woman out of you."

Sydney's mouth fell open.

"That's how he asked you to marry him?"

"Yes." Her mother giggled. And do you know what I felt Sydney?"

Sydney shook her head.

"Relief. And excitement. Because marriage meant a house and a baby."

"And a husband?" Sydney offered.

"He was a necessary part of the equation, yes. I knew it wasn't necessarily the love affair to end them all. I'd read romance novels, I knew I'd never swooned. I wasn't in love with him. Not the way you're supposed to be. But I figured a real-life husband was far more practical than a fantasy any day."

"Wow." Sydney blinked.

"Now hearing that might make you feel a bit sorry for your old Dad, but he wasn't innocent. The arrangement worked just as well for him. His parents, your Grandma and Grandpa Stone, you know how very old-fashioned they were. By marrying me, your Dad fulfilled his duty. He made them happy and escaped their strict rules, all at the same time."

"Those first few months we were married, Syd, oh we were both giddy with the freedom!"

"You lived in a little flat above the fish and chip shop on Alder Road and you were crazy happy," Sydney repeated the story she had always loved, trying to get her head around the new facts of what had come before.

"We did, and we were," her mother nodded. "We only did the dishes when we ran out of plates. We wore dirty socks and we never dusted a thing. We washed our clothes once a week, on Saturday afternoons. We'd take them to the laundromat and sit in the pub next door, running back and forth to transfer the clothes from the washing machine to the dryer."

"You were happy." Sydney didn't know if she was asking a question or simply stating a fact.

"We were very happy indeed," her mother nodded. "I was working in the bookshop and your father had started at the insurance company and even with our regular nights at the pub and eating takeaways, the money in our bank account kept growing and growing. So we got the grand idea to buy a house."

"Our house."

"Yes, Sydney, our house. It will always be our house in my mind too."

"I loved Saturday mornings. When the cartoons were on and the sun came into the lounge and I would lie on the carpet, watching the dust float in the air."

"Housework was never my highest priority," Sydney's mother mused. "My favourite room was yours," her mother reached across the table and held Sydney's hand. "I loved your little dressing table. And the stain glass window with its little yellow daffodils."

They sat in a companionable silence for a moment, lost in their own memories.

"What happened?" Sydney asked.

"You were everything we ever wanted. We marvelled at everything you did. Your first smile, the first time you slept through the night. The way you screwed your face up when you sucked on slices of orange. Your first steps."

"I get it," Sydney laughed. "I was an exemplary baby."

"Oh no you weren't," her mother laughed. "When you were five weeks old you screamed for three days straight. We took it in shifts walking you. Then we let you cry. Then we felt so guilty we rocked you for hours. We took you to the doctors. You screamed the surgery down. He was referring you to the hospital when you suddenly went very still, filled your nappy with the most foul smelling poo ever, then you closed your eyes and went to sleep."

Sydney laughed.

"Oh no, it wasn't funny," her mother cried. "We took you home and you slept for three days straight. Hardly fed. It was a nightmare. We hadn't slept from the screaming, then we lay awake, checking every half an hour to make sure you were still breathing."

"I'm not sure you're making your case for Grandchildren anytime soon," Sydney pointed out.

"The thing is Syd, in those early years, your Dad and I were focused on you. It's what happens when babies are around. They suck up all the attention and time and energy. And that's completely normal and there's nothing wrong with that if you've got a marriage built on more than convenience and a great fondness for each other."

"I see where you're going," Sydney told her mother.

"Then you'll see Sydney, that one day that baby bubble burst. You started sleeping through the night, then you went off to Kindergarten and learned to read and write. When there was time and space for your Dad and I to re-establish ourselves, it was very apparent to us both that there was nothing much left to salvage. Perhaps because there had never been much there to begin with."

"So why didn't you separate?" Sydney asked. "Get a divorce, like normal people."

"There always seemed to be a reason," Sydney's mother sighed. "Grandma Stone was still alive. Your Dad wanted to be there when you started school. Then the housing market took a hit so we couldn't sell. We both wanted to take you to Disneyland for Christmas."

"That was an amazing holiday," Sydney remembers. "We were happy. You were happy. Weren't you happy?" Sydney questioned her mother.

"It was the happiest we'd been, just us three. Your father and I were exhausted from chasing you around. You wanted to hug every Minnie Mouse you saw."

"I loved Minnie Mouse," Sydney grinned. "I was secretly planning on asking one of those Minnie Mouse's to come home with us. I was going to get you to buy me bunk beds for my bedroom."

"We never regretted our time together with you Sydney."

Her mother rose from the table. She took the pudding plates to the kitchen sink and rinsed them under the tap.

"The thing is, we came home from that holiday and we remembered what good friends we always were. And we just sort of carried on. We stopped talking about when we should separate. We stopped planning separate lives. We just sort of fell into a comfortable companionship."

"Did you know he was having an affair? You weren't suspicious?"

"We never talked about it. I never confronted him. But I probably knew before he did."

"What?"

"A few months after we got back from California, I was in the bookshop. It had rained all morning, but the clouds had cleared away and the sun was warm on my back. I was making a display for the new John Grisham book, and I looked out the window, and I saw them. She'd come out of the medical centre, she was the new receptionist. Your father had his head down trying not to get those ridiculous suede shoes wet in the puddles, and they crashed into each other."

"And?" Sydney asked.

"And they laughed at each other. She blushed. Your dad sort of hopped around laughing and pointing at those stupid shoes. And they should have carried on their separate ways. But they didn't. They just stood there laughing and chatting. Could have been a minute, could have been five. I'm not sure. I'd gone back to my display. But when I looked back across the road a while later, I saw his face. He was watching her walk away. And I just knew." Sydney's mum shrugged. "I thought, *she's the one*. And I guess I was sort of waiting, ever since that day, for him to come to me and tell me he was leaving."

"But he didn't." Sydney sighed. "He never said a thing. He just covered it up with lies. Business trips and networking weekends."

"But I lied too." Sydney's mother reached up to the cupboard above the fridge.

"Salt and Vinegar or Onion?"

"I don't mind," Sydney replied. "Wait, I want Salt and Vinegar!"

The crisps, deposited on the table between the two women, were eaten straight from the bag.

"You weren't the one having the affair," Sydney reasoned. "So how did you lie?"

"I lied by omission. I pretended not to know. I carried on the charade. Even though I knew, I didn't say or do anything. I'm quite ashamed of myself if I'm honest."

"Why?" Sydney asked. "Why did you keep pretending?"

"I can't really give you a reason that would justify my actions in a clear way. I was a little bit jealous. I liked my house. I liked my life. I didn't want to shuttle you between houses and have to negotiate Christmas and Birthdays and then see you meld into a new family. And your father was so careful. You're not going to buy it, but there was a mutual respect that had always existed between us. He never slipped up. He never left receipts lying around or tripped up in his stories. If I needed him, he was there. He always answered his phone. I appreciated that. And I thought to myself, if he's being this careful, maybe he doesn't want things to change either. And in lots of ways Syd, it was just easier that way. I always thought, when I meet someone else, when I fall in love, head over heels, heart pounding, can't live without him love, then we would do it. We'd sit down and tell each other the truth and make a plan to divorce. But my timing was off. Your Dad died years before I felt the kind of love that makes you do very silly things with crazy amounts of enthusiasm."

"You fell in love?" Sydney wiped the crisp crumbs off the table and watched them fall to the wooden floor. "You never said anything. When? And who with?"

"His name is Craig. We met at the markets last summer. He's a helicopter instructor with the army. He's sort of retired, which means he spends a little less time than he used to at the base."

"But you never mentioned him." Sydney struggled to keep the hurt from her voice.

"I know. To be honest, I've been nervous about talking about any of this with you. Craig's been banging on at me about ripping off the Band-aid. But you were so angry when your Dad died. And you seemed so happy with me coming to visit you in London. I didn't want to mess things up. I've kind of been waiting for the right time, waiting for you to come back. I thought, when Sydney is ready, she'll come back home. But I was wrong. Because you only had half the story. Here I was expecting you to find the path back home when you didn't even know you were going the wrong way."

Sydney nibbled around a potato crisp.

"What does he look like?" Her mother went to the bottom drawer in the kitchen and dug under the tea towels, returning to the table with a framed photograph of herself with her arm around a man wearing a blue-grey service uniform, two medals attached to the left side of his chest.

"He looks like Goose from Top Gun."

"It's the moustache. But he's in the air force, not the navy. And unless you have a great interest in avionics, I'd not bring up Top Gun when Craig's around."

Her mother's cheeks flushed a warm pink as she talked about the family farm Craig's brother managed, and the lovely new farmhouse Craig had built on a section of land there. He had a daughter, Bobby-Lee. She lived in Texas and was the result of a very brief fling with a girl from a really posh family.

"She didn't find out she was pregnant with Craig's baby until after her high school sweetheart came back from College and declared himself hers forever. So they pretended Bobby-Lee was his."

Sydney's mouth hung open.

"What?" her mother grinned. "You didn't think the Stones are the only ones with secrets hidden in the closet?"

"How did Craig find out about her?"

"Oh, well, the woman, Delia, she was honest with her fiancé about the pregnancy, and he still wanted to marry her. So they eloped and swore never to tell her family that Bobby-Lee wasn't his. That kind of backfired, because Bobby-Lee's grandfather lived till he was 90 something, so for a long time Bobby-Lee had an Uncle Craig, who sent her presents, and always came for Thanksgiving. And when her grandfather died, they told her the truth."

"Just like that? By the way, Uncle Craig is actually your dad. Happy Thanksgiving!"

"No Sydney. Of course it wasn't just like that. They did it gently. But she got very angry and ran away to New York. Wouldn't talk to her mother or father for a year. Then she turned up here in Cambridge, knocked on Craig's door one Sunday afternoon. She stayed a while. They talked a lot. She went home and there was more talking. Delia's parents were very hurt. There were some strong feelings that needed to be worked out."

"How is it now?"

"They're sickening," Sydney's mother laughed. "All happy families in that loud American, hug everyone and have another slice of sweet potato pie kind of way."

"You've met them all?" Sydney asked.

"Not Bobby-Lee, only her parents. They stayed with Craig for a night when their Mediterranean cruise got rescheduled."

Sydney took another crisp from the bag, turning it over in her hands, examining the sharp edges.

"I think that's why Craig's been so keen for me to get you back home. He's got this grand plan for Christmas at the farm, with all of us. Bobby-Lee and her boyfriend – he's a musician with grotty hair, but that's another story completely. Delia and her husband, and us. He loves the idea of a whole big family thing."

"I don't like sweet potato." Sydney wasn't sure how she felt about this sudden group of people falling into the category of extended family.

"We can have roast potatoes. Especially if it's Christmas. You don't have mashed potato at Christmas. You have lamb and roast potatoes and carrots..." Sydney's mother was listing the menu that had remained unchanged as long as Sydney could remember. A family tradition.

"So, Sydney. I know this has been a lot for you to take in. And I'm sure you've got a fair amount of processing you'd like to do. I know that's what the young people say and do before they're ready to get on with things." Sydney was only half listening. She was staring at the photograph of Craig.

"I just can't believe I had it so wrong."

"I didn't give you much else to believe." Sydney's mother shrugged. "But I think you should know that even though your father left a mess behind when he died, he wasn't the only one to blame. And I really don't want the decisions I made, the mad way I lived in a half marriage and then tiptoed around you after your Dad's death, to ruin your future happiness."

"I'm quite happy," Sydney tried. "I have an amazing career, and-,"

"What about this Denton boy?"

Sydney smiled at her mother's youthful reference.

"I think that's a fizzle," Sydney forced the corners of her mouth upwards. "Wasn't meant to be."

"Do you love him?" her mother asked. "You can tell me," she winked, "I won't tell anyone else."

Sydney promptly burst into tears.

"It doesn't matter because he's not in love with me and he just has lots of casual women, I've seen them, I looked them up on Google, and Florence told me he's never settled down, never even taken a girl home to their house."

"Who's Florence?"

"Justin Haig's mu, mu, mum," Sydney sobbed. "Denton basically grew up with his family."

"Okay. Who is Justin Haig?"

"He's the whi, whi, whistleblower."

"Right." Sydney's mum took her hand.

"You were at Justin Haig's house in New Zealand?"

Sydney nodded.

"We had breakfast biscuits." Sydney dabbed at the corners of her leaky eyes.

"This Florence, Justin Haig's mum. She's never met any of Denton Cole's girlfriends?"

Sydney shook her head, put her hands to her face, the tears she'd pushed down were now a gushing river.

"But Sydney darling. She met you. Denton Cole took *you* home."

"Well. Yes. But that was a practicality."

"You've never brought a boy home here either."

"So?" Sydney sniffed.

"So," her mother said, offering her a piece of kitchen paper towel and waiting while she wiped her eyes and blew her nose. "So maybe you are in love with him."

"But I can't be."

Sydney rested her head on the table.

"You need to tell him. Get it out there."

"That's a very risky suggestion."

"Listen to me Sydney Stone. Life is about taking risks. If I hadn't taken on old Maude's chickens when she died, I would never have needed an extra supply of leafy greens from the markets, so I wouldn't have been there, with my bum up in the air, choosing a bunch of leeks, when Craig tripped on a small pug and crashed into me, spilling hot chocolate over both of us."

"You have chickens?" Sydney sniffed.

"*Had* chickens. They're with the lord now. Thank god. Bloody things ate right through my marigolds."

"I don't know if I can do it, Mum. It might just be easier to stay here. Start afresh. Maybe I can go to the markets and fall in love with a nice vegetable grower. Or a beekeeper? The world needs more bees. I read about it somewhere…"

"The market gardeners' son is already married to a lovely woman who runs the popcorn stall. And the beekeeper is 73 years old. And he's gay."

"Right."

"Also. You can't stay here. I've got a guest coming."

"Who?" Sydney asked, alarmed at the prospect of losing her hideaway.

"His name is Lars. He booked me through Air BnB."

"But what about me?"

"You'll be fine," her mother smiled. "I've booked you on the 3 pm train back to London."

"You what?"

"I've got your ticket printed out already. It's in my handbag. You should probably get yourself ready. I'll pack you a sandwich to have on the ride back home."

"You're sending me home?"

"Yes, Sydney. I love you so much, and I love having you here. You are always welcome here. But you need to go home. It's where the heart is."

42

"I'm sorry if I'm calling at a bad time. Sydney's friend Matilda gave me your mobile number."

"I know who you are Mr Cole. I'm sitting here on the landline, just listening to the Passion Media hold music. It's not very good. Plinky-plonky rage inducing. I know you're just new there, but you should probably look at getting some Ed Sheeran or maybe Adele. She's got a lovely voice."

"I'll get on top of it, Mrs Stone."

"Call me Jocelyn."

"Okay, Jocelyn. I was wondering if I might be able to talk to Sydney?"

"Absolutely not!"

"Oh," Denton felt his heart plummet to his stomach.

"No way at all I could get her on the telephone right now to talk to you."

"Okay. What if I came to see her?"

"Terrible idea!" Jocelyn declared.

"Right. I see." Denton wasn't sure he knew what to do next. He hadn't considered Sydney would flat out refuse to talk to him.

"It would be a shocking waste of all our time if you came here."

"Yes, I see."

"Oh I don't think you do Mr Cole. She's on the train!" Jocelyn declared.

"Call me Denton. She's on the train?"

"Yes Denton, the train. You know – choo-choo. Tell me my daughter hasn't fallen in love with a nin-com-poop!"

"Sydney is on a train?" Denton's heart was picking up speed.

"Yes Dear, that's what I said."

"Is the train coming to London Mrs Stone?"

"It is Dear. Hurtling towards you. Unless she got on the wrong way. Then she'll end up in Scotland!"

"Sydney is coming back?" Denton asked.

"She is. I gave her a sandwich to eat on the way, but I think she might be quite hungry when she gets home."

"I can sort out some dinner." Denton was already pulling on his shoes.

"Not takeout," Sydney's mother advised. "Put some effort in."

"Pasta?" Denton offered.

"Good boy. That'll do. Now I better go. I'm taking Lars to Scrabble Club!"

43

The train doors beeped then slowly closed, and Sydney worked hard to return her mother's eager smile only until she was out of sight, then she sunk down in her seat.

The train was moving too fast, the world beyond her window whizzing past with a reckless disregard for Sydney's emotional readiness to step back into her old life. Or what was left of it.

She cursed herself for leaving her phone in the office. She had no desire to see if there were 168 voice messages, or to panic about how many may or may not have come from Denton Cole. But a game of Zombie Cupcake Wars or Bubble Witch would have helped distract her from her nerves.

At Baldock Station, Sydney decided she would go directly to Denton Cole's apartment. She would lay out her feelings, simple and clear. But by Hitchin, Sydney thought maybe that was too presumptuous. She would sneak into work and retrieve her cell phone. Then she would send him a text. She would tell him her mother had been struck down by the flu. And that she'd left her cell phone in the office. By mistake. And her mother didn't have a landline.

At Stevenage Station, she thought perhaps lying wasn't the best way to approach a relationship with Denton Cole.

By Finsbury Park she was in a complete panic, sweat beads forming on her forehead.

A relationship? How could she, Sydney Stone, single girl and glad to be so, suddenly be thinking of shacking up with Denton Cole? And she'd disappeared for days and what if he'd decided she was a flake and never wanted to see her again?

But when the train pulled into Kings Cross Station, she had a plan. Sydney Stone was going home.

She changed to the northern line.

She was going home to lock the door and close the curtains. At Bank Station, the sign said her train to Blackwall Station would arrive in four minutes.

"My train," Sydney whispered to herself. She was going home and there she would climb deep under the blankets and pretend that in the morning, she would know exactly what to do.

Sydney did not stop for milk or bread. She knew there were bagels frozen in the small ice box of her fridge, and she could drink black coffee in the morning. Or borrow milk from Alfie. Sydney was especially careful not to look at the headlines of The Daily Mail, The Metro, or The Times. She pulled the hood of her coat tightly over her head and hurried past the newsagents, out into the cool night.

It was after seven and Sydney joined the tail end of the after-work rush, overtaking most of the suited profess-ionals, tired from their days spent in cubicles under fluorescent lights. She power walked all the way home and stood breathless in the lift as it rose up to her apartment. Sydney slid her key into the lock and pushed open her front door.

Home safe and sound.

A rush of warm air and the glow of light caught her off guard. Sydney froze in the doorway, her handbag dangling off her arm. The television was on. She could see BBC news scrolling the latest stories across the bottom of the screen and hear the sound of her dishwasher being loaded. Or emptied? It must be Alfie and Cornflake.

"Is that you Alfie?" she called out. Of course it was her next door neighbour, he was the only other person who had a key. But the relief washed out and was replaced with a wave of panic. Alfie in the kitchen? He was barely able to work a toaster, let alone a dishwasher. Had she entered the wrong apartment? Sydney stared at the keys in her hand.

"You made it back!"

Sydney looked up and squeaked.

"I've made pasta. I was going to do an alfredo thing but you haven't got any eggs, and I forgot to buy them. So we're having very fancy Italian handmade pasta with ham and parmesan cheese."

Sydney couldn't move. Simultaneous emotions were fighting for attention. She was struck by an overwhelming urge to run and dive into Denton Cole's arms. To rub her cheek against the stubble on his chin, and press her lips into his.

But then a foot-stomping anger bubbled up.

Why is he here? In my home. Without an invitation. Her plan was ruined. Her time to think, *okay to hide*, had been taken away. She began desperately blinking to hold back the tears that threatened to tumble out.

"Sydney, you look a little pale, and you're blinking a lot. Are you okay?" Denton Cole was walking towards her. He was wearing a faded navy blue Yale University t-shirt and a pair of grey tracksuit bottoms. Tanned bare feet. Fiji feet. Now Denton Cole was standing in front of her.

Sydney decided his feet were the safest place for her gaze so she kept her eyes down.

"I'll take your coat. There you go." Sydney slipped her coat off her shoulders and watched Denton hang it in the cupboard beside the front door. Then quickly returned her eyes to his feet.

"You want to sit down. Or do you want a shower? Wash off the train travel?"

Sydney shook her head. She could not be naked in the apartment right now. Even if it was behind a locked bathroom door. And how did he know she'd been on the train? She wanted to demand an explanation, but she seemed to have lost the power of speech.

"Okay, well the couch is yours. I'll bring you a glass of wine. I'll put the pasta on. Ready in 8 minutes!"

Denton stood and waited until Sydney shuffled over to the couch.

"There we go!" Denton said when she perched on the edge of a couch cushion. Then he disappeared into the kitchen. Sydney held a hand out and watched her fingers shaking.

"Chardonnay?" Denton called out, and Sydney sat on her hands. Why hadn't she agreed to the shower? It would have given her a chance to work out what was going on.

What the hell is going on?

Denton Cole, the man Sydney had secretly fallen in love with, then run away from, was in her apartment.

"What are you doing?" she finally managed to whisper, as Denton placed a wine glass on a coaster in front of her.

"Cooking pasta." Denton raised his eyebrows and smiled, then disappeared again.

"Matilda wanted me to tell you she's got a lot to talk about in her appraisal next week." Denton placed a bowl of pasta in Sydney's lap. "I'll just get the pepper." Sydney took a bite of pasta. The sandwich from her mother lay squashed in the bottom of her bag. She'd been too distracted to think about eating on the train. She should be hungry.

"She wants to be your personal assistant. She also wants a pay rise. And fish in the reception area."

"Fish?"

"She wanted us to adopt guide dog puppies and keep them in a basket for guests and staff to play with. I talked her down to fish."

Sydney smiled.

"She's been worried. We all have."

Sydney nodded.

Denton picked up the remote control and scrolled through channels until he came to an episode of Friends. They finished their pasta without conversation, letting Monica's disastrous Thanksgiving fill the space.

"All done?" Denton asked. She nodded. She'd only managed a few bites but he didn't comment. He took the bowls to the kitchen. Sydney heard the tap running and the clatter of crockery in the sink.

Sydney didn't know what to do. Should she start with a proclamation of love? She took it as a positive thing, that Denton Cole was here in her apartment. That he said he'd been worried about her. But was that what he said? No, he'd said Matilda was worried. *That they all had.* Maybe he just wanted to be friends. Or what if he was here in a professional capacity? Covering the organisation in case she wanted to sue for emotional harm or wrongful dismissal?

"You're doing that blinking thing again." Denton turned off the telly and sat on the couch next to Sydney, an arm stretched along the backrest.

"I'm," Sydney thought hard about what to say.

"I'm sorry."

"Okay." Denton nodded, he lifted his arm off the back of the couch, scratched a spot of stubble on his chin, then returned the arm to its original position.

"Okay." *No, it is not okay,* Sydney thought. She wanted to cry.

"But it's not okay. Because I ran away. Right when our investigation was being unleashed. I left you to handle everything. And I didn't even, you know, say goodbye." Sydney could feel imminent tears.

"You did." Denton nodded again. "And you didn't. Say goodbye." He seemed quite happy to wait for Sydney to talk again. He stretched his legs out and continued watching her.

Sydney was flummoxed.

"It wasn't very professional of me."

Denton smiled. He looked very relaxed and it made her uptight.

"I'm sorry Denton. I don't know what you want."

He sat up, pulled Sydney into his arms and kissed her on the mouth. His lips talked their way across her own, his tongue teased her and Sydney felt a storm of electricity rise up between them.

Denton pulled away, holding Sydney at arm's length, their two bodies gasping for breath, affronted by the sudden separation.

"What I want, is for you to stop talking about work. I want to stop playing this game."

"What game?" Sydney whispered.

"This thing we've been doing." Denton was still holding Sydney by the arms.

"Look at me," he demanded when she tried to avoid his fiery eyes.

"You always do that," he cried. "You close yourself off. You disappear. Look at me." Sydney met Denton's gaze and the tears that had been threatening came thick and fast.

Denton pulled her into his arms and held her to his chest. He waited for her sobs to ease.

"I don't know what to say." Sydney croaked through her tears. "What do you want me to say?"

"I want to know how you feel about me. About us. Not the us that works together. Not the investigation. I want to see you Sydney." Denton held her tightly in his arms.

"I want you to stop hiding from me."

Sydney felt a wave of fear grow from deep inside. She closed her eyes and took a steadying breath. She didn't open her eyes, but her words came, sounding foreign and fragile, and Sydney would be hard pressed to believe they were her own if it weren't for her lips moving against Denton's chest as she formed each word.

"I'm in love with you Denton Cole. I think I have been from the first day you walked into my office."

Sydney waited. Her eyes tightly closed. Her heart hammering in her chest. When the silence reached an unbearable racket, Sydney peaked through her wet eyelashes.

"I'm still here," Denton smiled. Sydney bravely opened her eyes.

"Scary, isn't it." Denton used his thumbs to wipe Sydney's tear-stained cheeks.

"I'm a mess," Sydney whispered.

"I love you all wet and wild." And he kissed her again. He lay her down on the couch and wrapped her in his arms.

"And here's some information that might come as a surprise to you Sydney Stone, but I am absolutely terrified about how much *I* love you." Denton's hands were tangled in Sydney's hair, his kisses falling like gentle summer rain on her burning lips.

"When your mum said you were coming back home. I've never been so relieved in all my life. I love you Sydney Stone, but you need to know I have no idea how these proper relationships work."

"Neither do I," Sydney murmured, letting her fingers cover the familiar muscles of Denton's shoulders, travelling down his back, finding the edge of his t-shirt, and pushing it up so her fingers could traverse his warm smooth skin.

"But I'm told it's quite achievable. Normal people do it all the time." Denton left a trail of kisses along the length of her neck.

"We can get married," he offered. "Have a pile of babies. We can live in a castle if you want."

"Or in a caravan," Sydney replied, wrapping her legs around Denton, feeling him press against her. "Or a tent. I really don't mind, as long as we're together."

"Castle, tent, cardboard box." Denton was struggling to remove layers of clothing, throwing them over the side of the couch.

"As long as we're together."

"Happily ever after," Sydney smiled.

Epilogue

Sydney opened her eyes and blinked in the bright sunlight. She glanced sideways at her husband who had his head in her new romance novel.

"Nice nap?" Denton asked.

Sydney grinned. The past year had opened up a whole new world for Sydney. Waking up next to Denton every morning still made her giddy. Even with all the relationship revelations that came with sharing your life with another person.

She'd learned he got very grumpy if anyone got him out of bed before ten on a Sunday morning, and it had become apparent that Denton's cooking abilities started and ended at cheesy pasta.

"You seem very engaged in that book," Sydney laughed, adjusting her bikini top and waving to the attendant, who padded across the sand in his bare feet.

"Could I have another pineapple juice please," she asked. "And some chicken nuggets."

"We just had breakfast," Denton laughed.

"Blame the Cole cubs," Sydney smiled, rubbing her hand across her rounded belly. "Back to the book."

"I can't believe you read this stuff," Denton laughed.

"What page are you on?" Sydney demanded.

"Fifty-five," Denton murmured.

"Has Victoria seduced her riding instructor in the stables yet?"

"He's not going to fall for that," Denton scoffed. "He'd lose his job."

"Ah, but the heart wants what the heart wants."

"And these stories, there's always a happy ending?"

"The best ones often do. But keep on reading my love. We'll see what happens."

About the Author

Rochelle Elliot is a New Zealand writer of novels and short stories. She lives in Wellington, with her husband Aidan and her children Isabelle and Ashton. Their household is run by their sturdy cat Buttons (She's not obese - her mother had her tested!).

A sucker for a good love story, Rochelle has developed a passion for creating strong heroines, the kind who accidentally bump into romance while they're out building an empire or celebrating their promotion!

Rochelle's short stories have a distinctly New Zealand flavour, and have been read on Radio New Zealand, and published in magazines and newspapers. In 2012, her short story *No Returnsies,* took first place in the Cambridge Autumn Festival Short Story Competition.

In 2013, with the support and encouragement of her family, friends and community, Rochelle crowd-funded the self-publication of her first novel, *Lighthouse Love.* She has gone on to write Making Over Mabel (2014) and a selection of novelettes, embracing her Kiwi flair.

Rochelle brings together the defining relationships in our lives. Lovers, friends and family coalesce, with a sprinkle of humour, a touch of whimsy and a liberal load of lusty romance!

Acknowledgements

Being a self-published writer involves a lot of different tasks, some of which would be impossible without the encouragement, support and expertise of a bunch of fabulous people who invest a big chunk of their time and energy into seeing my books transported from file on an old blippy laptop, to 'hey, there's Rochelle Elliot's book on the shelf at the library!"

My husband Aidan. He's never afraid of a drop-cap drama or a hyphenation hullabaloo. The headers and footers, the correctly placed words on the cover – that's all him! I love you and I'm so lucky to have you on my team!

Cherie, my fabulous finder of faults, your keen eye and kind corrections take my writing to the next level. Thank you for your time and enthusiasm. You make me a better writer and for that I am so very grateful.

Caroline, who helps me come unstuck. In the best way! She can take an almost sentence and craft it into something beautiful, never questioning the importance of one word's placement in a book of over 65,000. Every writer needs a Caroline!

And my friends Helen and Michelle. When I stuck this book in a drawer at the start of this year, and declared myself *over it*, you never forgot it was there. And when the time was right you gave me a shove in the right direction. Your excitement and energy motivates me to keep doing what I love. Your belief in me reminds me to believe in myself.

And lastly, to my readers. Thank you. I hope you enjoyed reading Hidden Agenda!

www.ingramcontent.com/pod-product-compliance
Lightning Source LLC
Chambersburg PA
CBHW070117071125
35124CB00051B/2261